Praise for the

MW00425066

"A sassy, steamy read that had me racing to the next page to see if Samir would be on it. Mmm, Samir."
                    —*New York Times* bestselling author Chelsea M. Cameron

"*I See London* is fun, sexy, and kept me completely absorbed."
                    —Katie McGarry, award-winning author of *Pushing the Limits*

"Holy smokes, this book was very addicting. I loved everything about this book, from the beautiful cities of London, Paris and Italy that Maggie gets to see, to the swoon worthy guys that have captured her attention, jealousy, secrets, and of course the sizzling romantic chemistry."   —*Jess Time to Read*

"I read a lot of books, and I've read a lot of New Adult books that blend together, but weeks after reading it, I can still remember *I See London* vividly."   —*Book Labyrinth*

"I absolutely loved this book! It was different enough from others in its genre that it set itself apart from the beginning and it kept getting better as it went along."   —*Examiner.com*

LONDON FALLING

"Oh boy, I feel a book hangover coming on… *London Falling* is a brilliant sequel."   —*Martini Times Romance*

"I was so invested in these characters, I couldn't put the book down, yet I didn't want to finish because that meant I had to give them up. I still keep thinking about this book and Maggie and Samir weeks after finishing."
                    —*Kimberly Faye Reads*

"I loved the tension and burn between Maggie and Samir."
                    —*Teacups and Bookends*

"I already have read *and loved* *I See London*…and while I was sure that this ride couldn't get more crazy and deliciously epic…Ms. Cleeton proved me exactly how wrong I could be."   —*Shattering Words*

"I sat and thought for ages about how I could describe this book…it left me speechless, my thoughts incoherent. It was, in a word, AMAZING."
                    —*Tea Party Princess*

The International School series!

I SEE LONDON

Also by Chanel Cleeton

The International School Series

I SEE LONDON
LONDON FALLING
FRENCH KISSED

For a complete list of books by Chanel Cleeton,
please visit her website at chanelcleeton.com.

If you purchased this book without a cover you should be aware
that this book is stolen property. It was reported as "unsold and
destroyed" to the publisher, and neither the author nor the
publisher has received any payment for this "stripped book."

CANARY
STREET
PRESS™

Recycling programs
for this product may
not exist in your area.

ISBN-13: 978-1-335-00485-7

London Falling

First published in 2014. This edition published in 2024 with revised text.

Copyright © 2014 by Chanel Cleeton

Copyright © 2024 by Chanel Cleeton, revised text edition.

All rights reserved. No part of this book may be used or reproduced in
any manner whatsoever without written permission.

Without limiting the author's and publisher's exclusive rights, any unauthorized
use of this publication to train generative artificial intelligence (AI) technologies is
expressly prohibited.

This is a work of fiction. Names, characters, places and incidents are either
the product of the author's imagination or are used fictitiously. Any resemblance
to actual persons, living or dead, businesses, companies, events or locales is
entirely coincidental.

For questions and comments about the quality of this book, please contact us
at CustomerService@Harlequin.com.

TM is a trademark of Harlequin Enterprises ULC.

Canary Street Press
22 Adelaide St. West, 41st Floor
Toronto, Ontario M5H 4E3, Canada
CanaryStPress.com

Printed in U.S.A.

CHANEL CLEETON

LONDON FALLING

CANARY STREET PRESS

LONDON
FALLING

1

Maggie

I wasn't looking for Samir. At least that's what I told myself.

I shouldn't be looking for Samir.

"We spent most of the summer in Saint-Tropez. You should have seen the guys. There was this one guy…" Fleur took a sip of her soda, her brown eyes sparkling. She wiggled her eyebrows suggestively. "He was so fine. You would have died."

I flashed her an easy smile, my gaze glued to the door behind her. Classes started tomorrow. Where the hell was he?

"How was the US?"

I tore my gaze away from the cafeteria door, like a kid caught with her hand in the cookie jar. Which I pretty much was, come to think of it.

"It was fine." *Boring. Frustrating. Agonizing.*

I turned my head to the side. The entrance was just barely visible out of the corner of my eye. *Come on.* Three more students walked in, laughing and talking about their summer break. My heart sank.

"Are you listening?" Fleur's voice was impatient, two shades away from pissed off, as she nudged my plate. "You seem like you're somewhere else."

"I heard you," I lied with ease, turning my body toward the open doorway and glancing at the clock against the wall. The dining hall closed in fifteen minutes. If he was going to make our first family dinner back at school, time was running out.

I shouldn't have cared. I should have known better than this. I shouldn't have been sitting here waiting, my stomach in knots, my nerves frayed. I'd already made it through four months with only two one-line texts from him. What was another day?

Everything.

I tore my attention from the empty doorway, the gaping hole taunting me. "Is anyone else joining us?" I asked Fleur, my voice deceptively casual. I couldn't say his name, but I was desperate to hear it. He was a secret I both wanted to keep and needed to spill.

I'd spent the whole summer in South Carolina talking about him to my friends back home, until even my best friend, Jo, was sick of hearing about my boy woes. Sadly that was saying a lot.

"No idea where Mya is. She's been MIA practically all sum- mer. I think her parents' divorce is hitting her hard. Michael said something about the two of them going out to dinner with other friends."

Mya split her vacation time between her home in Nigeria and her family's flat in London, where her father worked for the Nigerian Embassy. Last year she'd discovered he was cheat- ing on her mother and apparently over the summer he'd asked for a divorce. Mya was spending most of her time with her mom and not speaking to her dad. She seemed to be handling it pretty well, all things considered. But still—Mya's priority right now was her family.

I waited for Fleur to continue, to say the one name that had been flooding my head all summer long. But in classic Fleur fashion, it appeared she was going to make me work for it.

"And Samir?" I kept my gaze trained on my plate, memorizing the china's webbed pattern, hoping she hadn't heard the hitch in my voice.

Fleur shrugged in that wonderfully French way that reminded me of him. A wave of nostalgia crashed over me. It had been four months, after all.

"No idea. You know how Samir is, you can't exactly predict what he's going to do next."

No kidding. Not being able to predict Samir's moves was exactly what got me into this mess in the first place. Not that I regretted our one night together. I just wished to hell he'd given me more to go on than a text the morning after, followed by a cryptic one in July. Even worse?

There hadn't even been a chance for me to casually interact with him online. Trust me to hook up with the one guy who seemed allergic to social media.

I tucked a loose strand of hair behind my ear, not bothering to resist the urge to smooth down any stray flyaways. My hair was just the tip of the iceberg; brand-new black sandals adorned my feet, their height more aptly suited to a nightclub than a university cafeteria. Relentless workouts at the gym, combined with endless overtime hours, had squeezed my curvy five-four frame into a pair of designer jeans so expensive, I'd been too afraid to eat for fear of spilling. A new black halter top completed the look that an hour ago I thought had screamed "I look good without trying to" but now felt more like "I'm desperate over here."

"Maggie!"

I jerked my head up. Fleur stared back at me, an annoyed expression on her face.

"Sorry," I mumbled, my cheeks heating.

"What is up with you?" Her tone was a mix of concern and petulance. Classic Fleur.

For the millionth time, I wanted to tell her. *Last semester on my last night in London I lost my virginity to your cousin and I can't stop thinking about it. Or him.* I wanted to confide in Fleur. But if I did, I wasn't just admitting to a one-night stand. It was so much worse. *Yeah, he was still with his girlfriend when it happened. No, I don't know if they're still together. No, I don't know if he likes me. Or if he regrets it. Or if he thinks about that night at all. No, we haven't talked in one hundred and twenty-four days save for two texts, but who's counting?*

"I'm sorry, I think I'm just jet-lagged." That, at least, wasn't completely a lie. My flight from Charlotte to London had been particularly brutal. I stared back at the clock. Five minutes left.

Unfuckingbelievable.

I'd been camped out here for like four hours. No way I'd missed him. Was he avoiding me?

I sighed, pushing back my chair. I knew when to admit defeat. "I'm going to head up to the room and go to bed."

"Can I join you?"

I froze, my entire body prickling with awareness. I knew that voice, that teasing tone. It had been haunting me for months.

"Samir!" Fleur jumped up from the table and launched herself at her cousin.

I turned, time moving in slow motion. Fragmented images and thoughts flew at me. Flashes back to that night—his body pressing into me, his hands molding my curves, his lips devouring mine—mixed with the reality of Samir in the flesh. My gaze ran over his body, drinking in the sight of him.

He'd cut his hair. The black curls I'd once run my fingers through were shorter now. The skin I'd kissed, tasted on my tongue, was a deeper tan. Whatever he'd done this summer, clearly he'd spent time in the sun. Impossibly, he looked better than I remembered. His shoulders looked broader, his body toned and hard. The memory of his naked flesh, his muscled chest, his abs…

I flushed.

Would I always look at Samir and see him naked?

It was an excellent trick and exquisite torture all rolled into one. Just being here—a foot away from him—was enough to tempt me. I ached to reach out, brush my fingers against his skin, and curl into that warmth.

And then I heard that voice again—sexy and sultry, the husky tone winding its way through my body, sending a shiver in its wake. I could drown in his voice.

"Hi, Maggie."

Samir

It was like being punched in the chest. Fuck me.

She sat there, inches away. I could smell her perfume; the memory of that subtle scent had been driving me wild for months. I remembered exactly what it smelled like on her naked body. Remembered kissing every inch of her gorgeous skin, nibbling on her, my tongue tracing patterns across her flesh.

The rush of arousal hit me like another punch.

"Samir? Are you paying attention?"

I jerked my gaze away from Maggie, taking one last look before turning to face my cousin. I slid a smile on my face, struggling to get my body under control. I'd known it would be weird seeing Maggie after... well, after seeing *all* of her. But this?

Somehow I'd missed the memo that seeing her under the harsh cafeteria lights, surrounded by the aroma of crappy food and the presence of other students, would make me want to take her back to my room and strip her bare. Hell, at this point a cafeteria table would have worked.

I wanted to bury myself in her body.

"Samir."

"Give me a minute, Fleur."

I needed a moment. A moment of quiet before I had to look back at her. I needed a moment to get my shit under control.

"I'm tired, Fleur. I just flew in from Beirut. Excuse me if my response time's a little delayed."

Fleur rolled her eyes. "There seems to be a lot of jet lag going around."

I looked over at Maggie. Her head was turned, her gaze focused on the plate in front of her, her face partially hidden by the curtain of her brown hair. I remembered all too well having her hair wrapped around my fist, pulling her head back, capturing those lips—

"Samir. Are you going to sit, or are you just going to stand there staring?"

"Chill," I muttered through gritted teeth, sliding into the chair next to Fleur so I could have a perfect, uninterrupted view of Maggie. If only she'd look at me.

"So how was Lebanon?"

"Fine." I needed to get Fleur on another subject fast. Lebanon was the last thing I wanted to talk about right now.

"How's your girlfriend?"

The word *girlfriend* passed so easily from Fleur's lips, sending a wave of dread through me.

I couldn't look at Maggie now. This wasn't how I'd imagined this going down. I needed a chance to talk to her—to explain in private, without Fleur and the rest of the damned school listening in.

I didn't want to look at Maggie. I *couldn't* look at Maggie. I owed her an explanation—an apology—so much more than I could give her. Instead I froze, unable to think of anything to save this moment.

Her head jerked up from the plate, the anger flashing across her face a knife slashing me open. But it was nothing compared to the hurt that followed, clouding her beautiful brown eyes. Shame filled me. Not for the first time, I wished I could go back and undo everything that had happened this summer. I wished things were different. I wished *I* were different. I'd never been one for regrets. Until now. Until her.

This girl brought me to my fucking knees.

2

Maggie

Girlfriend.

The word pierced me, knocking the breath out of me. I sat there, staring, watching it play out in front of me. It was one of those moments when my world lurched to a crashing stop.

I waited. Waited for him to laugh and say he'd broken up with her. Waited for him to look at me. Waited for something—some sign—to let me know I hadn't been an idiot all summer, lusting after a guy who didn't even want me. I waited for words that never came. My heart—the one I'd sworn was never engaged—broke a little bit.

I was such an idiot.

I'd known there was a possibility this would happen. I'd known it even when I'd gone to bed with him. He'd had a girlfriend then, and there had been no promises, no guarantees. Nothing beyond the way he looked at me, the way he touched me. He'd never given me the words, just the fire and passion that changed everything.

But the revelation still shattered me.

I escaped from the cafeteria in a mad dash, mumbling some

ridiculous excuse that had Fleur looking at me in surprise and Samir staring down at the floor. He should be staring at the floor. A strangled gasp pushed through the anger. *Months.* Months since we'd had sex, and not so much as a phone call or an email or a freaking message in a bottle. Just a text that had come in the middle of the night in July.

When he'd sent me that first text after our night together and I'd read those words—Last night was amazing. We should do it again. Often. See you next year. Xxxx—I'd actually believed it. Our one night together had been amazing. So amazing that four months later I was still reliving it in my thoughts and in my dreams.

And he was still with his girlfriend.

How could he? Did he sleep with his arms curled around her like he had with me? Did he hold her body against his? Did he kiss her lips like he'd kissed mine?

How could he do what he'd done with me with someone else, when I couldn't so much as look at another guy?

I pushed open the door to our room, anger and hurt flooding me, building to a stunning crescendo. I stopped short at the sight of Mya staring at me with a worried expression on her face.

"You seem upset."

"I've been better."

The three of us were roommates this year—me, Mya and Fleur. I'd felt guilty about leaving our old roommate, Noora, but she'd found an off-campus apartment and seemed happy with her new living arrangement. Moments like these I wished I had a single.

"Want to talk about it?"

"Not really."

Mya more than anyone would think I was an idiot for fooling around with Samir. She'd told me from the beginning that he had "bad idea" written all over him. She'd been right—and wrong. Mya hadn't been there to see how amazing he'd been when we'd lost Fleur in Venice during fall break. Or how kind he'd been the night I'd found out my dad was marrying a complete stranger. She didn't know Samir could look at you and make you feel like you were the most beautiful girl in the world. Or that he could kiss you like he was drowning and you were his lifeline. She didn't know he could make you laugh until your sides ached, or make you smile so hard your cheeks hurt.

It would have been easy to chalk up my night with Samir as a big mistake if he really were the player everyone seemed to think he was. I didn't blame them for thinking that. I'd seen the girls who fell into his lap at clubs. I wasn't stupid. The boy had moves—in bed and everywhere else. His rep was well-earned. But he was still *more*.

The *more* was what kept me up at night, reliving our conversations, basking in the memory of our kisses. The *more* meant I was basically screwed.

I pushed the golf ball–sized lump out of my throat. I wanted to be alone and yet I didn't. Sitting in this room, reliving that night with Samir over and over again in my head, was too much. There were ghosts here. Ghosts in every hallway, every stairway, in the cafeteria and common room. Memories of last year I couldn't seem to shake off no matter how hard I tried.

In the beginning, he'd just been this guy I'd met on my first day at the International School—a guy who, embarrassingly enough, had accidentally seen me naked. I didn't know then that he would become my friend, or be the one I'd share my first kiss with. And I'd never expected him to become someone I couldn't live without.

He'd been single for most of the year, so when he'd casually mentioned he was dating someone, it had been a shock.

"Do you want to go out?"

"Tonight? The night before our first day of classes? On a Sunday?" Mya looked at me like I had three heads.

I shrugged, the idea forming, taking root. Alcohol and dancing might be the only things that would make this disaster better.

"It's only the first day. At most we're going to read the syllabus. I bet none of our classes will even go past the first half hour." Not to mention the fact that over half the student body routinely blew off the first week of classes. "Besides, it's London, there are a ton of bars and clubs open on Sunday. It'll be fun."

"Okay, what have you done with the real Maggie?"

I flashed her an easy grin. "Maybe this is the new-and-improved Maggie."

I'd done the moping-over-a-guy thing for way too long. If Samir wanted to walk away and pretend nothing existed between us, fine. But I wasn't going to wait around for him. Last year I'd spent too much time obsessing over Hugh, the twenty-seven-year-old British bar owner I'd casually dated. Not to mention how much of my freshman year I'd spent in knots over Samir.

This year was going to be different. It had to be.

"Are you sure everything's all right?"

The concern in Mya's voice was what made her an amazing friend. She was the first person I'd befriended freshman year and was easily the nicest person I'd ever met. Unfortunately right now I needed less emotion, and more champagne and dancing on tables. I needed Fleur.

"I'm fine. I spent months in the US not being able to drink and hanging out with my grandparents. I love them and all, but I kinda need to have some fun. You in?"

Mya grinned. "Fine, I'm in. But it'll be your fault when I fall asleep in class."

"Fair enough."

I grabbed my phone and shot off a quick text to Fleur.

Drinks. Dancing. Tonight. No boys.

Ten minutes later, Fleur waltzed into the room. "So where are we headed?"

"You tell me. What's the new, hot place no one can get into?"

With a model's body and a socialite's wardrobe, Fleur was the epitome of trendy. Long, sleek brown hair, big brown eyes and the kind of tan it took a tanning bed for me to achieve made her a knockout. Her personality made her trouble—the kind you couldn't resist. Despite our rocky start freshman year, she was now one of my best friends.

Last year had been rough for her, and she didn't seem to want to party as hard as she used to, but she was still the go-to for social advice. I figured she needed to let off steam as much as I did.

"I like where your head is at. There's this place called Air."

"Seriously? What kind of name is that?"

"It's an oxygen bar."

I had to laugh at that one. These were the moments when I felt the furthest away from my unremarkable life back in South Carolina.

"Of course it is."

One of the benefits of my not-so-glamorous summer job in retail was the employee discount. At a school like the International School, being on scholarship made it tough, if not impossible, to keep up with everyone else. My bags weren't Gucci or Prada; my shoes weren't Jimmy Choo or Giuseppe Zanotti. But thanks to my discount, I had a whole new wardrobe of cute dresses. I would never look like I'd walked off the runway like Fleur, but it was good enough for me.

We were in full-on pregaming mode—loud house music blared through Fleur's computer speakers. I was more of a hip-hop fan, but I wasn't complaining. We'd gotten into this habit last year—pregaming in our room before a night out. Having Mya here as a roommate made it so much better. We traded hair and makeup tips, shared outfits, and did some dancing and drinking while we got ready.

I'd missed them desperately these past few months.

"You guys all set?" Fleur asked, a wide smile on her face.

This summer had been good for her. She seemed lighter, happier. Last year had been rough. Her boyfriend, Costa, had dumped her before the start of the semester for another girl at the International School, but then continued to fool around with Fleur, making her believe he really cared. I hadn't understood why she was so connected to him until she'd told me about her accidental pregnancy—and subsequent miscarriage. It had all come crashing down around her at the end of last year when Fleur had learned how fickle he really was, a devastating loss that had pushed her into a drug overdose. It had been a scary wake-up call for all of us, but one Fleur had seemed to need.

The Fleur standing in front of me was laughing and smiling again, some of the sadness erased from her. She finally seemed to be over Costa. Now I just needed to find her a nice guy— the right guy. Given how things had ended last semester, with him bringing her flowers in the hospital, I had high hopes for my friend George.

I grabbed my purse off the bed, weaving slightly as I walked. A summer of not drinking was catching up with me, and my normally low alcohol tolerance seemed even lower than usual.

I followed Mya and Fleur out of the room, excitement and anticipation filling me.

I loved nights like this—unplanned, full of possibilities. For me, London was one big adventure—you never knew what to expect or what the night might bring. It made you feel like you could do anything, be anyone. You could reinvent yourself in a city like this.

This time last year I'd been nervous and unsure of myself. The International School had been a glamorous, intimidating place that made me feel like an impostor, playing dress-up and trying to fit in. Now I belonged.

"Going somewhere?" a voice called out.

I looked up and my gaze instantly connected with Samir's.

Samir

I didn't know where to look first.

In the cafeteria I'd been afraid to sneak more than a glance at her, sure that if I did, the whole school would see what I wanted—who I wanted. But she'd left so quickly—fled when Fleur dropped her little bombshell—and I'd lost my chance. I wasn't going to make the same mistake again. This time I looked my fill.

Her brown hair seemed longer than it had been in May. It fell past her shoulders, the ends just barely grazing the top of her tits. Her dress, some sort of strappy thing, left little to the imagination—and I had a pretty vivid imagination *and memory*—and showed off her tanned, tight little body. It ended just under her curvy ass, exposing plenty of leg.

For a moment I couldn't speak. I couldn't look her in the eye. I was two steps away from maneuvering Maggie up against the wall and getting under that dress, audience or not.

"Girls' night," Fleur answered, oblivious to the tenuous grip I kept on my sanity.

I looked away from Maggie, my gaze traveling over the three of them. They were all dressed to kill tonight. Fleur smirked back at me. Mya's eyes narrowed slightly, and for one awful moment, I wondered if she'd seen my reaction. Maggie still wouldn't look at me.

"Where are you headed?" I asked Fleur, trying to keep my voice casual. I hated the tension running through my body, the possessiveness flooding me. It was a new experience, one that wasn't entirely welcome.

"That new club, Air."

Awesome. It was exactly the kind of place Fleur would choose. It would likely be full of B-list actors and athletes and flashy new money. In that dress, they'd be all over Maggie.

No way.

I couldn't help it. I had to know if she hated me. I turned my attention away from Fleur, my gaze lingering over Maggie's body, before reaching her eyes.

She flinched and looked back down at the floor.

I needed to explain to her about Layla. If she wasn't going to give me a chance to get close to her, I would take it.

"I'll come with you guys."

3

Maggie

I wished he would stop looking at me.

Actually, I wished he would go home. Or never have come out with us at all. I still didn't know how he'd managed it. One minute we were walking down the stairs, the next he was helping me into a cab, his hands grazing my bare shoulders.

I blamed Fleur. Besides being her cousin, he was also one of her closest friends, and she never did a good job of telling him no. Of course, a lot of girls seemed to have that problem where Samir was concerned—myself included.

I moved my hips to the music, tossing my head back. I wanted to lose myself in the beat, the freedom of it. For the first time in months, I felt like I belonged. I felt more like myself here in this nightclub in London than I ever had in a lifetime in South Carolina.

Summer had been awkward. My life back home was beginning to feel a lot like a shirt that was a size too small. I tried to make it work, tried to fit in. But there was a part of me that was always here, in London, wishing I could get back to the life

I left behind. Wishing I could get back to the person I liked, versus the shell of me I'd been in my hometown.

I'd missed this, missed feeling like I was a part of life, rather than like it was just happening to me.

This place was a prime example.

Here, waitresses served canisters of oxygen and fancy cocktails. Thanks to Samir, we were in the club's VIP section, girls dancing on the tables around us, people mixing magnums of champagne with oxygen. It was a surreal experience that felt like something out of a movie and yet somehow—thanks to my scholarship and, indirectly, my Harvard rejection—it had become my life.

I grabbed my glass of champagne, downing the remnants in one big gulp. The oxygen was supposed to be best when mixed with champagne or something—I couldn't tell much of a difference. But of course, the drink selection was the furthest thing from my mind. This time I stared back at him.

Samir lounged in his chair, whiskey and Coke in hand, his feet crossed at the ankles, propped up against the table. All he needed was a cigar to complete the portrait of satisfied male.

He'd dressed casually tonight, probably more out of haste than anything else. He wore a simple collared black dress shirt—a few buttons unbuttoned—and a pair of jeans. The shoes propped up against the table looked like Gucci or something equally expensive.

The more I drank, the more I wanted to undress him, one article of clothing at a time.

Samir used to be the one temptation I couldn't resist. And now that I'd had him, I wanted more.

I hadn't been able to really look at him earlier, surrounded by everyone. I studied him now, until our gazes locked and his eyes widened slightly.

Shit.

I looked away, nerves pounding. I was playing with fire,

dancing around the heat and the flames. But wasn't that part of the excitement? Deep down, in places I didn't want to admit to having, wasn't that part of what I liked? The thrill of the chase—the ecstasy and agony of wondering if he still wanted me, if he lay awake at nights turned on, fantasizing about me, or if he woke from dreams that seemed more like memories—of naked flesh and heat and release.

I couldn't resist—I glanced back over at him.

He sat at the table, nursing his drink, his eyes hooded. This time, he wasn't looking at me.

Since we'd arrived, scores of girls had come over to the table, flirting with him. He'd ignored every one. He was taking this girlfriend more seriously than I'd thought.

We'd all criticized him for being a player and yet, here he was, faithful to someone far away. A better person would have been happy for him. It just made me want to drink more.

I turned my body slightly, sneaking another peek at him. He stared back at me, unsmiling, his gaze unwavering. It was the staring equivalent of a game of chicken, one he would probably win.

A girl walked over to the table, a sultry grin on her face. What was this, number six for the night? If anything, Samir's lack of interest seemed to spur them on. I had no doubt he'd become a competition to them—the prize they all wanted to win.

The girl leaned down, her long blond hair brushing against Samir as she whispered in his ear.

My stomach clenched. It was harder than I'd anticipated, watching him with someone else. I hated that I even wondered, but the thought flashed through my mind: *Has he slept with her, too?* I wasn't prepared for the spark of hurt I felt—irrational as it was—at the sight of another girl so physically close to him. I held my breath, waiting for his reaction, wishing I didn't care.

He waved her off, his gaze connecting with mine. Something that might have been embarrassment flickered in his eyes before it was replaced by the same smug expression I'd come to know as classically Samir.

I glared back at him.

The girl remained at his side. I knew I'd regret what I was about to do, but I couldn't resist. It—all of it—was just too much.

"He has a girlfriend, you know. He's devoted to her. So you might as well not waste your time." I wanted to hurt him, wanted to make him feel small, the way he'd made me feel. It was petty of me, but I was pissed off and spoiling for a fight.

The girl turned to face me, but I barely spared her a glance. My words weren't for her. This time I met his gaze dead-on. Challenging him.

Samir's eyes darkened. He stood and brushed past the girl, his gaze locked on me. As difficult as it was, I held his stare. I was done being the girl who backed away from a fight.

He moved toward me, coming to stand before me, inches separating our bodies. He was just tall enough, and close enough, that I had to tilt my head up to meet his gaze. It was the closest we'd been since we'd slept together, and my body knew it. My skin felt overly warm, desire pooling, spreading throughout my limbs. My body had terrible judgment and all too often around him, my mind followed suit.

For a moment, neither one of us spoke.

Samir leaned into me, his chest brushing against mine. I struggled to keep myself from swaying forward, from sinking into him. His lips brushed against my ear and a tremor ran through me. I clenched my hands into little fists.

You can look, but you can't touch.

"Come with me."

I shook my head, taking a step away from him. I wanted to act like I didn't care, like his presence didn't affect me. But I couldn't. Self-preservation became infinitely more important than my ego. I couldn't be this close to him again. Not when it hurt too much, made me want too much, made me reckless.

"We need to talk."

"There's nothing left to say."

"Isn't there? Are you just going to avoid talking about it?"

"Funny you should mention wanting to discuss what happened, considering you didn't talk to me all summer."

"Maggie—"

"No. You don't get to talk now. You sent me texts. One that made me think you didn't regret what happened between us. And then that cryptic text in July. 'Are you okay?' That's what you had to text me?" My voice rose with each word.

"I was worried about you. I didn't know what to say."

"Really? Really? You were worried about me?" I laughed bitterly. "Was that in between the time you spent with your *girlfriend*?"

I didn't know who I was angrier at, him or myself. Sure, he'd cheated on his girlfriend, but I'd been right there with him. I was the one who had been stupid enough to believe our night might have meant something. I was the one who had spent all summer obsessing about him, imagining seeing him again, preparing for it. More than anything, I was angry that I'd let my guard down with him for even a moment. I wasn't making that mistake again.

I turned away. Samir reached out, grabbing at my hand, pulling me back toward him.

"Don't touch me," I snapped.

"Do you want to do this now? In front of everyone? Come with me." He tugged on my hand, curving his fingers on my wrist. They lingered for a moment, just over my pulse, stroking there.

"No."

"I need to explain." His voice was raw. "Please."

"Don't do this to me," I whispered, forgetting I was sup-

posed to be putting on a brave face. He had no idea how he af-
fected me, what this whole summer had been like for me. He
had no idea what the mere touch of his hand did to my body.
Or about the hope I had to beat back to keep from having my
heart crushed again.

I couldn't take a chance on him, couldn't risk the near cer-
tainty of what it would feel like to have my heart broken by
him. Because now that I'd had him—even just for one night—
I knew he wasn't someone I would be able to walk away from
whole.

Samir

I was screwing this up so badly it wasn't even funny.

I'd never been here before, never had to plead with a girl.
Clearly it showed.

"Just give me a few minutes. Just a few minutes alone, and
then you don't have to talk to me again." I swallowed. "Please."

For a moment she didn't answer me—it felt like an eternity.
I'd blown it, I got that. But she had to forgive me. Maybe I
didn't deserve it, but I needed her forgiveness. I needed her,
however I could get her.

Finally, she nodded. "Okay."

I clung to that word like a lifeline.

I reached down between us, grabbing her hand. She flinched
against me, but didn't move away. We stood there for a moment, frozen. It felt strange holding her hand again after all this
time. Strange, yet right.

I led her through the club, my hand pulling her along like a
magnet. The crowd was thick tonight, especially for a Sunday,
but I elbowed my way through.

I stopped in front of the girls' bathroom, hesitating for a moment. Then I pushed open the door.

Behind me, Maggie protested, but I ignored her. The words

had been inside of me, pushing to get out, for months now. I needed this chance to explain. Hurting her was inevitable, always had been. Hadn't I known, even the morning after, that I couldn't keep her?

It didn't matter how much I wanted to.

The startled bathroom attendant gaped at us—specifically, me. "You can't be in here."

Despite her protests, I doubted this was the first time something like this had happened here.

Two girls washed their hands in the sink, their faces avid with interest, but besides them, the bathroom was empty. I pulled out my wallet, peeling off some cash and handing it to the attendant.

"Can you give us five minutes? Please."

She hesitated for a moment before glancing down at the money, and then back at me. Her gaze drifted behind me, focusing on Maggie.

"Is everything okay?"

"I'm fine," Maggie answered, her voice unusually quiet. "We just need a place to talk."

Something tumbled in my gut.

The woman looked back at me before nodding. "Fine. Five minutes." She ushered the other two girls out, leaving Maggie and me alone.

Five minutes. It was a safe amount of time. Short enough to ensure I kept my hands where they belonged—off of her. Long enough for me to explain why things were the way they were.

But the second the room emptied, my words dried up. I was finally alone with her, and I didn't have a thought in my head.

"You wanted your chance. You got it. Talk." Maggie's voice trembled slightly. "You have five minutes, and then I'm gone."

That was the part that scared me the most. I didn't want her to leave, but I couldn't give her enough to make her stay.

Story of my life. Always close, but never quite good enough. Definitely not good enough for her.

It made sense to start with the most important thing I had to say.

"I fucked up. I'm sorry."

4

Maggie

No shit.

"That's what you have to say to me? You fucked up?" He didn't respond. He just stood there, staring at me, his expression blank. "Seriously. That's the best you can do?"

"Look, I know this is coming out all wrong. And I'm sorry. I know you deserve better than this. I'm trying to tell you I'm sorry. For all of it."

"What do you mean 'all of it'?"

"I should never have let things get out of control with you. I should have known better. You're you and I'm me, and I should have known better."

I didn't even know what that meant. We were both speaking English, and yet I needed a dictionary to understand what he was saying.

"You regret having sex with me?"

I pushed away the slice of hurt that knifed through my heart. I'd deal with that later.

Samir closed his eyes. I waited, staring at him, wishing he would just end this. It was like there was still a cord linking us, a tether tying me to him, and if I couldn't have him, then I wanted nothing between us. I'd rather have nothing than live with the memories that gave me hope. They made everything worse.

"Just say it. Say you're sorry we had sex. Say you regret it. Say you wish it never happened. Just say it and let me go." My voice rose with each word, tears filling my eyes. I spun away from him. There was no way I was going to let Samir see me cry. No way I ever wanted him to know I was tangled up inside, that just standing here with him was gutting me.

"I can't."

I turned again. Samir stared back at me.

"I can't say I'm sorry. I'm not sorry, okay? I'm not sorry I kissed you. I'm not sorry I had you in my bed. I'm not sorry that some nights I wake up from a dream of how fucking good it felt to be inside of you. I'm not sorry that every time I look at you, all I can think about is how badly I want to be inside of you again. I'm not sorry I cheated on my girlfriend. And as much as I know it makes me the biggest bastard on the planet, I'm not even sorry that I was your first. I fucking love that I was your first."

I couldn't speak. I couldn't think.

"But I am sorry. I'm so sorry. Because I can't be what you want or what you need."

I just stared at him.

"I don't want to hurt you. I know—I should have told you I'm still with her. I should have explained it to you."

"Why?" It was the only word that filled my head, the only word that escaped from my lips. But there were other words there, too, stuck in between my head and my heart. Words I could never say.

Why her and not me?

Story of my life.

Samir

I tensed. "I don't want to talk about Layla." I hated even saying her name in Maggie's presence.

"Why?" Maggie repeated.

"Because you don't understand. I have responsibilities to my family. Expectations. Layla's father and mine have been political allies for a long time. My mother and her mother are best friends. Our mothers have practically been planning this since we were born."

Maggie was silent for a moment. I desperately wished I could read the emotions brewing in her beautiful brown eyes. She looked down at the floor, and I couldn't see anything anymore.

"Do you love her?" she finally asked.

A pounding noise sounded on the other end of the door.

"Just a minute," we shouted in unison.

Maggie looked up at me. "Well. Do you love her?" Her voice cracked a bit. "Are you happy with her?"

She asked the question like my answer mattered. But I didn't know how to answer that one.

"No. I don't love her. And she definitely doesn't love me. But we both understand what's expected of us after we finish university." I hesitated, torn between needing to be open with her and not wanting to be so honest that she thought I was completely irredeemable.

"I like you, Maggie." She flushed. "But you need to know, what you see with me is pretty much what you get. I can't walk away from my life. I can't promise anything other than a good time. I don't have anything else; everything else isn't mine to give."

Maggie

He was warning me off. I got it.

I didn't know what to say anymore, didn't know what to

make of him. I couldn't spend the whole year like this. We had the same group of friends, the same major. We went to a really small school. Even London felt small when you considered that we frequented the same places, liked the same restaurants. I couldn't avoid him even if I wanted to.

"Okay. Let's just forget this all happened. No one knows about it. It was a onetime thing. We feel awkward now, but I'm sure if we just give each other space, that feeling will eventually go away."

Samir was silent for a moment. "That's what you want?"

No. "Yeah. That's what I want."

"Okay." He hesitated for a moment. "Friends?"

I wasn't sure. Friends seemed a bit optimistic. Right now, I just didn't want to feel like I was dying inside every time I saw him.

"Something like that."

5

Maggie

"How was your first day?" Michael asked. He sat down across from me at the dinner table, tray in hand.

"It was good. Classes were interesting. No major disasters. You?"

"Boring as hell." He grimaced, poking at his food. "What is this? Is it just me, or has the food gotten even worse this year?"

"It's definitely worse," Fleur announced, sinking down into the seat next to mine.

"Did you manage to make it to any of your classes today?" I teased. When I'd left for mine this morning, she'd been curled up in bed, fast asleep.

Fleur rolled her eyes. "Yes, Mom. I went to half of them."

"Didn't you only have two?" Michael interjected.

"Yes. So what?"

I shook my head, affection and exasperation filling me. "So technically you only made it to one class."

"Or I only skipped one," Fleur countered. "I'm improving."

I laughed. "True. I guess it's a matter of perspective."

"What's a matter of perspective?"

Heat rolled over me. *Do not look up. Do not look up.*

Samir stood over me, a smile on his face. Our gazes held for a moment before he sat down next to Michael, directly across from me. I stared down at my plate like it was the most interesting thing in the world.

Do not look up.

I hated my reaction to him, hated that he made me this uncomfortable.

"What did I miss?" Samir asked.

Thankfully Fleur answered for all of us. "Maggie and Michael giving me shit over my attendance—or lack thereof—for the first day of classes."

Samir laughed. "Nice to see little has changed since last year."

Bad choice of words. This time I did look at him. And glare. Apparently he was right. Little had changed. He still had a girlfriend. In the light of sobriety, I was still kind of pissed. I might have agreed to put things behind us, but that didn't mean I had to like it. Or him.

"How was your day?"

I mean, why did he have to sit with us? Didn't he have other friends? Where was Omar? If we were going to do "just friends," I needed a break. He needed to disappear, just for a little while, long enough for me to get my head on straight.

"Maggie?"

My head jerked up. Samir shot me a quizzical look. "I asked how your day was."

I blinked. Why didn't he just announce to the entire table that we'd boned? Samir didn't ask people how their day was, and everyone knew it.

"Fine." My voice came back as an awkward squeak. "It was fine."

"Any hot guys in your classes?" Fleur asked, thankfully oblivious to the undercurrent of nerves and awkwardness swirling around the table.

My face heated. "Not really. There aren't any hot guys in the International Relations department."

"Really? Not a single one?" Samir drawled.

We had the same major. It was petty of me, but I couldn't resist the urge to take a jab at him.

"Nope. None whatsoever." I took a sip from my drink, annoyance filling me. "It's a shame, really. I've heard the finance guys are pretty hot. Maybe I should take some finance classes." I flashed a smile that was all teeth and no joy.

Fleur grinned. "The finance guys are pretty fine."

I leaned forward, some perverse part of me wanting to screw with Samir. "Have you seen Alessandro Marin yet? He looks amazing this year. I saw him in the hall, and he was wearing this gray shirt and jeans. His body—"

Samir stood up, pushing back from the table and lifting his tray. A scowl marred his handsome face.

Fleur frowned. "Where are you going?"

"Out. The food sucks tonight." He shot me a look that said everything. He was pissed, and he knew what I was doing.

I flinched, staring after his retreating back, a sinking feeling in my gut. I hadn't lied when I'd said I wanted things to be normal between us. But everything felt so messed up. I was angry, and I'd never had much success resisting the urge to screw with him. But I also missed him. I couldn't imagine my sophomore year without Samir in it. Somehow we needed to find a way to get past this thing between us.

"Speaking of guys—what's the deal with George?" Fleur asked.

I blinked, tearing my gaze away from Samir. "Excuse me?"

"George. The residence life guy. The one who brought me flowers in the hospital. Aren't you friends with him?"

I felt like my brain was struggling to keep up with the conversation. "Yeah. He's nice. Why?"

"I don't think he likes me very much," Fleur announced.

I'd seen the way George looked at Fleur, so I wasn't so sure about that. "Why?"

"I ran into him today and I said hi. He looked at me like I had two heads. It was totally weird."

Michael snorted. "At least one guy is immune to your charms."

"Only you, baby, and that's because you play for the other team."

Michael laughed. "True. But if I were straight, I'd definitely try to get in your pants."

Fleur blew him a kiss. "That's because you have exquisite taste." She turned her attention back to me. "Seriously though, what do you think his problem is? It was kind of rude."

"I don't think you should take it personally. He's just shy."

"I guess. But I said hi. It wasn't a big deal. How hard would it have been for him to say hi back?"

Given Fleur's reputation? I tried to be diplomatic. "I think you may intimidate him."

Fleur rolled her eyes. "Not that Ice Queen shit again."

"He may have mentioned it once or twice."

"I'm so sick of that stupid nickname. And the asshole who gave it to me," she muttered.

"And who was that?"

Fleur scowled at me. "Someone not worth talking about."

"It *was* well-earned," Michael teased.

I shot him a look. After everything Fleur had been through last year, I was scared of anything that might send her into a re-bound. I alternated between wanting to treat her with care and trying to act like everything was normal. She wouldn't really talk about what had happened—about me finding her on the floor surrounded by pills—but she seemed better. I still couldn't get the image of her lifeless body out of my mind.

"I'm not an ice queen." The hurt in Fleur's voice surprised me.

"I know you're not," I answered. "But maybe you should try letting everyone else see that, too."

"So what, I'm supposed to smile at everyone and start talking about my feelings all the time? I'm not that girl."

"Tell me about it," Michael joked under his breath. I elbowed him. "What? She's not. We all know it."

"You're fine. Exactly as you are."

Fleur made it hard for people to get close to her. There was the public version she gave the world—the girl who kept a tight circle of friends, wasn't accepting of new people and appeared to glide through life, looking down on us mere mortals. Then there was the private Fleur—the friend I'd gotten to know and love—who was fiercely loyal and protective. The girl who made you laugh and could show you the time of your life.

She was quiet for a moment. "Maybe I'll see if George wants to grab coffee or something. I never did thank him for bringing me those flowers."

George was one of the sweetest guys I'd met in London. But I also knew Fleur. She was my best friend and I loved her to death, but she was still a bit of a mess. George wasn't exactly the kind of guy you practiced on.

"Be careful with him, Fleur. He's a nice guy."

A flash of hurt crossed her face. "And what? You think I can't handle a nice guy?"

"No. I think you need a nice guy more than anything. But George has had a crush on you for a while now, and he's my friend, too. I don't want to see him get hurt." I knew firsthand how it felt to want someone you knew was out of your league, how much it hurt when they didn't want you back. "Just be careful. Please."

6

Maggie

We celebrated the end of the first week of school by heading out to a bar in Soho that Fleur had been dying to go to. I dressed casually in a pair of skinny jeans and heels paired with a red halter top. I didn't put too much thought into my outfit because it was supposed to be just the girls. Until Fleur invited Samir and Michael along.

If this continued, I was really going to have to find new friends.

It was already 11:00 p.m. when we arrived and crammed into one of the few tables left, my body squished in between Mya and Michael. Fleur and Samir sat opposite us.

The bar was pretty low-key, just on the edge between trendy and seedy, situated next to a sex shop with a very interesting window display. We didn't come to this part of town a lot, but for some reason, the change fit my mood. Less baggage going to new places.

It had been a weird week. School was great. I had some of the same professors from last year for my IR classes, and thankfully

I was almost done with my prerequisites. Next year I would be able to completely focus on taking courses for my major.

I loved having Mya and Fleur as roommates, and being back in London was amazing. But I couldn't help but feel like something was missing. It wasn't hard to figure out what that "something" was. I'd been avoiding Samir and I blamed the five days since I'd last seen him for the fact that I couldn't take my eyes off him or stop thinking about how good he looked, sitting there across from me.

He looked like he hadn't shaved in days. His face was covered in sexy stubble that made him look way hotter than I was ready to handle.

Mya nudged me. "You okay tonight?"

"Yeah. Just thinking."

"You seem quieter than normal."

My cheeks heated. "I'm fine." Somehow I managed a smile. "I'm a little tired."

It was awkward as hell pretending things were normal between me and Samir. I didn't want to have to look at him, was afraid I still couldn't without wearing my emotions on my face. I kept thinking if I just waited, if time passed, one day I would see him and not feel like I was at the peak of a roller coaster, my body poised to hurtle to the ground.

They said time healed all wounds. Or something like that. But then I saw him, and suddenly time didn't matter anymore.

"Want to dance?"

My head jerked up.

"Want to dance?" Samir repeated.

I waited to see if anyone would notice. But Fleur and Michael were deep in conversation about something, and Mya was playing with her phone.

Dancing seemed like the worst idea I could think of. I could barely stand to look at him. How was I supposed to handle being in his arms, my body pressed up against his? How was I supposed to pretend I didn't want more than a dance?

But I never could resist him.

I rose from the table and took the hand he extended.

Samir

I led her to the small dance floor, her hand clutched in mine.

I didn't feel like dancing. It was, if anything, a pathetic excuse for me to touch her. If everything weren't so fucked up, I would have laughed. How many times had I barely crooked my finger and girls had landed in my bed? Getting laid had never been a challenge for me. Here I was, *not* getting laid, trying to avoid it, in fact, yet desperate to hold a girl's hand. Maggie's hand.

I pulled her against my body, wrapping my arm around her waist. She was flush against me, and I was hard, and I knew she knew, and I didn't care.

I needed this. Just for a moment. Just a dance.

She didn't speak, which was fine with me. Talking seemed to complicate things with us. Everything I tried to say either stuck in my throat or came out wrong. I was scared to speak at all, worried I would only make things worse.

For now, I had her exactly where I wanted her, her gorgeous body pressed up against mine, and I couldn't resist the urge to move my fingers a little higher, up from her waist to the bare skin exposed by her top's open back. Her skin was warm beneath my touch, silky smooth under my fingers.

For a moment, I imagined it was just the two of us. That I could reach up and untie the strings at her neck, pulling her top down, baring those gorgeous tits to my eyes and hands and lips. I wanted to cup them, run my fingers and lips all over her nipples. I wanted to taste her in my mouth, to drown in her scent.

Maggie shot me a strange look.

I coughed, wondering if she'd caught me staring at her,

struggling to put the image of her naked body out of my mind. "Sorry."

The song ended, but I didn't release her. Another song started up and I couldn't resist keeping her in my arms, maneuvering her out of sight of our friends. I was stealing time with her, minute by minute, trying to borrow a future we could never have.

"I didn't see much of you this week." I didn't add the rest of it—*I missed you*.

For a moment, she looked embarrassed. Then she shrugged. Did she know how often she did that now? My lips twitched. Somehow she seemed to have picked up my shrug.

"I was kind of avoiding you."

"Avoiding me?"

She nodded.

"I thought we were doing the friends thing."

She met my gaze and held it for a moment. "I don't know how to be your friend."

"We were friends before…" I thought of all the times we'd kissed, from that first night at Babel to our trip to Italy. I thought about our "kissing lessons" and playing strip rummy in Paris. Of all the times I'd wanted her, all the times I'd been desperate to have her. Okay, so we'd been friends who kissed. I might have wanted her in my bed from the beginning, but still, I hadn't acted on it. That had to count for something. "Sort of."

Her lips quirked. "Sort of."

Those two words perfectly summed up the ambiguity of our relationship…or whatever it was.

"I want to be your friend." Besides Fleur—and she didn't totally count, since she was family—I didn't exactly have female friends. But I wanted to be friends with Maggie. It wasn't nearly enough, but it was better than the alternative. "Can we start over?"

She sighed. "What is this, like our fourth fresh start?"

"Maybe."

"What did you have in mind?"

"I have no clue."

"Me, either. But it doesn't seem like it should be this hard."

I knew what she meant. "Fine. Let's not let it be hard then. Let's act like everything is normal between us. Like things are the way they used to be."

Let's pretend.

"How are your classes?" I asked her.

"Good. Yours?"

"Boring." I flashed her a grin, unable to resist. "You look beautiful tonight."

She blushed, and my heartbeat sped up. "I don't think friends are supposed to say things like that."

"You mean Fleur didn't tell you that you looked good tonight?"

Maggie considered this. "Actually, Fleur told me I looked fucking hot."

"Well, she's right, but beautiful seemed friendlier." I winked at her. "See? Trying."

"I thought you didn't do that."

"Do what?"

"Try."

"If you think that, then you haven't been paying attention." She shook her head. "What are we doing here?"

"Not fucking?"

That startled a laugh out of her. I'd missed hearing her laugh.

"Has anyone told you you're kind of impossible?" she asked me.

"Yes. You. All the time. But you like it. A lot. You can't resist my charm." I was determined to tease whatever awkwardness lingered between us out of her. Even if the teasing bordered on flirting.

"You're not nearly as charming as you think."

"Maybe not, but you like it."

"Maybe I do." She shook her head, resignation filling her eyes. "This is so fucked up."

It was, but it was also us. I'd take it any way I could get it. I'd take her any way I could get her.

7

Maggie

"Are we going to talk about it?" Mya asked, looking up from her dinner.

"Talk about what?"

"Last night. You and Samir."

"What about me and Samir?"

"You guys have been weird ever since this semester started. Half the time you won't look at him, and he looks at you like you're a tall glass of water and he's dying of thirst."

"That's ridiculous." I struggled not to react even as her words sent a funny thrill through me. "That's just how Samir is. You know that."

"Come on. He didn't talk or dance with one girl last night. Hell, he didn't even check anyone out."

"He has a girlfriend. There's nothing between me and Samir."

"You sure about that?"

"Yes."

She looked totally unconvinced. There was only one way

this could get worse. "You haven't said anything to Fleur, have you? About your suspicions?"

Mya shook her head.

"Please don't. There's nothing going on." *Anymore.* "I swear."

The last thing I needed was for Fleur to think I was somehow involved with her cousin. I wasn't sure if she'd be pissed or feel sorry for me. Probably a combination of both.

"I won't. Just promise that if you ever need to talk, you'll tell me."

"I promise."

"Promise what?" Fleur slid into the seat next to me, a tray of food in hand.

I flushed. "Nothing important. How's your day going?"

"Good. By the way, George is going to sit with us."

"Seriously?"

"I invited him. He said yes."

Mya and I gaped at her.

"What's the big deal? You both told me I needed to find a nice guy. In fact, I seem to remember both of you bitching at me because of Costa." My jaw dropped. Fleur never said his name.

"We didn't think you would actually listen to us," Mya answered.

"I didn't ask him to marry me. I invited him to eat dinner with us. It's only a big deal if you make it one."

Or if George made it one. I was happy for them, but worried at the same time.

"Hi, Maggie."

I looked up to see George standing in front of us, an uncomfortable expression on his face. I stood and gave him a hug.

George was a member of the residence life staff and one of the few British students at the International School. He was tall, blond, and cute in a boy-next-door sort of way. And he was totally, completely head over heels for Fleur—a fact he'd managed to hide from me until she'd landed herself in the hospital last spring.

"Come join us."

I slid my chair over, making room for him at the table. He fumbled with his tray for a moment before settling into the seat next to mine. I felt a pang of sympathy for him. It wasn't too long ago that I'd felt the same way—nervous, awkward, completely intimidated by the International School glitterati.

The George I'd gotten to know last year was confident and fun. This version was... different. Fleur seemed to reduce him to a pile of nerves.

We talked for a few minutes about our summers. Finally, Mya shot me a look, wiggling her eyebrows suggestively toward Fleur and George.

What? I mouthed.

Suddenly Mya coughed loudly. "I think I'm going to head to the library and do some studying."

Ahh. "Yeah, me, too." Fleur shot us both a look filled with suspicion. George just looked uncomfortable.

I grinned, grabbing my tray and pushing away from the table. "See you guys later."

Mya and I walked out of the cafeteria together.

"Okay, it's a little weird, right? Fleur and George?" she asked.

"I guess. I mean, I figured he had a thing for her last year. I just wasn't sure if she'd ever be interested in him. He's a great guy, but yeah, he's not exactly her type. Although George would be a billion times better for her than Costa ever was." My eyes narrowed. "Where is Costa, anyway? I haven't seen him around this year."

"You didn't hear?"

"Obviously not." I'd been so consumed by my current situation with Samir that I'd barely paid attention to the usual International School gossip.

"He transferred."

"Really?"

"Yeah. The rumor is that his parents pulled him out of school and sent him somewhere in the US." Mya lowered her voice, stepping closer to me. "You absolutely cannot tell Fleur, but I heard his parents found out he got a girl pregnant while he was here, and they flipped out."

Horror filled me.

"Seriously, though, that's supersecret. You can't tell anyone. Especially Fleur. I don't think she could handle it right now."

It was a minute before I could formulate a response. Because I knew something Mya didn't and I had a pretty good idea of who the girl in question was. Fleur was going to freak out. I didn't know how to break it to her, but she had to know what people were saying before someone blindsided her with it.

Mya gestured toward the library. "Do you want to come study?"

"Go on ahead. I'm not in a studying mood."

I wanted a chance to talk to Fleur. If she was going to hear about Costa from someone, I wanted it to be me.

Samir

I hit "end" on my phone, shoving it back into my pocket.

My conversations with Layla were always like this— awkward. I'd known her most of my life, and we'd seen each other at enough events, but we'd never really been friends or anything. She was nice, but we had nothing in common and I suspected I made her just as uncomfortable as she made me. She seemed about as into our "relationship" as I was.

I was trying to do this right. Trying to be a good boyfriend and call her to see how she was doing. I was trying. But I sucked at it, and I was so sick of trying.

I pulled a cigarette out of my pocket, fumbling for my lighter. Then I saw her, and a slow smile spread across my face.

I couldn't help it; the damn thing just appeared every time I caught sight of her.

She sat on the steps, her knees pulled up against her chest, her long brown hair falling all around her.

"Hi."

Maggie's head jerked up and her lips slowly curved. Any lingering awkwardness evaporated with that smile.

"Hi."

"What are you doing out here?" I walked up to the top step where she sat.

"Waiting for Fleur."

I sank down next to her. "Is everything okay?"

She hesitated for a moment, and I knew whatever answer she gave wouldn't be completely the truth. I hated that there were things she didn't seem to be willing to trust me with.

"Yeah, everything's fine."

"I don't believe you."

"I know. But I can't talk about it."

I was silent for a moment. "Just tell me this at least—are you okay?"

"I'm fine."

I lit the cigarette, positioning my body so the smoke would blow away from her. I knew she didn't like this habit of mine and I tried not to smoke around her, but I needed a cigarette right now, needed something to take the edge off after my conversation with Layla.

"Where is Fleur?"

"In the cafeteria with George."

I made a face. "Sorry, but you know that's the worst idea ever."

"It's not," Maggie protested. "He's a good guy. He really seems to like her."

I loved Fleur, but I'd had a few classes with George. There was no way he could handle someone like Fleur. She'd chew him up and spit him out without even meaning to. The hope in Maggie's eyes was the only thing that had me refraining from saying so.

People like Fleur and me were too fucked up for nice, normal people. We hurt them without even meaning to, let them down without even realizing it. We should come with a warning label.

"You're matchmaking."

"Maybe."

I grinned, reaching out and tucking a stray strand of hair behind her ear. I'd never thought cute could be sexy before her, but she was so adorable I couldn't resist.

For a moment, my fingers lingered against her skin.

The pink shade on her cheeks deepened. "Thanks," she mumbled.

"My pleasure."

"Are you like this with everyone? Or am I just lucky?" she asked, her voice tart.

"Like what?"

"Turning every word into a proposition?"

I laughed. "Only for you, babe."

She shoved me playfully and all I could think was, *Don't ever take your hands off of me. Please.*

We faced off across from each other, her hands on my chest. She was close enough that if I just leaned forward, I could kiss her. Our breath mingled, our faces nearly touching. Her fingers curled into the fabric of my jacket, holding me in place. I didn't move. I just sat there, staring at her. Waiting to see what she would do next, wondering how I would respond. There was an invitation in her eyes that made me want to close the distance between us. There was a defensiveness in her stance that held me back.

Suddenly Maggie broke the connection, looking away from me. She reached down, grabbing her bag. I sat there, watching her, my hands at my sides, struggling not to reach out and take what I so desperately wanted.

Whatever had passed between us disappeared as quickly as it had flared. Its absence left a chill in the air.

"I'm going to head back to the dorm," Maggie announced.

"I thought you were waiting for Fleur."

"I better go before you do full-on proposition me here on the steps."

Her words were light, but her eyes and her voice were sad. I knew what she was trying to do, hated faking it with her. But I played along. It was easier not to be serious with her.

"I bet I could have you naked in three minutes flat."

She laughed, the sound filling the air. "Come on, Samir. It would take at least ten."

"Then it would be the best ten minutes of my life," I answered honestly.

She turned away for a moment, hiding her face, before looking back at me. "I'll see you around."

I wanted to ask her to stay. I wanted to keep joking with her, talking with her, anything to keep her near me. I wanted to strip her naked on the steps. I wanted it all, and I had a right to none of it. So, I simply nodded.

"See you around."

I watched her walk away, her hips swaying and hair swinging, and I couldn't help but feel like her departure had taken all the laughter out of the air.

I sat on the steps, staring out at the sky, taking another drag from my cigarette. It was all I could do to keep from calling her back to me.

8

Maggie

It took me ten minutes to get my shit together after seeing Samir out on the steps. Twenty before I was able to think about something other than how good it felt when he touched me, how easy it had been to laugh around him. It took me opening a book to clear my head. I was still reading when I heard the door opening.

Fleur walked into the room.

I wasn't even sure how to start this conversation. I didn't know how Fleur was going to take it, or if she was even strong enough to hear it right now. But she deserved to hear it from someone who cared about her rather than someone looking for a piece of gossip.

"Nice job back there in the cafeteria. Way to be smooth."

"It was all Mya."

Fleur shot me a look. "Sure, it was."

"How did it go?"

Fleur sank down on the bed across from me. "It was good, I think. I don't know. He's nice. Quiet. I've never been with a guy like that before. But he's also so shy. It's hard to get him to talk."

"I think it's you. Honestly, I've known him for a year now, and he's fun. I think you intimidate him."

Fleur frowned. "I'm not trying to."

"I know. But I think he has this image of you built up in his head."

She sighed. "I just wish he would let go a bit. I think I could like him if he were more relaxed with me. Half the time we just stare at each other, and he doesn't even talk. And when he does talk, I have no clue what he's talking about. He's so smart. I feel like an idiot around him."

Surprise filled me. "You're not an idiot."

"Well, I feel like one. Did you know he's a history major?"

I nodded.

"He talks about all these old wars; I've never even heard of half of them."

"I don't think knowing about old wars makes you smart."

"I'm fairly sure it does in his book. And I can't help but feel like he thinks I'm a moron."

"Fleur, he doesn't."

"His friend does."

"Which friend?"

"That guy Max. The American one."

"I don't know him."

"Oh, come on. You totally do. He's the super-boring guy with the underwear model's body. I swear, you can practically see how cut his abs are through his T-shirts." She shrugged. "He works out at my gym."

I cracked up. "Definitely don't know who you're talking about."

"Whatever. We've had a few classes together, and he's a total dick. He got pissed at me one time because I was texting in class next to him. Said it was distracting."

As nice as George was, I had a hard time believing he'd be friends with a dick. "It is a little annoying when people do that."

Fleur glared at me. "It was microeconomics. Do you know how boring microeconomics is?"

I laughed. "Fine. Fair enough. I'm sorry I questioned your right to text."

"Whatever. I like George. I think. Despite his tendency to talk about old wars and his bad choice in friends."

"If that's not a ringing endorsement…" I joked.

Fleur chucked her pillow at me. "Laugh all you want. I'm trying here. You told me to find a nice guy. I'm trying to find a nice guy. It's not as easy as it looks."

Tell me about it.

"What about you?"

"What do you mean?"

"Well, now that the Hugh thing is over, what's next? Any cute guys on the horizon?"

I grimaced. "Not even kind of."

Fleur sighed, leaning back on her bed. "We're a fine pair, aren't we?"

Yep, we both put the "fun" in dysfunctional when it came to romance.

It was now or never. "I need to talk to you about something. I don't want you to freak out and I hate having to tell you this, but I also don't want you to hear it from anyone else."

"Okay."

"There's a rumor going around here that Costa had to transfer out of the International School because his parents found out he got a girl pregnant while he was a student."

Fleur paled.

"No one knows who it is," I continued, "and it's a really quiet rumor. But I thought you should know."

"Oh my god."

"No one knows it was you. And with Costa gone, there's a good chance no one will ever find out."

Fleur shot me a horrified look. "This cannot be happening. That was over a year and a half ago. How are they just now finding out about it? How did they find out about it at all? Why the hell do they even care?"

"I'm so sorry."

"Do you know how bad it will be if this gets out? You've seen what the gossip here is like. Let's be honest, people *hate* me. This is exactly the kind of story that's going to spread around school like wildfire."

She was probably right about all of it, and I had no idea what to say to make her feel better.

"You can't freak out. You don't even know if anyone knows it was you. Costa may not have told anyone. And besides, even if it does get out, you have nothing to be ashamed of. What happened to you could have happened to anyone. No one has the right to judge you for having sex with your boyfriend. You didn't do anything wrong."

"Someone thinks I did." Fleur reached into her bag and took out her phone. She pulled something up on the screen and handed it to me.

Shock filled me at the words on the screen. It was an email from an account that looked anonymous. The email was two lines.

I know your secret. Fifteen thousand pounds buys my silence.

I met her gaze. "When did you get this?"

"A couple days ago." Fleur's expression was grim. "I thought it was a stupid prank or something. I didn't know what secret it could be referring to. But if someone knows about the baby, maybe this is related."

"Do you think it's from Natasha?"

Costa's current girlfriend hated Fleur. If I were going to start somewhere, I would start with her. I didn't know if she'd ever figured out that Costa had been fooling around with Fleur last year, but if she had, it would be a game changer.

"I don't know. She hates me enough. I thought about confronting her, but if it isn't her, I don't want her to realize she could have ammunition on me. I don't want to give her the satisfaction of thinking I'm rattled by this."

Her words were tough, but the look on her face said it all. Fleur was hanging on by a thread.

"You can't tell anyone. I'm not ready for anyone else to know about it yet."

"Not even Samir?"

"No one can know. Promise me."

"I think it would be better if you have help with this. But if you don't want me to say anything, I won't. What are you going to do?"

"I don't know." Tears welled up in Fleur's eyes. "I can't talk about it. I can't talk about the miscarriage. I can't talk about any of it. You don't know what it was like. No one does." A sob escaped. "I just want to move on. I want to put all this behind me and move on. I thought it would be easier with Costa gone. But no matter how hard I fucking try, I can't."

I hurt for her. I joined her on the bed, wrapping my arms around her while she cried.

"It's going to be okay," I whispered. "We all have your back. You don't have to talk about it if you don't want to. You're right—what happened is no one's business. But you have people who love you, and you aren't alone in this."

Fleur wiped at her eyes, pulling away from me. "Thank you. I know. It's just hard." She sighed. "Do you think I don't know people talk about me? That every time I enter the room everyone whispers about how I'm the girl who overdosed last semester. They all think the worst of me. They all think I'm just some party girl who deserves everything that's happened."

Fleur wasn't well-liked, and she had a reputation. It was tough. She was easily the most beautiful girl at the International School. Add in the gobs of money that kept her in Manolo Blahnik and Fendi, and she wasn't exactly the most sympathetic figure. And Fleur knew she was gorgeous. She walked around campus like she owned it. Even with the current gossip going around, I'd yet to see her duck her head or give an inch. If not for the fact that she was currently sobbing in my arms, I never would have imagined anyone could hurt her. Which was silly, of course. I knew better than anyone—the most painful scars were the ones we didn't show the rest of the world.

"The people who love you—me, Mya, Michael, Samir— we'll always be here for you. I promise."

"Thank you," she whispered, offering me a weak smile.

"For what it's worth, I think you're the strongest person I know."

Fleur laughed. "I find that really hard to believe."

"No. You are. You face the world head-on. You don't apologize for yourself; you don't let life get you down. You're human. You make mistakes. Bad shit happens to you. But every morning you wake up ready to conquer the world—and you look fabulous while doing so. You're an amazing friend. And I love you."

I didn't say "I love you" a lot. I told my grandmother I loved her, and that was about it. My dad had never said it. Maybe my mom had when I was younger, before she'd left without looking back. I didn't really remember. But in that moment, I knew I loved Fleur. On the surface we were so different. She was everything I wanted to be at times—strong, confident, fearless—and yet I saw so much of myself in her. She got me as very few people did. I was close to her in a way I would never be with Mya.

Fleur and I shared an understanding. Because underneath all the differences, on a fundamental level, she knew what it was like to not feel worthy of being loved.

And I, better than anyone, knew how much that could fuck you up.

9

Samir

I hesitated, my hand pressed against the wood-paneled door. *Walk upstairs. Do not go into the common room. Don't. Just don't.*

We were both night owls. I knew how much Maggie liked to hang out in the common room watching TV. I had a TV in my room, and yet last year I'd always found myself down here. This year, I'd been trying to avoid it. There was an intimacy to hanging out with Maggie at night. An intimacy that started out on a couch and ended up in bed.

It had been hours since I'd seen her on the steps, and I couldn't get the image out of my mind. She'd looked lost, and whatever was bothering her seemed to be wearing on her.

I pushed open the door, striding into the one room I'd avoided since coming back to London. In part because of the danger of being around her like this, and in part because I wasn't sure I wanted to confront the memories. This was where everything had changed, and it all hit me at once.

Just being in the common room reminded me of that night. Made me remember what it felt like to have her. It reminded me of the feeling of her legs wrapped around me, her ass in my hands, her tongue in my mouth. But the memories weren't the only reason I'd been avoiding this room. The other very big reason sat curled up on the couch, dressed in a sweater and shorts, her legs bare.

Her surprised gaze met mine, and for a moment a flash of unease crossed her face.

"Hi." Her voice was soft and smooth, filled with just the barest hint of the Southern accent I knew she hated, but I secretly loved.

"Hi," I echoed. It was 2:00 a.m. We had the common room all to ourselves. A wiser man would have turned and left. My feet carried me toward her.

"Can't sleep?"

She shook her head, wrapping the sweater tighter around her body.

"You?"

"Same."

I didn't add that I couldn't sleep because I'd spent the last hour in my bed, reliving the memory of her there. It was torture having the same room I'd had last year. Absolute torture.

"Are you just going to stand there? Or do you want to sit?"

Actually, I'd like to bury myself in your body.

"Sure."

I sank down on the couch next to her, careful to keep some space between us. It hit me at the exact same moment that a blush spread across her cheeks—

This was *our* couch. This was the couch that had started it all.

Minutes passed with silence between us. It wasn't comfortable silence. It was agonizingly awkward, but I literally couldn't think of one thing to say to her.

She ran her hand through her hair, the silky strands slipping through her fingers. The scent of her shampoo filled the air. She smelled like vanilla and cookies. I was instantly hard and strangely hungry.

"How is everything?"

I struggled to concentrate on her question. "Fine. Good."
Better now. "I was surprised I didn't see you in any of my classes."

Maggie grinned. "I have mostly morning classes."

"That explains it, then."

"Is it weird, knowing this is your last year of university?"

"I don't want it to end." I laughed at my words, realizing
how big a cliché I was. The boy who didn't want to grow up.

"I know what you mean."

I hated the sadness in her voice. "Rough time at home this
summer?"

"I don't know. It wasn't one thing. It was just…everything. I
felt so trapped there. I love my grandparents. I mean, seriously,
they're amazing. But I can't be myself. I'm this other person.
This girl who doesn't rock the boat and says 'yes, ma'am,' and
'no, sir' and plays by the rules. And it's not that I want to cause
trouble for them—I just sometimes don't want to have to be
that person. I don't want to have to pretend everything's fine
when it's not. That I'm not angry, when I am." Her voice was
raw. "I'm so tired of pretending. So tired of working so hard to
be good. It's exhausting pretending to be someone you're not."

Her words gutted me. With each word, something unraveled within me. I'd never heard anyone say exactly what I always felt. I knew what it was like to feel trapped in your own
body, like you were playing a role you desperately wanted to
break out from. I hated that she felt that way.

"You don't have to pretend with me."

Her eyes widened slightly.

I shrugged, embarrassment filling me. "I'm just saying. If
we're going to be friends, then you shouldn't feel like you can't
be yourself with me."

"You sure about that?" she asked, and I was relieved to hear
the teasing note in her voice. "I've been known to give you a
hard time."

"I don't mind."

She laughed, the sound full and rich. "Really?"

"Really." I nudged her with my knee. "It's nice. I like being friends. I've missed just hanging out."

What was wrong with me? This shit just kept coming out of my mouth, and there wasn't a damn thing I could do about it.

"I missed hanging out, too."

"See? We can do this, right? Be friends." I just had to keep my dick under control. So far, so good.

"True." She tucked her legs up to her chest, her body curling up into a little ball. She looked so comfortable, so perfect just sitting there. I shifted on the couch slightly, my leg brushing against hers. Okay, yes, maybe I did it on purpose, but I couldn't resist.

Besides, as long as I didn't kiss her, as long as I didn't run my hands under her sweater, caressing her skin, stripping that sweater off, all would be good.

I could do friends. Especially if it meant I could touch her. Even just a bit.

Maggie

The second his leg brushed mine, a wave of heat spread through my body. It was weird. I was still annoyed about the girlfriend thing, still pissed at him on some level. At least I had been. But now, sitting next to him on the couch, I didn't really care. There was something comfortable between us, underneath the tension and the awkwardness. It had been there last year when we'd barely known each other. It was the thing that made me share more with him than I did with most people.

I could be myself with Samir. I'd missed that. In between the butterflies and the nerves and the desire to pull out my hair, there were these moments when I felt peace. Maybe the sex stuff just complicated things. Maybe we were just supposed to be friends.

His leg was still there, resting near mine. Samir's face was turned away from me, watching the TV. Did he realize where his leg was? Did he even care?

Was this in the friend code? I had no idea what the rules were for a guy you were friends (ish) with, then slept with, and were then friends with again. But then again, I wasn't the one with the girlfriend. Even though I knew it was wrong, it felt too good to walk away from. I wouldn't move closer, but I wouldn't pull away—

"You look really uncomfortable," Samir said, a smile tugging at his lips.

My body was contorted in a weird angle, my leg the only part even close to him.

"I'm fine."

He sighed, raising his arm to the back of the couch. "Come here." He gestured to the space beside him.

"I'm okay."

"I promise I can stand you sitting next to me. We're friends right? Friends can lie beside each other on the couch and watch movies."

I pulled a face.

"They can. Come on. Just think of me as Michael. You'd lie next to him."

"Yeah, but I wouldn't be worried about Michael getting turned on by me sitting next to him."

"I can behave," he protested. "Come here."

I wasn't stupid. I knew by now that I couldn't control myself around him. I knew staying away from him was in my best interest and his. I knew better than to let myself get close to him, than to let him inside. And yet, as hard as I tried to resist, he was like a magnet pulling me closer. He made me reckless, and I'd never been reckless before him.

I shifted on the couch, moving my body closer to his. He closed the distance between us, tucking me against his body like a puzzle piece snapping into place.

"Comfortable?"

Not even kind of.

It was the worst kind of agony. I was close enough to smell his cologne, feel his strong body beside mine. His breath tickled my ear. His hands hovered dangerously close to places that burned for him. He was so close—and yet so far.

"Yep."

He pulled me even tighter against his body, a sigh escaping his lips. We both stared at the TV, neither one of us speaking.

There was nothing to say. We flirted around a line, dipping a toe or two over and then jumping back again. We played with fire, dancing on the precipice of something we couldn't come back from.

I was so afraid I would fall.

10

Samir

"Why are you being so weird?" Fleur asked me in French.

Most of the time we spoke in English at school—but sometimes, when she wanted to talk to me about something important or private, she switched to French.

I moved down the hallway, my strides impatient. I wasn't in the mood to get harassed by Fleur. It was the second week of classes and things were still a mess with Maggie. I was still a mess.

"I'm not being weird."

"I've barely seen you all semester."

"School has been back for a few weeks. It's hardly been 'all semester.'"

"Well, I didn't see you much this summer, either."

I'd tried my best to check in on her, but much like my life, my summer had not been my own. "I told you, I was working for my dad. We couldn't all spend the summer on a yacht in the South of France."

I was being an ass. I was angry and taking it out on her, which wasn't fair. I couldn't seem to control it, though. This gnawing frustration had been building, and was infinitely worse after seeing Maggie in the common room. I'd thought allowing myself small doses would be enough. Turned out it only made things worse.

"You seem on edge. Snappy."

"I'm not on edge."

Okay, maybe yes, I was a little on edge. I'd been chain-smoking like a maniac, and tension coursed through my body.

"You look like you need to get laid."

I froze in midstep. "Excuse me?"

Fleur fisted her hands on her hips. "You do. You definitely look like you're hurting for it."

"I don't want to talk about it. I have class in like five minutes and then I'm hanging out with Omar."

"I feel like you're avoiding me."

"I'm not avoiding you." I was, a bit. But it was hard being around her with the whole Maggie situation going on. We were trying to act like nothing had happened between us. I didn't need Fleur getting involved. "We'll hang out, I promise. Let's make a plan for next week."

"Want to go bowling?"

I stopped in my tracks. For like the millionth time today, Fleur had completely caught me off guard. "Excuse me?"

"Bowling. Tonight. In Holborn. There's a group of us going."

"Bowling?"

"It might be fun."

"Okay, you're asking me why *I'm* being weird? Since when do you bowl?"

"George is going."

"George?"

She flushed. "He's nice."

"Sure he is."

I knew Fleur had changed after her overdose, but I hadn't realized she'd basically had a lobotomy. If Fleur was going bowling, then hell had officially frozen over. Although I wasn't sure what was weirder: that she was going bowling, or that she was going bowling with a guy like George.

"He *is* nice. You should give him a chance."

"That's not what I do. You either. What gives?"

"I'm turning over a new leaf. Maggie suggested it. I think she may be onto something. Besides, you know how Maggie is. Once she gets her mind on something, there's no turning back."

I did know Maggie. Maybe better than anyone. That was the problem. She was frustrating and exciting and confusing. She was hard to read and impossible to forget. And she was killing my sanity.

"Are you coming or not?"

"Definitely not. I have no desire to bowl. I'm pretty sure there isn't any amount of money you could give me to make me even consider it. Besides, George is not my idea of a good time. The guy's less exciting than a trip to the dentist. I don't care how *nice* he is."

Fleur glared at me. "Fine. The rest of us will have fun without you."

"Is this a group date?"

"I told you. Maggie's the one pushing us to go out. She organized it."

Motherfucker.

"Maggie's going?"

"Yeah, it was her idea. She thought it would make George more comfortable to do something on his terms."

How was I going to tell her I wanted to go now?

My resolve was crumbling. Maybe it had never been there to begin with. My efforts had been half-assed at best. At a school this small, it was difficult enough to try to avoid Maggie, harder still when I didn't want to.

"Makes sense." I hesitated for a moment, not used to having to explain myself. "Okay fine, if everyone else is going, I'll go."

"Are you serious? After all that, now you want to go?"

"I didn't say I wanted to go," I lied. "But I'll go."

Fleur's eyes narrowed. "Are you just going to make fun of George?"

"No."

"Seriously, you have to promise not to make fun of him."

I was surprised she even cared—it was unlike her to be this concerned about someone boring like George.

"Fine. I promise."

There was one reason I was going bowling, and it had nothing to do with George.

Maggie

"You guys ready?"

There were six of us—me, Michael, Mya, Fleur, George, and George's friend Max. Max was a year ahead of me and though I hadn't met him before, he seemed nice enough. Hopefully, his presence would make things a little less awkward for George.

I loved bowling. Jo and I bowled all the time in South Carolina. I wasn't any good, but it was a ton of fun. Plus, I couldn't resist the idea of Fleur in rented shoes.

"We're just waiting for one other person," Fleur called out.

"Who?" My body collided with someone. I looked up—

"Me." Samir grinned, and my heart lurched like a boulder tumbling off a cliff. "Sorry I'm late."

"You're going bowling?"

His smile deepened. "Yes."

"Bowling? Like rented shoes and pizza and eighties music? Bowling?"

He laughed, the sound reverberating through my body, all the way down to my toes.

"Why?"

Samir draped an arm around my shoulders, pulling me toward the door. "It sounded like fun."

I looked up at him. "Okay, who are you and what have you done with Samir?"

Fleur laughed behind me. "That's what I said."

Samir leaned down, his lips grazing my ear as if he were telling me a secret. "Maybe I'm not here for the bowling. Maybe I'm here for the company."

Our gazes met. For a moment, I couldn't breathe. There was something in his eyes that made me think he wasn't teasing. This felt like full-on flirting. More than pretending to be friends.

I let him maneuver me down the steps before he finally released me. I immediately missed the feel of his arm around my shoulders, of my body near his. I struggled for nonchalance, trying to put some space between us, trying to get my silly, racing heart under control.

Mya shot me a look, linking arms with me. "Still sure nothing is going on?"

"Nothing at all," I lied.

We walked toward Gloucester Road tube station, heading for the Piccadilly line to Holborn. It was late enough that the streets were crowded with people on their way home from work. We walked as a group, occasionally separated by the stray pedestrian marching toward the station. I spent most of the time talking to Michael about his semester. He had a new boyfriend and had been spending most of his time with him. The rest of the group was quiet.

We all piled onto the tube, mashed against each other in the melee that was standard for London. I usually tried to avoid the Piccadilly line at rush hour when you got the truly awful combination of pissed-off commuters and wide-eyed tourists. Everyone sort of existed in a simmering rage, fueled by frequent delays.

By the time we got to Holborn and up to the street level, I felt like I'd just run a mile.

We walked toward the bowling alley, conversation picking up now. I checked out for a bit, my attention completely focused on my surroundings. I loved Holborn. For me, it was London at its most academic. It was the home of the London School of Economics, the Holy Grail of IR. They had these amazing lecture series that were open to the public; sometimes I'd go and listen to their world-class speakers. I'd sit in the audience and pretend I was a student there, doing a master's.

"Daydreaming?"

I turned and grinned at Samir. As an IR major, he understood what this place meant better than anyone.

"Maybe."

"Are you going to apply your senior year? You should."

"I might. It's competitive, though."

"True. But you're smart. You at least have to try."

He matched his pace with mine, walking beside me down the street. We'd broken off from the others; I wasn't sure if he'd meant to do it or not. For a few minutes, neither one of us spoke. His shoulder brushed against mine a few times, that alone filling me with anticipation.

"Fleur wearing rented, fake leather shoes. Highlight of your night?"

I giggled. "Definite highlight. I'm taking a photo."

He grinned, and for a moment it felt like we were sharing a secret.

"She must really like him."

"Why do you say that?"

He shrugged, a little smile on his face. "Because we all do things that are out of character when we really like someone."

I froze, my heart stumbling in my chest. "We? I thought that wasn't your style."

"Maybe I'm not the guy I used to be. Maybe I never liked

anyone enough." He paused for what felt like an eternity. "Until now."

I stared back at him, unable to formulate a response. I wasn't sure what that meant, and part of me was afraid to ask. Something was up tonight. There was something different between us. I couldn't read him, couldn't guess what he wanted. It felt like we were always a beat out of sync.

We walked the rest of the way to the bowling alley in silence.

"Hey, Maggie." I turned at the sound of Mya's voice. "We're forming teams. Why don't you and Max team up?" She shot me a knowing look that wasn't even kind of subtle.

Samir stiffened beside me.

"Sure."

I smiled at Max. He was cute, with dark brown hair and green eyes. He had that all-American look I'd become familiar with back home. He did look built, although sadly I couldn't make out the outline of the famous abs. I'd have to take Fleur's word for it.

I could see why Mya thought we would be a good fit. We had the American thing in common, and he seemed nice enough. But I wasn't that girl. Stupidly, maybe, all my attention was focused on the brooding and off-limits boy beside me.

We all got our shoes and headed toward the lanes. The bowling alley was upscale, with almost a nightclub feel to it—so different from the rundown place I bowled at back in South Carolina. Fleur looked predictably put out by the whole thing, but surprisingly, she seemed to be trying. Samir hadn't even bothered renting shoes. He'd decided he would just watch. Which I soon discovered meant he would watch *me*.

The first few games went by quickly. Max was easily the best in the group, so it wasn't a surprise when we immediately took the lead. Fleur was hopeless. But even she settled into the spirit of it all and was soon laughing with the rest of us.

And all the while I could feel Samir's eyes on me as he sat at the table, slowly nursing his whiskey and Coke.

Samir

It made her happy—bowling.

Her smile lit up the room and her laughter filled it, and I wanted her so badly it hurt.

I'd never met anyone like her. She didn't seem to care that we were in a bowling alley. She was just as happy here as she was sitting in the VIP section at a club. She treated life like everything was an adventure, and found pleasure in the littlest of things. I couldn't remember the last time I'd felt like that. Couldn't remember the last time I'd been so taken by something or surprised by anything. Couldn't remember feeling that kind of happiness—

Except with her.

I sipped my drink, the whiskey burning a hole down my throat. Maggie grabbed her ball and walked up to bowl. I couldn't stop staring at her legs, at her ass. She looked ridiculously hot in her orange shoes.

That guy who was friends with George—Matt or something—walked up next to her. Right behind her. My eyes narrowed as she turned back and said something to him. He laughed.

I didn't like him. He was American and tall and built and looked like he should be working on a farm or something.

He followed Maggie up to the bowling lane, positioning his body behind hers, showing her how to roll the ball. His hands gripped her hips, his arm moving with hers, mimicking the release. She wriggled her hips for a moment, and I swear my heart stopped beating. He grinned at her, still not moving his motherfucking hands from her body, and I saw red.

11

Maggie

"Yes!"

A perfect strike. I pumped my fist in the air, dancing in the lane. I grinned at Max, giving him a high five.

"Thanks for the advice, partner."

"Happy to help."

I turned and my gaze traveled over the group before finally connecting with Samir. His gaze was fixed on me, his stare unblinking. There was something there—a heat that had the smile slowly slipping from my face.

There were times when words seemed to fail us, when we communicated best without them. This was one of those times. I knew that look. It was the same look he'd given me that night. The same look I'd seen when he was inside of me. Whatever friend truce we'd agreed to disappeared with that look. I couldn't pretend I hadn't seen it, just like he couldn't pretend that whatever was inside of him wasn't pushing to get out.

I needed air.

I mumbled some excuse to Max and headed for the door, avoiding Samir's gaze. I was afraid if I looked at him now, everything would change. I couldn't keep pretending, but I wasn't ready to share us with everyone. When it was secret—forbidden—it was safe. If it was a secret, I could tell myself it wasn't real. That I wasn't falling for him. That my heart wasn't completely at risk. That maybe I hadn't already lost it months ago.

The second I pushed open the door and the cold air hit me, I sagged against the building, letting out a harsh breath. I closed my eyes. I couldn't lose control like this. Not now. Not in front of everyone.

We were just friends. I'd said so myself. He had a girlfriend. He'd already nearly broken my heart once. I couldn't put myself through that again. He was a bad idea. A really, really bad idea.

I heard footsteps, and suddenly the energy around me changed. I squeezed my eyes shut, fighting the urge to open them. Because suddenly I knew that when I did, he'd be right in front of me.

I didn't think we could be just friends anymore.

Samir

Somehow I managed to wait a full minute before going after her. Maybe two. But then I couldn't wait anymore. She pulled me toward her, and I was done resisting.

Seeing Max with her—

I wasn't jealous. I knew her. Knew what she wanted, knew the way she looked at me was different from the way she looked at everyone else. I was just angry with myself. Angry I'd put us in this situation, that things between us had gotten so bad. I didn't want him touching her, didn't want anyone touching her but me. I hated that she was just within my reach, but always unattainable, hated that she wasn't mine.

I stopped in front of her, taking a moment to look at her, really look at her, without feeling the pressure to pretend I didn't feel what I felt. Her brown hair fell past her shoulders.

Her skin was pale, a hint of color on her cheeks. Her lips were red. I ached to kiss them.

I reached out, placing my palm against the brick wall behind her. She sighed. I leaned forward, our bodies close but not touching, her scent surrounding me.

"Maggie." I said her voice like a prayer. For what, I wasn't sure. I wanted to beg her to release me from this hold she had over me, plead with her to let me kiss her.

Her eyes flickered open. The desire I saw there made my mouth instantly go dry.

I leaned forward slightly, my body just barely brushing hers. Her eyes widened. I rested my forehead against hers, our lips inches apart.

And suddenly I had the courage to give voice to the thoughts that had been taunting me for months.

"I still want you. I never stopped wanting you. I'm afraid I never will." The last part escaped in a strangled whisper. I was done playing around, done denying myself the one thing I so desperately wanted. I was weak and I needed her. Nothing else mattered.

I rocked forward, my body pushing hers against the wall. It felt good to be this close to her, to feel her body beneath mine. But I wanted more, always more with her. Nothing ever seemed to be enough.

Maggie

I was drowning in his voice and his words. With each word, my composure slipped some more. I wanted him. I'd never stopped wanting him. I'd wanted him for so long that I honestly didn't remember what it was like to not want him. Hearing him say he felt the same way was impossible to ignore.

My chin tilted up, our gazes locking, our lips so close that if I just leaned forward a bit, my mouth would graze his. What would it feel like to kiss him again? To give myself over to the pleasure of his lips and hands? To feel him hot and hard inside me, filling me, pushing into me until our bodies were one?

Our breath mingled, lips hovering just an inch away from heaven. His body pressed against mine, his legs brushing against me—every inch of him was hard. It was enough to make me forget why this was a bad idea. It was enough to tempt me to want more, to give myself over to the pleasure I found only in his arms. It was enough to have me moving forward, putting my mouth on his.

It had been four months since we'd kissed, and yet the second our mouths fused together something clicked into place. I opened my lips, and his tongue slid into my mouth. His hands grabbed my ass, pushing me back against the brick wall, and I found my nirvana. We kissed like we might never kiss again. His mouth plundered mine, his tongue possessed me, his teeth scraped my skin. He slid a thigh between my legs so I rode him, the friction between us sending a shock of heat through my body. He cupped my ass, pulling me harder against him, tearing his mouth from mine. He kissed his way down my neck, his hands moving up to brush against my breasts, seeking my nipples through my top. I moaned against his mouth.

He pulled back, staring at me, his gaze full of promise and want. It took a moment for me to calm my breathing, to come back to earth.

"Maggie."

Samir stiffened. I froze, the sound of my name breaking through the haze of lust and heat.

Max stood behind Samir, staring at us, his eyes wide. "It's your turn to bowl."

Heat flooded my face as sanity returned. We were all over each other on a crowded London street. Maybe Max didn't know Samir had a girlfriend, but still. Nothing about this was a good idea.

"Thanks," I answered, my stare never breaking contact with Samir's. There was so much I wanted to say to him. So much lingering between us. But as usual, I didn't know how to even begin. "I should go back in."

"I can't keep doing this," Samir answered, his voice low. "There's still too much that's unresolved between us. We need to talk."

"I know."

He was right. The tension in the air was ridiculous. We'd been dancing around that night, but no matter how hard we tried to ignore it, it wasn't going away, and our world was too small for us to try to pretend like the other one didn't exist.

Samir pulled away from me with a frustrated sigh.

"You should go in first. Mya's already asked me questions about us. I can't deal with anyone else finding out. Not now. Not yet."

He didn't answer. For a moment I thought he was going to press the issue. But instead, he just nodded and walked away.

I sagged against the wall, struggling to get my emotions under control. My heart raced, my nerves a live wire. Why was it that being around Samir always made me feel like I'd just jumped off a cliff?

"Everything okay?" Max asked. "I didn't mean to interrupt…" He flushed. "I didn't realize you guys were together."

"We're not. Please don't tell anyone about this."

"I won't." He shook his head. "That guy's a jerk. I'll never understand what girls see in him."

"He's not bad." I didn't expand. I felt silly trying to explain what Samir was like. "You just have to know him."

"He looked like he was ready to take my head off for talking to you. I wasn't hitting on you with the bowling thing. Honestly. I was just trying to help."

"I know."

He was quiet for a moment. "Why do you hang out with

all of them?" He gestured toward the bowling alley. "Do you ever get sick of the constant shallowness? I mean, Fleur doesn't have one intelligent thought in her head. And Samir Khouri?"

I could guess how we must all look to Max. He ran with a completely different crowd—honestly, besides George, I wasn't even sure he had friends. Fleur and Samir had a reputation. It just wasn't the whole story.

"Fleur's one of my best friends, and I promise you, she's a lot more than people give her credit for."

He didn't look convinced. "She's going to crush George's heart. He's a good guy. He doesn't need a girl like Fleur screwing around with him just because she's bored. He said you guys were friends. Can you honestly tell me he's not going to get hurt?"

I sighed, some of my annoyance softening. I understood wanting to fight for the people you loved.

"I don't know. I can't even begin to predict how their relationship is going to play out, but neither can you. That girl, the one you seem to think is some heartless man-eater, just spent last year getting her heart crushed by a guy who wasn't good enough for her by half. I don't know if George is the guy for Fleur or not, but I know she's trying. What more can she do?"

As much as I loved Fleur, I'd be lying if didn't admit I was a little worried for George, too. But I hated that people always assumed the worst about her and I hated that she didn't try to change that perception.

If I'd learned anything at the International School, it was that appearances were deceiving.

Samir

"Where's Maggie?"

"No idea."

Mya shot me a look that left no doubt that she didn't believe anything I said. For some reason, she always made me a little nervous. Fleur was usually too self-involved to pay attention to other people, and Maggie calling me on my bullshit was nothing new. But Mya looked at me like she knew I wasn't all I was cracked up to be. And Maggie was right; Mya was starting to notice things were different.

Mya smirked. "Maybe she's with Max. They'd make a cute couple, right?"

"Sure." I struggled to keep a pleasant expression on my face.

"They're both American," Mya continued. "He's really smart. Nice. Quiet, too. Shy. Kind of like Maggie. If you think about it, they're really perfect for each other."

Is she really trying to needle me? What had happened to my rep? People used to be afraid of me—reluctant even to talk to me. Thanks to Maggie, I had somehow become *approachable*. Hell, Mya was even giving me shit.

"I doubt that." I should have ended the conversation there. But today seemed to be my day for not doing what I should. "Maggie's not shy," I continued. She was the furthest thing from shy. She just wasn't in-your-face flashy, so people tended to overlook her. Which was stupid. Especially when I couldn't take my eyes off her.

"She's funny and not afraid to call you out on your shit when need be. She's strong. And even though she doesn't know it, she's confident. She knows who she is, and she owns it. She doesn't apologize for herself or shirk away from standing up for what's right. She takes chances all the time. She's tough. Don't underestimate her."

Mya gaped at me. Her gaze drifted to a point over my shoulder. I turned. Maggie stood behind me, a dazed expression on her face.

For a moment, neither one of us spoke. I wasn't sure what I was feeling. No small measure of embarrassment. A fierce sense of protectiveness that was new and beyond uncomfortable. I hated when people talked about Maggie as if she were some delicate flower. She was the strongest person I knew, and I was sick of people underestimating her.

"I guess I was wrong," Mya said, before she turned and walked away. She might as well have disappeared. Everything for me was Maggie.

I struggled to speak, but once again the words wouldn't come. I blamed the languages swirling in my head rather than the girl standing in front of me.

"Thanks for that." Maggie's lips curved into a heartbreakingly gorgeous smile. "You made me sound quite fierce."

Her smile deepened, and I was dazzled.

Again, I grasped for words, and none came. English had never been hard for me. I'd been speaking it long enough that I rarely found myself at a loss for words. But sometimes, when I was tired or my emotions were high, I found myself speaking and thinking in French or Arabic.

I had a ton of words for her now, things I'd never said considering I'd never felt like this about anyone before.

Those words scared me. I'd never been here before, and I felt unmistakably out of my league.

12

Maggie

Little by little, I started to relax around Samir. It was weird. Something had shifted between us outside the bowling alley—that kiss changed everything. Any doubts I'd had about what he wanted from me had been instantly erased. He wanted me just as much as I wanted him. I just wished I knew what happened next.

"So is it just me, or is watching them together the most awkward thing ever?" Samir whispered in my ear, his breath teasing the back of my neck. He'd been joking with me, teasing me, all evening long.

My gaze drifted to where Fleur walked next to George. "They're fine. Stop giving them a hard time."

Samir snorted. "He blushes constantly."

George did look a bit red. "He's British. He's pale. It's not his fault."

Samir just shook his head. "I hate to say it, but you just might be the worst matchmaker ever."

I elbowed him. "We'll see."

"Care to make a wager?" Samir murmured, his lips grazing my skin.

I instantly flashed back to our card game in Paris over spring break last year… that wager had ended with me stripping naked before him.

"Remembering?"

I flushed. We were walking way too close to each other, his body nearly touching mine. It was hard to think when he was this close to me. Hard to focus on all the reasons why we couldn't be together, when all I cared about was how much I wanted to be with him.

Subtlety seemed to have gone out the window. Our friends were up ahead, deep in conversation, but still. Here we were, on display for everyone to see.

"Move away."

"No. I like it here. I like having you close, being able to smell your perfume, the scent of your shampoo. Vanilla?"

I flushed. It totally was. The husky tone of his voice sent a shiver down my spine.

"You smell good enough to eat."

"You're such a weirdo." My lips twitched. "Try to refrain."

"What if I don't want to?" Samir teased. "You know how bad I am with delayed gratification. Or maybe I'm just very, very good."

"Stop it," I hissed, trying desperately to ignore the flush of arousal that ran through my body. I was so turned on—I had been all night—that all it would take was him touching me for my not-so-firmly held restraint to go out the window.

"I'm not doing anything." Samir lowered his voice. "Yet. But I'm thinking of doing a lot. I'm wondering if I touched you right now, if I slipped my fingers inside of you, would you be wet?"

Heat flooded my body.

So much for friends. So much for everything.

"I thought we were going to be good."

"Fuck being good."

Samir

We walked back to the dorms, everyone talking and laughing. I walked next to Maggie, purposely letting my hand graze hers. Her breath caught for a moment. I waited, all of my concentration focused on the point where our flesh met. Everything seemed to hinge on this moment—whether she'd pull back or keep her hand there. I'd shocked her earlier with my honesty. Now I could see her playing the same game she so frequently did—hovering between desire and caution. But she didn't move away. Something—relief, triumph, possibility?—filled me. Heart pounding, I moved my hand just an inch. I squeezed her hand, wrapping my fingers around hers. She squeezed back, her fingers grasping mine like she never wanted to let go.

"Do you guys want to watch a movie or something?" Fleur called out.

It took me a minute to realize she was talking to us. Another moment before I realized that all it would take was Fleur turning around to see Maggie's hand clutched in mine. I didn't let go.

"No."

"Yes," Maggie answered simultaneously, yanking her hand out of mine, leaving me reaching for thin air.

Fleur turned around, staring at us.

Maggie moved away from me, putting even more distance between us. "A movie sounds great."

I groaned. Watching a movie with a room full of people was the last thing I wanted to do.

"I'm in," Mya answered from up ahead.

Awesome.

"Sounds good," George agreed. "You in, Max?" Max nodded.

Maggie shot me an innocent look. "Doesn't a movie sound like fun?"

My eyes narrowed. She knew how badly I wanted her. I was pretty sure her playing hard to get would kill me. Was she even playing hard to get? Maybe I'd misread all her signals. Maybe she wasn't interested in picking up where we'd left off. Maybe I was losing my mind.

"I think there are other things that might be more fun," I responded, my voice low, my expression deceptively bland. "Other activities we could do."

Maggie elbowed me again. "Stop it," she hissed.

Mya turned around and shot us a look. There was no way she was buying that something wasn't going on between me and Maggie. I hated to be the one to break it to Maggie, but she was going to have to talk to Mya sooner rather than later.

Mya sent me a mocking smile. "Are you sure you're not going to join us, Samir?"

Twice in one night?

"You know, you're right. A movie sounds great."

Her expression was knowing. "I'll bet."

Maggie shot me a disapproving look.

"What?"

"What was that?" she whispered as we fell back from the group.

"I don't think she likes me very much."

"No shit." Maggie was silent for a minute. "She knows something's up, right?"

"Oh yeah. Definitely."

Maggie groaned. "This is so bad."

"Why do you care? Tell her the truth if you want."

"What if she tells Fleur?"

"She's one of your best friends, I don't think she's going to tell Fleur. Besides—" I stopped walking and turned to face her "—why do you care if Fleur knows?"

"Are you serious? She's going to freak out."

"She might not care. And even if she does, it's none of Fleur's business. We're both adults."

"She's definitely going to care." Maggie looked down at the ground. "It's embarrassing, okay?"

"Are you ashamed of me?"

I struggled to keep my voice casual. Tried to tell myself I didn't care what her answer was. I'd honestly never really cared what girls thought about me. When I wanted a girl, she pretty much always wanted me back. If she didn't, I could always turn on the charm and change her mind. I may have had very few useful skills in life, but my ability to get a girl into bed was my best one.

Except Maggie seemed immune to my charm. I could tell she liked the clubs and the champagne and the VIP status, and the jet, and all the shit that came with being a Khouri. But it didn't give me a free pass with her. She didn't treat me any differently because I had money. In a way she was almost impossible to impress. Which just made me want to impress her more.

"I'm not embarrassed of you."

"Then what?"

"I'm embarrassed of me." Her voice was strained. "Of what I did."

The look on her face sent a flicker of unease through me. "You shouldn't feel guilty."

If anything, what happened between us had been my fault. I'd known better. I was the one with the girlfriend. I was the one who'd fucked everything up.

"I knew you had—*have*—a girlfriend. There's no excuse for what I did."

I hated this. "Not your fault. I'm the only one who should feel guilty. Not you. Never you."

"That's sweet, but I don't think life works like that. You don't get to just take all the blame. I knew what I was doing when I went to bed with you. I knew we were probably hurting people. And I did it anyway. It's on me just as much as it's on you."

We'd gotten completely separated from the group now, but I didn't care. We were a block away from the school, and I was greedy to have more time with her. It always felt like this, like I was stealing time with her, and no matter how fast I was, it always slipped through my fingers.

"Of course, I can take all the blame. You know I always get my way," I joked, desperately wanting to erase the sadness from her face. I reached out, linking my hand with hers. It was dangerous to touch her this close to the school, where anyone could see us, but I couldn't not touch her.

"We can't do this."

I ignored her, my hand still linked with hers.

Maggie leveled a stern look at me, but her hand stayed in mine. "I'm serious, we can't. We're going to hurt people. We've already hurt people."

We couldn't undo what we'd done; the only thing we could do was change where we were headed.

"What if things were different?"

"What do you mean?"

"What if it were just the two of us? No one else. Would you want me?"

Suddenly it felt like the most important question I'd ever asked, and I hadn't even meant to ask it. The words had slipped out before I'd had a chance to hold them in. An eternity passed before she answered.

"I don't know."

Maggie

I didn't mean it the way it sounded. Would I still want him? Of course. I wanted him now. I'd wanted him last year. I'd wanted him even when I hadn't wanted to want him. But even if Samir didn't have a girlfriend, would I take a chance on him? I didn't know anymore.

My answer would have been different back in May. Before I'd heard he was still with his girlfriend. Before he'd hurt me. Before I'd really realized how much I liked him. Back then, I hadn't understood what being a Khouri really meant for him. I hadn't understood his responsibilities or the inevitability of him returning to Lebanon. Now, it just seemed like there was no point to even trying. He'd be gone in a few months. He had a future that was set—the furthest thing from mine. I didn't see a way around that.

I was scared, and yet I hated the hurt that flashed across his face.

"I didn't mean it like that."

He just stared at me, that same expression in his eyes.

"I don't know. I don't know how to explain what I feel. I'm sorry. I'm not very good at this."

I wished I were better at it. Wished I'd dated in high school or knew what I was doing. But truthfully, this didn't feel like dating. This thing between us was heavy, and emotional, and intense. It had been from the beginning. No one had told me how to handle that.

"I'm sorry," I repeated.

Samir closed the distance between us, bringing me to his side. I stiffened for a moment before relaxing into his arms.

"I want to tell you something," Samir whispered, his voice hovering near my ear.

With him this close, I couldn't find any words.

"There hasn't been anyone else since you."

Everything stopped. A wave of emotions crashed over me— hope, joy, fear, relief. I just stood there like an idiot while Samir pulled away and stared down into my face.

"I just thought you should know."

13

Maggie

I didn't even know what we were watching. Something with zombies, maybe—a horror flick by the look of it.

There hasn't been anyone else since you.

The words ran through my mind on a loop I couldn't forget or erase. Honestly, I'd never considered the possibility that Samir might not have had sex with his girlfriend this summer. Or that there hadn't been anyone else. As far as game changers went, it was a big one.

He kept staring at me. Even through the darkness, I couldn't ignore the weight of his attention.

We were all in the common room. As far as I was concerned, it might as well have just been me and Samir. He sat on the couch opposite mine, so close and yet once more out of reach.

Samir pulled out his phone, looking as restless as I felt. I wasn't sure why he hadn't left yet. It was obvious he didn't want to be here; he spent more time watching me than the movie.

My phone beeped.

"Sorry," I told the room at large.

I stared at the screen, my heart pounding madly.

I'm bored.

My lips twitched as I looked over at Samir. He had his phone out again, his fingers typing.

My phone pinged again.

"Sorry." My cheeks heated as I put the phone on silent. I snuck a peek at everyone else, but no one seemed to notice or care.

Entertain me.

I fought back a grin, typing my response.

No.

It was a minute before my screen lit up again.

You haven't been watching the movie.

How do you know?

A few seconds later—

I've been watching you not watch the movie.

I ignored the flare of heat, the ball of hope, longing and lust that rolled through me.

I know. You shouldn't. Everyone's going to notice.

Samir read my text and looked up, sending me a grin that had my toes curling. A minute later—

Don't care. But if you're worried, maybe we should go somewhere private. Xxxx

My heart pounded. I was more scared now than I had been the first time. This no longer felt like a one-off. This was becoming something big. Something I wasn't ready for. My screen lit up.

Come up to my room. We can watch a movie...

My phone pinged once more.

Or something.

Minutes passed. My fingers shook as I typed out my response.

Ok.

Samir

I made sure to leave first, making some bullshit excuse about being tired.

I headed up to my room, tension coursing through my body. I was beginning to care less and less about keeping this a secret, but at the same time, I wasn't exactly sure what we were doing, and I didn't want everyone butting in until Maggie and I figured it out.

I let myself into the room, shutting the door behind me. I turned on the light, grabbed a pile of clothes off the floor and shoved them into my wardrobe. My gaze settled on some candles sitting on my dresser. I used them to keep the smell of smoke out of my room. I hesitated before grabbing my lighter and lighting them.

I wasn't sure how to play this one. She had to know "want

to watch a movie" was code for sex. But I didn't want her to think this was some kind of booty call, that all I wanted from her was a casual hookup.

I hoped candlelight conveyed that message better than I could.

I was nervous. Sex had never made me nervous before.

A knock sounded at the door.

I turned on the TV and flicked off the lights. I swung open the door. Maggie stared back at me, a small smile on her face. For a moment, I couldn't speak.

"Can I come in?"

"Yeah. Of course. Sorry." I was an idiot. I moved out of the way as she stepped over the threshold, closing the door behind her with a soft thud.

She looked nervous standing there in the middle of my room. She fisted her hands on her hips, and I wondered if she was thinking of the last time she was here.

I knew I was.

I wanted to touch her, but she looked unsure of herself, ready to bolt. There it was again, the constant push and pull. Everything was somehow easier and harder with her.

I didn't want to fuck this up.

I settled for safe. "Want to watch a movie?"

Maggie hesitated for a moment, nibbling on her lower lip. I wanted to take her mouth, to suck on those pretty lips of hers, to nip at her, listening to those throaty little moans she loved to make. She'd been in my room a total of two minutes, and I was already hard.

"What kind of movie?"

I wracked my brain for a moment. I couldn't have cared less. Something that involved the lights off and her body curled up in bed next to mine.

"Pick one," I suggested, gesturing to the TV.

She scrolled through the options. "How about this one?"

"Looks good to me." I had no idea what she'd picked.

I managed to start the movie and turned back to face Maggie. She stood at the foot of the bed, staring at it. It was so weird having her here, remembering having her in my bed. It felt like we were in two different places. On one hand, I'd seen her naked, explored every inch of her body. On the other, there was this wall of awkwardness between us. We were strangers, and yet we weren't.

I stared at the bed. It was the only place to comfortably sit and watch TV, but I was pretty sure if I got her in bed, I wasn't going to be able to keep my hands off her.

I sighed. "I can sit on the floor or something, if you want to take the bed."

As soon as the words left my mouth, I cursed myself in Arabic, French *and* English.

"You don't have to sit on the floor."

Maggie sat down on the bed, moving up to rest her head against the pillows. I slipped in beside her, careful to leave some room between our bodies. I didn't know what she wanted, couldn't read her.

So I waited, relying on patience I'd never known I had.

14

Maggie

All I could think about was his body lying next to mine. He was so close, inches away, and yet those inches felt like they might as well have been a mile.

There was something about the darkness, something about being back in his room, in his bed. It felt like we were in our own little world where nothing else mattered. There were ghosts here, memories of that night that cropped up with the slightest shift of his body, the smell of his cologne, the feel of the sheets against my skin.

I would have bet my life that neither one of us was even kind of watching the movie. We'd been "not watching the movie" for an hour now. Neither one of us had spoken, and yet it felt like we'd been having a conversation between us, hidden in the dark.

For an hour we played the game. I accidentally-on-purpose touched his foot with mine. His shoulder shifted, grazing me. My hand reached out, settling next to his, only our pinkies touching. Each touch was deliberate, a move in an elaborate game of chess. Each move took us closer and closer to each other. The air was thick with tension and anticipation. My breasts felt heavy, my nipples tight. If this was foreplay, I didn't know how much longer I could last. It felt like we'd already had a lifetime of foreplay.

I shifted slightly, turning to face him.

He smiled at me. "Hi."

"Hi," I whispered back. There was enough light in the room that I could just make out the shape of his face. His lips were inches away from mine.

A new kind of tension filled the air between us. I could feel it in my bones, could see it in his eyes. Impatience filled me.

"You're not going to make the first move, are you?" I asked.

"Nope."

"Why?"

I wondered if I would be able to hear his response over the mad pounding of my heart.

"Because I don't want to pressure you. I don't have answers for you. I don't even know what promises I can make. I want you, more than I've ever wanted anyone. That's all I've got."

There would be time for conversations later. I knew we had to deal with things. We had to figure out what, if anything, was between us. But for now, the elephant in the room pushed everything out. I wanted him. He wanted me.

To hell with everything else.

Samir

The moment she kissed me, my heart stopped.

It was different from all our other kisses, and yet the feel of her lips was so familiar—soft, smooth, lush.

I wrapped my arms around her, levering my body over hers until her body sank into the mattress. I settled between her legs, pressing against all that softness. I nipped at her, pulling her bottom lip into my mouth, sucking on it, tracing my tongue over her full mouth.

She moaned.

"I've been thinking about this for months," I murmured against her mouth. "I wake up in the night, hard, wanting you. Wanting this." I ran my hands through her hair, pulling her head back so I could see her face.

I nipped at her neck, tasting her there, leaving kisses on her soft skin. Before this night was over, I wanted to run my hands and mouth over every inch of her gorgeous body. Impatient, I reached for the hem of her shirt, pulling it up over her head, dragging the fabric across her skin until her torso was free.

I froze, staring down at Maggie, bared before me. Whatever memories I'd had—and I'd had plenty—the reality of her naked flesh was impossibly better. Her skin was a creamy white, offset by a sheer blue bra that just barely allowed a glimpse of her rosy nipples.

I groaned. She was so fucking hot—and for tonight, she was mine.

My head bent, I nipped at the edge of the lace, dragging the bra's edge down. My teeth scraped against her bare skin, grazing her nipple.

Her hands reached out, gripping my head, her fingers threading through my hair, pulling me closer to her. There was no shyness in her. Just fire.

I arched my hips, pushing against her softness, enjoying the moan that escaped from her lips.

I wanted to devour her. I wanted to bury myself inside her, to lose myself in her mouth. I wanted to sink into all that creamy softness.

I leaned back, fumbling with the clasp of her bra.

"*Merde.*"

I'd gotten plenty of girls' bras off before. For some reason hers felt like a labyrinth I couldn't find my way out of.

"Here." Maggie pushed my hands away, reaching behind her back. I should have been embarrassed, but I was so grateful to finally see her gorgeous tits that I couldn't have cared less.

She stripped the bra away, baring herself to my gaze, no trace of shyness in her expression. Gone was the girl who had been nervous our first time together. At some point the dynamic between us had shifted, and now I was the one who felt like a virgin. The knowing gleam in Maggie's eyes, the way her body responded like it craved my touch, was enough to have me begging for it.

I stared down at her naked skin, a lump in my throat. Her hair fell around her shoulders, the strands long enough to tease at her nipples. I couldn't resist. I leaned down, capturing one in my mouth, tugging it with my lips, sucking hard, loving the taste of her. My hand reached out, stroking her other breast, molding its shape in my hand. She was destroying me, inch by inch.

Maggie

He was killing me.

I clung to my sanity by a thread, my body's needs having far outstripped any rational thought. This was what it felt like to lose control. This was the memory that had been plaguing me for months—invading my thoughts and dreams.

He was better than I'd remembered, and I was determined to reap the rewards of his years of experience.

His mouth at my breast, sucking on my nipple, had my hips thrashing. His teeth grazed the tight bud in an exquisite mixture of pleasure and pain. A moan escaped my lips, fueled by the desire gathering between my legs, flooding my body. His lips left my skin, the cool air hitting me instantly. He reached down between us, his knuckles grazing my stomach. I arched my back, giving myself over to the feel of his hands on me, to the sweet torment of his fingers. His hand continued its descent, caressing, teasing, before dipping lower and unbuttoning my jeans, dragging the denim down my hips with agonizing slowness.

The contrast of sensations nearly overwhelmed me. The fabric against my skin was rough, the touch of his hands, finger-light, teasing my flesh.

"Don't stop," I whispered, pleading. "Whatever you do, don't stop."

He pulled my jeans off, throwing them onto the floor. Then he was back on the bed, joining me, his body hovering over mine, his mouth back at my breasts.

I moved between us, my hands sliding down his stomach, reaching the snap of his jeans. I dipped lower, running my palm against the outline of his arousal. He hissed.

I unbuttoned his jeans, starting with the top button, revealing another one, and then another, dragging my fingers downward, tracing that hard line. When I finally reached the last button, I pulled at his jeans, tugging at them with an impatience I didn't bother to hide.

Samir moved out of my reach, standing next to the bed, staring down at me. The sight of his long, tanned fingers mesmerized me as he slipped the jeans from his hips until they pooled near his feet. His boxers came next. With the same unhurried effort, he pulled the cotton down—the whole time, his gaze pinned to mine. His boxers fell to the floor in a heap next to his jeans.

For a moment I could only stare. His skin was tan, his body lean but sculpted. His shoulders were broad without being overwhelming, his collarbone a sharp line I wanted to run my tongue along. His chest was sprinkled with dark hair, his stomach flat, the indent over his hips faint.

His lips quirked in a little half smile. "Like what you see?"

I shook my head, a smile forming. "Trust you to be cocky even during sex."

"I thought you liked it when I was cocky." He reached down, grazing the inside of my thigh, moving higher, higher—

My hips arched off the bed as his hand reached the edge of my lacy thong. His fingers teased the fabric there before dipping lower, caressing my skin before sliding into my body in one smooth stroke.

Suddenly I couldn't think at all.

Samir groaned. "You're so fucking wet. You feel incredible."

He played with me, minutes passing, each touch taking me closer and closer to the edge. He moved his fingers, slowly, lazily, making little circles deep inside me—curling, stroking, seeking—

The orgasm ripped through me, leaving my body sensitive, a tremor filling me.

His fingers slid out of me, the pounding in my chest an urgent beat. He moved toward the nightstand, grabbing a condom, rolling it on before coming to join me on the bed.

"I bought these earlier today," he confessed, his expression sheepish. "I hoped—"

I fused my mouth with his, smothering the rest of his words. I'd never wanted anything as badly as I wanted this.

Samir reached between us, his hands shaping my legs, exploring, moving higher until he reached my hips. He bent his head, his lips following the path his hands had taken. I arched my back, pushing my body against his, wanting more, anything, everything. His hands grazed my hips as he reached down, pulling my lace thong off my legs. The fabric sliding down my bare skin sent another shiver through me.

His gaze met mine, and for a moment we just stared at each other. I didn't know what I felt. Lust. Longing. Despite the intensity I knew sex between us could bring, I couldn't resist. Being with him felt right. Not just because the feeling of his hands and mouth on me was the single hottest thing I'd ever experienced, but because of the look in his eyes when he stared at me. He made me feel like I was everything.

No one had ever done that.

"You okay?"

I nodded.

For a moment, his body hovered over me, his skin against mine.

"You are the most beautiful thing I've ever seen," he whispered. And then he plunged into me, filling me, pushing me over the edge.

I drowned in him.

15

Samir

"Hi."

Maggie's eyelids fluttered open, a smile slowly spreading across her face. My chest tightened.

"Hi," she whispered, rubbing her eyes. "What time is it?"

I tore my gaze away, looking at the clock on my nightstand. "Seven." I'd been up for three hours watching her sleep, wondering what the hell I'd done and how we could move forward from this. If things were normal, I would have woken her up with my lips on hers and my hand between her legs. I would have made her come with my hands and mouth, taking her over the edge. But things weren't normal. As much as I loved waking up with her, I felt like the world's biggest ass.

"Are you okay?"

I forced a smile. "Better than okay."

"Are you sure?"

I nodded, even though I was lying. I wasn't sure of anything anymore. Part of me wanted to keep her in my bed forever. Part of me needed her to leave now. I needed space, time to think.

What the hell happened last night?

The first time we slept together, I'd known things were different with her. There had been something about it. Maybe it was the fact that we were friends. I'd never slept with a girl I was friends with before.

But this time—

I hadn't thought anything could be as good as it had been between us back in May. I'd been wrong. It was better.

The fact that I'd wanted to hold her in my arms afterward just complicated everything between us. I didn't know what I wanted anymore. We couldn't continue the way we'd been. I couldn't pretend there wasn't something between us. I wanted her in my bed, in my arms. I wanted to know no one else would put his hands on her.

I needed time to figure things out.

"Are you sure you're okay?" she asked, pulling back slightly.

I didn't know what to say. I needed to deal with the Layla situation. And given the expectations she had, I needed to do it in person.

Maggie

The spell had been broken. Whatever had made Samir throw caution to the wind last night seemed to have been replaced by something I was afraid to name as regret.

Last night had been special. I knew it, I'd felt it. I may not have been experienced with guys, but I'd seen the way Samir had looked at me, the way he'd touched me, demanding and reverent. Last night had meant something to him.

This morning it was like there was a different Samir in bed with me. The walls were back up. And it hurt.

I could read the writing on the wall. He regretted it. The truth of it hit me like a glass of cold water to the face.

I pulled the sheets back, climbing out of bed.

"I have to go."

Samir sat up, the white sheet slipping low on his stomach. The flash of skin was enough to send a wave of desire crashing through me.

The look in his eyes, though, changed desire to confusion. *How could he look at me like that one moment and be cold the next?*

"Don't be upset. Please." The frustration broke through his voice. "I just need some time."

I shook my head, the truth of it hitting me. I could give him time, but what would be the point? We'd been doing this dance for over a year now. It wasn't getting better. The obstacles weren't going away. He wasn't choosing me. He'd never chosen me. What kind of person did it make me that I kept coming back for more?

"I can't do this anymore."

"Do what?"

"This." I gestured between us. "Sex. Kissing. Touching. Any of it. All of it."

He didn't answer me.

"This isn't working," I continued. "It has never worked. I can't be your friend. I can't pretend like that's all there is between us. I can't pretend you and I haven't been more to each other."

"Maggie..."

The first tear slipped down my cheek. Horror filled his eyes.

"We're not good for each other. Can't you see that?"

"That's not true."

I shook my head, rubbing at my eyes to clear my vision. "It is true. Can you honestly tell me you don't feel guilty? That you don't regret what we did?"

"I don't regret it."

Pain knifed through me. "Well, I do. I can't be that girl. I can't be the girl you screw around with. I can't be the girl you keep on the side who gets whatever pieces of you are left when your girlfriend is done with you."

With each word that left my lips, I realized the truth of everything I said. My entire life I'd always been someone's second choice. My mom hadn't loved me enough to stay; my dad hadn't loved me enough to come home. There was always something that mattered more than me, always something chosen over me. I wanted to be someone's first choice. For once, I wanted to know what it felt like to have someone fight for me, to have someone stay.

He'd made his choice. He could have ended things with his girlfriend over the summer. He could have chosen me. But he didn't. He stayed with her. He chose her and now he wanted me on the side. It wasn't good enough. It was time I started valuing myself more.

Every time I came back to him, every moment I gave more of myself to him, I lost something. Something I was never going to be able to get back. He was taking pieces of me with him, stripping me to the bone, leaving me raw and exposed.

He was breaking my heart.

16

Maggie

"You wouldn't believe the day I've had."

My head jerked up as Mya walked into the room. I rubbed at my eyes, hoping she wouldn't notice I'd been crying for the last few hours.

She froze, her gaze raking over my appearance.

"What happened?" she asked.

"Nothing."

"Okay, that's enough. We're talking about this."

"Talking about what?" I forced a smile. "I'm fine. I'm just not feeling great. Allergies or something. It's no big deal."

"Bullshit."

I gaped at her.

"I'm not an idiot. It's obvious. The only reason Fleur hasn't figured it out is that, well, she's Fleur. And she's got so much shit going on in her own life she can't be bothered to notice what's going on in everyone else's."

It was true, if not a bit unfair.

"What's going on between you and Samir? And don't lie

to me. It's obvious something's up, and it looks like you need someone to talk to more than anything."

I thought about denying it. I wanted to deny it. But I also desperately needed someone to talk to right now. Mya, more than anyone, wasn't likely to judge.

"We had sex."

It was a moment before she spoke. "When?"

"The first time?"

"There's been more than one time?"

"Yeah. Twice. The first time was in May."

"Ohmigod. You've been keeping this a secret since May?"

I nodded.

"Does anyone else know?"

"A friend from home."

"Okay, back up." Mya sank down on her bed. "How long have you liked him? How did it happen?"

I knew she meant well, knew she was trying to figure out where things stood, but her questions felt like pouring salt on a raw wound. I needed to talk about him and yet the last thing I wanted to do was relive everything between us. It felt weird opening up after keeping it a secret for so long. I struggled to explain feelings even I didn't understand.

"I don't know. I didn't even like him at first. I mean, I thought he was hot and everything, but he was such an ass. But we kissed, that first night when we all went to Babel—the night of the boat party. It was nothing—just a kiss." An amazing, earth-shattering first kiss that had haunted me for the better part of last year. "I was drunk, and he was Samir and I'd just moved to London and it was my first kiss and it was amazing. Then, little by little, things changed, and we started making out."

"Ohmigod. When, where?"

I winced. I felt like I had a whole secret life. "Lots of places. Italy. Nights out."

"But what about Hugh?"

I sighed. "I liked Hugh. But with Samir…" I shrugged. "It was just different with Samir."

"You like him. A lot."

There was curiosity there, but not the condemnation I'd feared. Yet.

"Yeah. I like him. A lot." My voice cracked.

"What about the girlfriend?"

"I don't know."

"Did you guys have sex again last night?"

I nodded.

Her lips twitched. "Well, fine, I have to ask. Is he as amazing as he seems to think he is?"

I snorted, before my eyes filled with tears. "Is it possible he's actually better?"

Mya moved forward, wrapping her arms around me. "You have it bad, don't you?"

I nodded, too miserable to answer.

"Well, give me a minute to think about this one. In all fairness, I totally expected you to say you'd kissed or something. I wasn't expecting full-on sex." She was quiet for a moment. "He was your first, wasn't he?"

I flushed. "Yeah."

"Regrets?"

The answer surprised me, but it was the truth. "Not one."

"What are you going to do now?"

"No idea. Stay away from him? Try to pretend none of this ever happened."

"Do you really think you can do that?"

"I'm going to try."

"Why don't you give it a chance to see if the two of you could work together?"

"Because we can't."

"Have you tried?"

"It's kind of hard to try, when it's all one-sided." I struggled to push past the hurt building up inside me. "I don't know what he wants. When we're together, I think I know. But then everything just seems to fall apart."

"Have you tried talking to him about it?"

"Yes. Not really. We talk, but things just always seem to get jumbled between us."

I didn't know how to describe it to her. I'd always known Mya to be so calm with guys. I didn't know how to explain to her that my brain temporarily stopped working when I was around Samir. Sometimes I couldn't think past the rush of being with him.

"It's complicated," I answered, figuring that was the safest and easiest answer.

"I'm sorry."

"Me too."

Mya grabbed her purse off the bed. "Come on. I know exactly what we need."

"What?"

"Pedicures. I promise it'll make you feel better."

"Okay."

"And Maggie?"

"Yeah?"

"Just so you know, I think he really likes you, too."

I hated the hope her words brought. I hated that I cared. More than anything, I hated that I didn't know if she was right.

"Where have you guys been?"

I closed the door behind me and Mya. Fleur lounged on her bed, flipping through *Vogue*.

"Pedicures," Mya answered.

I felt uncomfortable looking Fleur in the eye. I hated lying to her. Felt terrible that now Mya knew about Samir and Fleur didn't. And yet I couldn't tell her... because she would freak out. Absolutely freak out. But the more time that passed, the worse the consequences of her not knowing were going to be. If it were anyone else, I would have told her by now. But it wasn't just anyone. It was Samir, and with Fleur, that was going to change everything. I didn't want her caught in the middle of us. I feared, if it came down to a choice, she would choose him.

"I should have gone with you. I have a date with George tonight."

"Seriously?"

"Yeah. An actual solo date." She frowned. "I had to ask him. Does that still count?"

I laughed. "I think so. What are you guys doing?"

"Dinner and a movie. It seemed safe. We're okay as long as we don't have to talk very much."

"He's still being shy?"

"He seems perpetually shy."

"Do you guys even have anything in common?" Mya interjected.

I shot her a look.

"What? I'm just saying. What do you even talk about?"

"Not a lot." Fleur sighed. "I thought this was what it was like with nice guys. I thought it was supposed to be quiet. I thought this was normal." She stared at me like I had all the answers to the nice-boy riddle.

"Don't look at me. I have no idea what it's supposed to be like. I'm not sure I know much of anything about guys—nice or otherwise."

"This is why I'm single," Mya announced. "You both spend all of your time obsessing about guys. You could probably take over the world if you spent the same amount of time worrying about things that really mattered."

She had a point.

"Maggie hasn't been bad this year," Fleur protested. "Now that the Hugh thing is over, she's not obsessing over anyone."

Inwardly, I winced.

"Maybe you both need a distraction." Mya's gaze darted from me to Fleur. "We need something to look forward to that doesn't involve guys. This semester has been boring. We need to shake it up a bit."

"Shake it up how?"

"Fall break."

I grinned. "Not another epic trip. I don't think my liver, bank account or sanity can handle it."

"Weak. I'm talking about a trip to Spain. The three of us. We could go to Marbella."

A slow grin spread across Fleur's face. "That's actually a really good idea."

"I don't know…"

Mya shot me a meaningful look. "It could be just the chance you need. A break to get away from things and figure out what you want. It's a good chance to clear your head. Besides, I need a reprieve from all of the shit with my parents."

"I'm definitely in," Fleur announced. "Maybe we could invite Samir. He seems kind of down lately. He could probably use this trip as much as we could."

I froze. *No way.*

"I'm not going if Samir goes," I blurted out.

"Why?"

Oh god.

The most spectacularly awful cocktail of emotions flooded me. Guilt. Guilt for lying to Fleur, for having sex with a guy who had a girlfriend, for not feeling as guilty as I probably should for having sex with a guy who had a girlfriend. Fear. The same yawning fear that had me worrying Fleur would find out about me and Samir. Now was my chance to say, *I don't want Samir to go because he was inside me less than twenty-four hours ago and I don't know how to deal with seeing him right now.*

But I didn't say that. I didn't say anything.

"Because it's a girl trip," Mya interjected.

Fleur frowned.

"Look, I don't want to fight about it, okay? If you want to go to Spain, fine, I'll go," Mya responded, totally taking one for the team. "But no Samir. He makes things uncomfortable."

Fleur sighed. "Fine. We'll go to Spain. No Samir."

17

Maggie

I picked up my phone, scrolling through my messages. *Nothing.* It had been five days since Samir and I had sex, and I hadn't seen him once. The less frequently used, logical part of my brain knew he was doing what I'd asked. Unfortunately, when sex came into the equation, logic flew out the window.

"I can't fit everything."

I stared at the massive pile of clothes next to Fleur's Louis Vuitton luggage. "Big surprise."

She rolled her eyes. "I need to look hot in Spain."

"I thought you were dating George."

"I am dating George. But we haven't had the exclusivity talk, and it's only been a few dates. That doesn't mean I can't flirt, does it?"

"Don't look at me. I'm not exactly an expert on the dating rules."

"We need to find you someone in Spain. Your dry spell has been going on for way too long." Fleur's eyes lit up. "I know! What about Max? We can double date."

"Seriously?"

"I know, I know. He's kind of boring and a bit of a jerk."

I couldn't help but laugh. "I don't think he's boring or a jerk. He's just a little quiet."

"See, you already like him. And he is kind of hot, if you like beefy American guys. Have you noticed the abs?"

I grinned. "I have noticed the abs, although not as much as I'm beginning to think you have. He's nice. But I don't like beefy American guys, and I promise you, he's not interested in me."

Fleur groaned. "Maybe Mya will date him then. He's always around when I hang out with George. I need someone to take him off my hands."

"This is less about my love life and what, more about your boredom?"

"Maybe."

I snorted. "Thanks."

"Sorry, not sorry. I don't like him. He makes fun of me and he's a giant pain in the ass."

"He makes fun of you?"

The few times I'd hung around with Max he seemed like a nice enough guy. I couldn't really see him being mean.

"Well, maybe not out loud, but he makes these faces when I talk. Like I'm boring him. He thinks I'm stupid."

"He doesn't think you're stupid."

"He does. I don't get why George even hangs out with him."

"Maybe because they're friends. Maybe people wonder why I'm friends with you," I teased.

She grinned at that one. "Please. People think you're lucky to be friends with me."

I laughed. "You're such an asshole. You want my advice? Be nice to George's friends. I talked to Max the night we all went bowling. He's not a bad guy. Give him a chance."

"You're too easy on people."

I grinned. "Compared to you? Maybe."

"Can you blame me? If anything, I wish I'd trusted people a little less." She shut her eyes for a moment. "Have you heard any more about the Costa rumor?"

"No."

It was weird that it hadn't gotten out more. Stranger still that Mya, one of Fleur's closest friends, was the one who'd first heard it. It was beginning to feel less like normal International School gossip and more like a coordinated plot against Fleur, and I couldn't help but wonder when the other shoe would drop.

"Did you find out who Mya heard it from?"

I'd done as much investigating as I could without raising suspicion. Unfortunately, there wasn't a ton to go on.

"She heard it from that girl Amara. You know the one, she was in our bio class last year."

"Who'd she hear it from?"

"A friend of a friend. You know how it is. The trail disappears within the labyrinth of International School gossip. I'm worried the more we poke at it, the more likely they'll figure out why we want to know."

"Do you think Natasha knows?" Fleur's expression filled with distaste.

Costa's girlfriend. The girl he'd left Fleur for.

"I'm not sure. Do you think he would tell her?"

"I don't know. I want to think he wouldn't, that he's better than that. But apparently nothing I thought about him was right. If it was Natasha, then he's doing everything in his power to ruin me. She hates me—she's always wanted Costa, even when he was mine. If she does know about the baby, there's a reason she's not spreading the news right now and I promise you, it's not out of the goodness of her heart. She would do anything to see me look bad in front of the whole school."

That was what I feared.

"Do you think she's behind the blackmail? Have you gotten any more emails?"

"No. I don't know if it's Natasha or not, but it definitely sounds like something she would do."

"You could try talking to her," I suggested, knowing the odds of success weren't great.

Fleur sighed. "I don't know. I'm not kidding. She hates me. And that's even without her knowing Costa and I fooled around last year." She grimaced. "I'm trying to change things. I'm dating George now. I barely go out. I read for most of my classes. Fine, some of my classes. I don't want to be the girl who had the drug overdose. I'm sick of people seeing me as just some stupid party girl. And if this gets out, nothing I do will even matter."

"You didn't do anything wrong," I protested. "It wasn't your fault. You had sex with your boyfriend. Since when is that a crime?"

"It won't matter. I'm the Ice Queen, remember? Who doesn't want to see me taken down a peg or two? I can't even say I blame them. I'd probably do the same thing."

"You wouldn't."

She shrugged. "Whatever."

"You wouldn't. You're usually too self-absorbed to gossip about other people," I joked, struggling to lighten the mood.

That cracked a small smile on her lips. "True."

I walked over to her side of the room and gave her a hug. "It'll be okay. I promise. If it does get out, we'll deal with it."

A ringing sound interrupted us. I stared down at my phone. "Sorry. It's my grandmother. I need to take this. I just sent her the info for my flight home in December."

Fleur nodded. "I'm going to grab dinner with George, but I'll hook up with you later."

I hit "accept."

"Hey, Grandma."

"Maggie! I was worried I wouldn't be able to catch you. How are you? It seems like it's been weeks since we talked."

Guilt filled me. It had been weeks. I'd been so busy with

school and my friends and everything going on with Samir that I hadn't thought to call home, hadn't even thought about my life in South Carolina. How long had it been since I'd talked to Jo? Too long.

"I'm sorry. School has been hectic. Did you get my email about Christmas break?"

"I did! I just showed your grandfather. We're so excited to see you."

"I'm excited to see you guys, too."

"Have you heard the good news?"

"No. What's up?"

"Your dad's coming home for Christmas."

For a moment, I couldn't speak. I wasn't sure how I was supposed to respond to that. I guess I was supposed to feel happy. Part of me—the only part that could claim any naïveté where my father was concerned—was happy. But it was just for a moment, one that slipped away when I remembered the years of broken promises, the years that had gone by without seeing him, and the new wife he'd sprung on me months ago.

"That's great, Grandma."

I felt an irrational urge to cancel my plane ticket. I wanted to see him... sort of. I wanted to see him if things between us could be different. I wanted to see him if he was going to start being a real parent, rather than someone who just flitted in and out of my life as if I were a virtual stranger. I wanted to see him if it wouldn't hurt so much.

"He's bringing his wife home with him. He wants everyone to meet her."

Now I wanted to cancel my ticket.

"She sounds wonderful," my grandmother continued, oblivious to my complete and utter freak-out. "She's in the military, too. Isn't that great?"

"Yeah, really great," I echoed, sinking down on the bed.

"I know things have been rushed, sweetie, but I can't help

but think this is going to be a really good thing for you and your dad. I know she's just going to love you."

I found that hard to believe. I knew nothing about her. My dad had called to tell me he'd gotten married, and then I hadn't heard from him for months. When we finally did talk over the summer, it had been brief. He'd gone straight from his deployment to an overseas remote assignment in South Korea. While there had been talk of him coming home to visit in between, I hadn't held my breath, and he'd never made it. It was so typical that the first time I heard about him coming home was from my grandmother. He hadn't called since the summer, and I didn't have a way to reach him other than an email address he rarely used.

I knew my grandparents were happy that he'd married again. His marriage to my mother was a disaster that had ended in her abandoning her child and husband, so I didn't blame them. But I was still angry. Maybe it was petty of me, but I couldn't deny it. I was angry because he was taking a second chance at having a family, one he'd never given me. I was so young when my mother walked out on us, I didn't remember anything else. I didn't remember if we had been happy or acted like a normal family or any of it. All I knew was the *after*, the part where my grandparents had done the best they could to raise me when I was dumped on them like a piece of unwanted luggage.

The thing was—I didn't want to be angry anymore. I just wanted to be done. I wanted to not have to think about it anymore. That was the best part of being in London. I could forget here. I had my own life, one I'd chosen and one that made me happy, one where I felt for the first time in my life like I belonged. I didn't want to go back to feeling like the little girl who was unwanted by both her parents. The girl who was impossible to love.

18

Maggie

We flew into the small airport in Málaga, Spain, our flight crammed with British tourists who obviously had the same idea we did. The plane was smaller than any I'd ever flown on, the seats so cramped that Fleur struggled to open her copy of *Tatler*. The plane was my fault. It was cheap and easy, if not very comfortable. By the time we landed, Fleur was bitching about not flying private, and Mya and I were halfway drunk. A driver met us at the airport and took us to the hotel in Marbella, our luggage crammed into the small sedan.

Mya and Fleur chatted during the car ride. I stared down at my phone, scrolling through my text messages. Still nothing from Samir. It had been almost a week. I hadn't seen him since I woke up in his bed.

This was the trouble with liking a boy. On Saturday I'd convinced myself he was bad for me, and I needed to stay away. By the following Wednesday, I missed him so much I didn't care. I wasn't sure if that said more about my impulse control or my heart, but either way I was screwed.

I grimaced, thankful for the sunglasses covering my eyes. I hated asking, but I couldn't stand the suspense.

"Have you seen Samir lately?" I asked Fleur, struggling to keep my tone casual.

"Not for a few days. He's in Lebanon."

"He's *what*?"

"He went back a couple days ago. Monday maybe. Since we had the end of the week off, he didn't think it would be a big deal to miss a few more days of classes."

Had he always planned to go back to Lebanon? Why had he slept with me right before he went to see his girlfriend? How could he not tell me?

"Was it a planned trip?" Mya asked.

Thank god. I owed her one for voicing the question I was too devastated to ask.

"I don't know. He told me about it after he'd already left. I just know he's there until tomorrow." She frowned. "How much longer until we're at the hotel?"

I heard Mya answer her, but I had no idea what she said. I turned away from both of them, staring out the car window, fighting back anger and tears. Maybe I'd been wrong all along. Maybe I wasn't special; maybe he'd lied to me about everything with his girlfriend. It didn't even matter, really. She had the title. She was someone official in his life, someone he didn't hide under the cover of night. He didn't text her in secret or fuck her in private only to disappear the next day.

How was it that I was smart in most aspects of my life and yet clueless when it came to relationships? I'd made myself a casual hookup and he had taken what I'd offered and given nothing in return. I should have demanded more. I shouldn't have been willing to settle for pieces of him when I wanted all of him.

I stared out the window, the Spanish countryside passing us by. The southern coast of Spain was beautiful, such a departure from the crowded London streets. This close to the water we were surrounded by palm trees and sand and small white Mediterranean-style houses with sunny ocean views peeking through along the drive. There was something so peaceful about the scenery—at least it should have been peaceful. The weight on my chest made it difficult to breathe.

I heard Fleur and Mya chatting away, but I made no effort to join in. Let them think I was sleeping—I didn't care. I couldn't keep doing this. The secret of what had happened between me and Samir was becoming too much, and suddenly I just wanted it gone. I needed to stop making this *something*, so it could be nothing and I could finally be free.

"I had sex with Samir. Twice."

All conversation stopped.

Fleur turned, her gaze boring into me.

"Excuse me?"

"I had sex with Samir," I repeated calmly. "Once in May. The other time Friday night."

Fleur gaped at me. "I thought you didn't like Samir," she finally sputtered.

"Sometimes I don't. Sometimes…" My heart clenched. "Sometimes I do." The truth of it pushed me on. "Sometimes I think I more than like him. I don't know. It's complicated. It's really complicated. And stupid. I've been keeping this a secret for months now and I just can't keep lying to you or pretending it didn't happen. It happened. I need it to not happen again."

"Why?"

"Because I think I'm falling for him, and he has a girlfriend, and I don't know what he wants or feels. Sometimes I think I catch a glimpse, but he's impossible to read. And I'm so scared he's going to break my heart."

Fleur turned on Mya. "Why aren't you as shocked about this as I am?"

"I knew," Mya admitted. "She told me a few days ago."

Fleur whirled on me, hurt flashing in her eyes. I knew she

was thinking of all the secrets between us—secrets she'd trusted me with—and now the one I wasn't a good enough friend to trust her with.

"You told Mya and not me."

This was exactly what I'd feared. "It wasn't like that." Although it was exactly like that. "I wanted to tell you, but I know how close you and Samir are." It hurt to say his name. Especially now that I knew he'd gone from sleeping with me to visiting his girlfriend. "I didn't want you to get upset. I didn't want you to be mad at me."

"Really? Or did you just not want to admit that the whole time you were judging me about the Costa situation last year, you were doing the same thing?"

I deserved that.

"You said you had sex with Samir in May. But before that—that wasn't the first time you kissed, was it?"

"No."

"This wasn't just one drunken night, was it?"

I shook my head, hating myself.

"How long have you guys been fooling around?"

"Since first semester last year. Since the beginning."

"The whole time I was helping you with Hugh, the whole time we were becoming friends, you were lying to me about your relationship with my cousin. And god, he's just as bad. He never mentioned anything either."

"I asked him not to."

"Why? He didn't have a girlfriend last September. Why the secrecy? Were you using me to get to Samir? This whole time—our friendship—was it just a ploy to get closer to him?"

"No! How could you think that?"

"You lied to me. He lied to me. You're two of my closest friends, and you both lied to me. How do you think that feels?"

"I was wrong. I know I was. I'm sorry. So sorry."

Fleur ignored my apology, narrowing her eyes. "Why were

you fooling around with Hugh when you could have had Samir?"

"That's just the point. I never *could have had* Samir. He never let me think I had a chance at anything with him. He never seemed interested in anything other than hooking up. That's why I didn't tell you. The whole thing was just casual. At least it was supposed to be."

"Then what changed between you guys? What made you look like this?"

"I don't know." It was hard to explain. A bunch of little, nothing moments that somehow, when strung together, turned into something life-changing, something that changed me.

"I got to know him better. You were right. He's a good guy. He has moments when he can be a total dick, but he also has times when he can be really sweet." Tears welled up in my eyes. "Everything just got out of control. I wanted to tell you, but it snowballed, and things kept getting bigger and bigger and I didn't know what to do."

"I can't believe you didn't tell me. After everything I shared with you. I told you things I haven't told anyone else." Her voice cracked. She was right. I deserved everything she threw at me, and my only explanation was, *I fucked up.*

"I didn't know how to tell you this. You're right; I was worried you would judge me. I did give you a hard time over Costa when I had no right to. I just didn't know how to explain because it was Samir. I didn't want you to be in the middle of both of us, I didn't know how you would feel about everything. I know I've completely fucked this up, but you're one of my closest friends and I never meant to hurt you."

"Are we friends?" Fleur asked. "It sure doesn't sound like it."

"Are you going to ignore me the rest of the trip?"

Fleur glared at me across the room. Our hotel was small but fancy. Right now, the room felt too small. Shortly after we'd checked in, Mya had left to go call her mom and see how things were going. I was pretty sure she'd also done it to force me and Fleur to talk to each other.

"Maybe."

"Why are you being like this?"

She'd been freezing me out since I'd told her about Samir. In classic Fleur fashion, she hadn't been subtle about it, either.

"I don't know. Why are you such a bad friend?"

"I wasn't trying to be a bad friend," I hissed through clenched teeth. "Why didn't you tell me about Costa to begin with? Because you were embarrassed. Did you ever think maybe that's how I felt about Samir? I knew I was doing something wrong, and I wasn't proud of it.

"I know you love him. I know he's one of the people you're closest to. I didn't know how to talk to you about him. The more time that passed, the harder it became. In the beginning I was afraid if I told you, I'd lose you as a friend. Then as time went on, everything just became so complicated. I didn't know how to talk about it because I didn't know how I felt.

"And let's be real here. You push. You would have pushed me about it. You would have wanted to know how I felt about Samir and where things were going, and I wouldn't have had answers. I just wasn't ready to deal with it."

"And now?"

"I still don't know how I feel."

"I don't think that's true. I think you know exactly how you feel."

"Then maybe you understand."

Fleur sighed. "Yeah. I guess I do. I just need a moment to wrap my head around this. I didn't think—" She shook her head. "I just didn't think he'd get involved with someone like you."

That stung. "Gee, thanks."

"No. I didn't mean it like that. I just…" Fleur sighed again.

"You're not the kind of girl you just fool around with. He knows better. Especially now. His parents want him to get married when he graduates. There's a plan in place that has been there for years—"

"And I don't fit into that plan."

"I'm sorry." She stood up and walked over to the bed, sinking down next to me. She reached out and squeezed my hand. "I don't want to see you get hurt."

I believed her, but it didn't make it any easier to hear.

"I think we're a little past the point of worrying about me getting hurt."

"I'm sorry I mentioned him going to Lebanon."

"You had no way of knowing." I attempted a half-hearted smile. "Why wouldn't he go visit his girlfriend? It makes sense. It fits. I'm the one who doesn't fit."

"It's not like that with her. He doesn't love her. He never has."

"Oh, I know. Or so he tells me. That doesn't make it hurt any less."

She nodded. "No. I suppose it doesn't."

19

Samir

I loved being back in Lebanon. I hated being home.

The second my plane touched down, I felt a sense of belonging I never felt anywhere else. I loved France, loved Paris. And after almost four years in London, I loved it there, too. But Beirut was home.

Even in November the weather was perfect—warm enough for a T-shirt and jeans. I looked out at the water on the drive to my father's office, wishing I could escape to the sun and the waves. I needed to decompress after my conversation with Layla, needed to take the edge off before I faced my father.

But I also needed to get back to London. So instead of staring out at the ocean, I stared at my father's office door, nerves and tension filling me. No one else made me feel like I could never quite measure up.

His secretary flashed me a smile before I walked through the door, probably for good luck. I was going to need it.

My father didn't even bother looking up as I walked in. He was busy, and I was an unwelcome reminder that his legacy was in jeopardy.

"What are you doing home?" he asked, greeting me in Arabic.

Hi. How are you? I'm fine, thanks. You?

"I had a couple days off from class." He didn't invite me to sit. Flashes of my childhood, standing before him, reciting my litany of misdeeds, passed before my eyes.

"What did you want to talk to me about?"

This was not going to go well. "I broke up with Layla."

Which made this the second awkward conversation for me today. Somehow I'd figured this one would go a hell of a lot worse than the first. Layla had handled our breakup with calm and grace, which just made me feel like an even bigger ass.

She'd find someone else—we both knew it. She was beautiful and from the right family. Her parents would find her a better match. I didn't doubt I was easy to replace—for her and for them. But at the same time, I'd broken a commitment I'd made, and regardless of what my father thought, my word meant something to me.

I waited for the explosion, waited for the disappointment and anger I'd known my whole life. He was silent. The silence almost felt worse. I felt the need to fill it with *something*.

"It wasn't working. I'm not ready to settle down."

A combination of anger and disgust flashed across his face. I hated that it was like looking in a mirror.

"I'd hoped you'd outgrown these childish antics."

I clenched my jaw. It was always like this with him. Everything I did was wrong; nothing was good enough. I would have said he hated me, but hate would require too much effort. I was just a colossal fuck-up in his eyes.

"Do you think this is just about you? That your decisions don't affect anyone else? Did you consider how much this means to your mother? To Layla's?"

I struggled not to flinch. "No, sir."

"You're twenty-three. This is your last year of university.

It's time for you to settle down, get serious about your life. Do you think you're just going to graduate and come back here and live the way you do in London?"

I shook my head, fighting back the anger building inside of me. I wanted to walk away. But he was right—I didn't have much of a plan. I'd never had one. They always told me what to do, and I either did it or fought it. And eventually I always caved anyway. As long as he controlled the money, he controlled me. We both knew it, too.

I would come into my trust fund in a few months when I graduated. It was enough to live on, enough to be comfortable. But compared to what I was set to inherit—millions, hundreds of millions—it was nothing. And I was the only male left to take over everything when my father died. Our legacy mattered.

"Answer me."

I'd forgotten what this was like. Forgotten the clammy hands and the pit in my stomach.

"No, sir."

"The damage is already done. You want to spend the next few months screwing around London? Fine. But you will get married when you come home. To someone who understands the importance and responsibilities that will come with being your wife."

Inwardly I shuddered. "Yes, sir."

"You have a responsibility to this family, Samir." He made a sweeping gesture around his office, his little kingdom from which he ruled with an iron fist. "When I die, this will all be yours. I expect you to earn it."

"Yes, sir."

He dismissed me with a curt nod. I walked out of his office, the weight of my future hanging around my neck like a burden I couldn't shake off.

My phone rang. I looked down at the caller ID. *Fleur.*

"This isn't a good time."

"Tough."

I stifled a groan. There was something in her voice—an edge. She sounded more pissed off than normal, and suddenly I had a pretty good idea of why she was calling. Or maybe it was just my own guilty conscience getting in the way.

"How could you have hooked up with Maggie?"

Shit.

"Fleur—"

"Look, I get it. I know how you are. I've seen you with girls. But Maggie is different. She doesn't deserve for you to string her along and break her heart. She's been through enough. What the hell were you thinking, having sex with her, and then going to see your girlfriend? That's tacky, even for you."

"Thanks, Fleur."

I struggled to keep my temper in check. Between everything with Maggie and my dad, I felt close to losing it.

"She's my best friend. Out of everyone for you to mess with, she's the one person I'm not okay with. She deserves better."

"I agree."

"Then why did you have sex with her?"

I lifted the phone away from my ear, Fleur's voice shrill through the other end of the line.

"It wasn't exactly planned," I muttered through clenched teeth. "And I'm trying to fix it now."

"How?"

"I broke up with Layla."

A long pause filled the line. "I'm not sure if I should be happy about that or not."

"What's that supposed to mean? I didn't think you were a fan of me and Layla."

"I'm not. But I like the idea of you and Maggie even less."

I wasn't totally shocked. Fleur was fiercely protective of Maggie. I'd always thought it was a good thing, since Fleur was one of the most loyal people I knew. But now that it was Fleur standing in between me and Maggie, she was starting to feel like a pain in the ass.

"Why?"

"Because you're going to break her heart."

I was afraid of that, but strangely enough I was just as afraid of what would happen to *me* when this thing ended. I'd never felt the way I felt about Maggie before. I'd liked my last girl-friend before Layla, and when she'd cheated on me, I'd been upset. But it was nothing compared to what I felt at the idea of Maggie cheating on me or the tightness I'd felt in my chest every time she'd gone off with that British asshole.

"I would never hurt Maggie."

"Maybe not intentionally. But you will hurt her. She's not like us. She's romantic and sentimental. Things matter to her. People matter to her. What matters to you, Samir?"

I couldn't argue with some of her points. I wasn't sure I was the best guy for Maggie. But I cared about her. A lot. I wanted to be better for her. I wanted to try.

I had to ask, especially given the chance I'd just taken. "Do you think I'm one of those people? Do you think she cares about me?"

"Don't put me in the middle of this."

I laughed. "Really? I thought you just did that yourself."

"She's my friend."

"She's my friend, too. She's tougher than you give her credit for. Maggie does just fine on her own. Trust me—she knows how to handle me."

"And in the future—when you go back to Lebanon for good? What are you going to do then? What is she going to do? How is she going to handle that?"

I wanted to brush her off, but I couldn't blame Fleur for asking the same questions that had been nagging me all along.

"I don't know. I don't have all the answers. I wish I did."

"You have to tell her. You have to explain to her that whatever this thing is between the two of you, you aren't going to be around forever. She needs to be able to make the choice before she decides if she wants to be with you. She needs to understand."

"I will."

"I still don't like it."

"I know. I know you love her. But it's not your choice to make. It's hers and mine."

"At the first sign of you hurting her, I will kick your ass."

I grinned and repeated, "I know." I looked back at my watch. "Now that the interrogation is over, will you let me go?"

"Why are you in such a hurry?"

"I'm trying to get a flight back to London tonight. My dad's kind of pissed with me over the whole breakup with Layla, so the jet isn't an option."

"Are you coming back to talk to Maggie?"

"Yeah. It's not the sort of conversation I want to have over the phone. I need to explain to her about Layla and everything else."

"Well, we're not in London."

"Where are you?"

"Marbella."

I could feel the beginning of a headache coming on. "Let me guess—that was your idea?"

"Mya's actually, I just encouraged it. By the way, I don't think she likes you very much."

"Tell me about it. Does Maggie know I went to Lebanon?"

"Yes."

Fuck. "Thanks, Fleur. Way to help me out."

"It's not my fault you suck at this. Why didn't you just explain what you were doing before you left for Lebanon?"

"Because I didn't want her to think it was just me stringing her along. I've fucked up enough. I wanted to wait until it was done so she would believe in it, in me, in us."

"Well, if I'd known that, I wouldn't have said anything. But in my defense, all of this happened before I knew you were boning Maggie."

I bit back a curse. "Okay, I'm changing my ticket. I'll meet you guys in Marbella."

"You better hurry. Maggie's looking pretty hot in Spain. She's going to be a hit with all those Spanish guys—"

"I hate you."

She was still laughing as I ended the call.

20

Maggie

Spain wasn't what I'd expected. Marbella was nice—full of elegant shops, bars, and restaurants. The focal point seemed to be the marina—filled with fancy boats and gorgeous views of the water. But there were way more British people than Spanish. It almost felt like we hadn't left London at all.

"Where are all the Spaniards?" I asked Mya after we walked past yet another group talking loudly, their British accents noticeable.

"It's more of an expat haven. Lots of Brits come here for vacations. It's becoming what Ibiza used to be."

We were at the marina tonight for a party hosted by friends of Fleur's. On their yacht. Yet another experience I'd never thought I'd have.

I wrapped my pashmina around my shoulders, wishing desperately that I'd ignored Fleur's advice and worn pants instead of borrowing one of her dresses. We may have been in southern Spain, but it was still November and there was a definite chill in the air.

"Stop wrapping yourself up like an old lady. The dress is better without the scarf."

"It's freezing."

"It's not that bad." Fleur reached out, fussing with my hair.

"It is a little cold," Mya interjected. "Maybe we should just go to a bar or something."

Fleur gestured at the marina, the boats illuminated, some with strings of white lights. "And miss this? Come on. We don't get to do this in London."

She had a point. "I just wish it were warmer." My eyes narrowed. "Tell me again why you got to wear pants and I had to dress like this?"

"Because you never know who you might meet. I'm dating George. I can look but I'm not doing anything else."

"I didn't realize the depth of your feelings for George extended to fidelity."

Mya snorted.

Fleur glared at both of us.

We followed her up the boat ramp. She exchanged air kisses with her friends, and we all introduced ourselves. Fleur's friends seemed nice, but it soon became obvious they had the same vague air of friendship as most of the people I'd met through her. It was hard to tell how long they'd been friends or how any of them had met. They'd just gotten to know each other through some random party in some country no one remembered, and now met up whenever they happened to be in the same place.

This seemed to be a common thread with the international elite. Their ties were tenuous and yet they all greeted each other as though they were the best of friends. Fleur slipped into the scene with ease, but she wasn't totally herself. Her smile was brighter, her laugh louder than usual, and she just seemed more *on* than normal, as if she were trying to convince everyone she was having more fun than she really was.

"You seem a little off tonight," I commented as we grabbed a drink from the bar. We'd lost Mya to some old friends from boarding school. It was good to see her so happy after everything going on with her parents.

"I guess I wasn't as in the mood for a party as I thought I was," Fleur answered, her gaze surveying the crowd. She was restless tonight, a bundle of nervous energy.

"We can leave if you want." I sipped a glass of champagne. "Preferably before I get hypothermia."

"I'm okay. Ignore me. I'm just in a weird mood tonight." She grinned. "Sorry about the dress."

"Eh. If I were going to get hypothermia, this would be the dress that would make it all worthwhile."

I turned away from Fleur and stared out at the marina, at the vast expanse of lights. I felt like I was living someone else's life. Would I always feel this way? No matter how much time I spent in London, there was always a part of me that felt like I was playing dress-up. As strange as that feeling was, I couldn't help but think maybe it was a good thing. I wasn't entirely ready for this world to suck me in.

"You aren't having fun." I nudged Fleur. "What's up?"

"I don't know. It's always the same old parties, the same people, the same everything. It's like my life is on a constant loop." She shrugged. "That seems stupid, right?"

"Not at all. You've been through a lot. It makes sense that you would come out of it a bit changed. Now you're dealing with this shit with Costa and that email. It's a lot for anyone to have to deal with. But you know if you ever need to talk, I'm always here."

"Thanks."

Mya walked toward us, a smile on her face. "I've been looking for you. Have you guys danced yet? The DJ is amazing."

"I don't think either one of us is in a huge dancing mood,"

Fleur answered. She grinned. "But I did notice James Duncan's here."

"Seriously?"

"Who is James Duncan?"

"The older brother of a girl we went to boarding school with. Very cute. And if I'm not mistaken, there were some rumors he and Mya once shared a very hot and heavy kiss."

"Go, Mya."

"It was like five years ago. But the kiss was pretty amazing." Her eyes sparkled with mischief. "Maybe I should go reintroduce myself."

"Definitely."

I raised my champagne flute. "To old flames."

Mya's glass clinked with mine. "Wish me luck."

We both watched her walk away, disappearing into the sea of dancers. I turned my back to the crowd, facing away from Fleur, staring out at the water. My thoughts drifted to the one person who always seemed to occupy my mind. I missed him. Wished he were here with me, his arms wrapped around me, his fingers linked with mine. I wanted to talk with him, to laugh with him.

I pulled out my phone, staring down at the screen.

No new messages.

I wanted to text him. I didn't even know what I wanted to say anymore. His absence was an ache inside me. I tried to ignore the pang in my chest, tried to tell myself I didn't care. I failed miserably.

These were the moments when I hated his girlfriend the most, the moments when I felt the weakest, when my resolve wavered. Because I wanted him—and not just at night. Not just in those moments when we fell into bed together. I wanted to walk into parties on his arm. To stare at the stars with him, as corny as it sounded. I wanted more than I had.

I wanted it all.

Fleur turned to me, a wide smile on her face. She lifted her champagne flute in the air, clinking it with mine. "Here's to new flames." She put her arms around me, pulling me into a hug. "I told him if he hurt you, I'd kill him. I still think you deserve better, but if he makes you happy then that's what I want for you. Give him a chance to explain." She stepped back and winked at me. "And tell me all of the hot details later."

She walked away, gliding through the crowd. I stared after her, confusion filling me.

My phone beeped. I looked down at the screen again, my heart pounding at the sight of his name there—

Turn around.

What? I reread the words, once, twice, as my heartbeat kicked up a notch. And then I turned.

Samir stood in front of me, close enough that I could have touched him. He was dressed in a white shirt, a black jacket, and a pair of dark jeans. He clutched a bouquet of pink peonies in his hand.

I opened my mouth to speak, but no words came out. My brain fired rapid thoughts—What had Fleur meant? What was he doing in Spain? Were those flowers really for me?—but all I could do was stand there and stare. All around us, people talked and laughed, music blaring from the DJ booth. It all faded away. All that mattered was me and Samir. All that mattered was the look in his eyes.

He stepped forward, closing the distance between us, holding out the bouquet.

I took the flowers from him, speech still eluding me. Everything seemed to be moving in slow motion.

He reached out, his fingers running through my hair, catching a stray strand and tucking it behind my ear.

And then he was kissing me, and I knew everything had changed.

21

Samir

I'd intended to wait before kissing her. Before putting my hands on her, really. But then I saw her standing there, the stars behind her, wearing a dress I wanted to peel off her body, and I literally couldn't stop myself.

I had to kiss her.

The second my lips touched hers, I felt the same click I always felt. We'd kissed enough that there was a familiarity there now. I knew the shape of her mouth, the taste of her lips. Yet each time, I felt as if I were wading deeper and deeper into uncharted territory, discovering a new part of her.

Kissing her felt like drowning, the waves crashing over me, pulling me under. I was losing control, inch by inch. Forgetting myself, where we were, anything, everything but the feel of her mouth on mine, the feel of her body—her bare skin, beneath my hands, in my arms, everywhere.

She broke away first—

"What was that? What are you doing here? I thought you were in Lebanon?" Her voice was breathless, her lips swollen from the kiss. It just made me want to kiss her more.

I'd never been a big kisser. For me, kissing was just a pre-lude to sex. But with Maggie—everything was different with Maggie.

"I was in Lebanon. Fleur told me you were here. So now I'm here."

"Why?"

It was ridiculous that this made me nervous, but it did. It was all or nothing.

"I can't stay away from you. I was an idiot to let you leave my bed that morning. I want a chance to start over. To really start over. I want to be with you."

She studied me for a moment, not speaking. The wind whipped around her, her brown hair flowing over her shoul-ders. I would never really understand what it was about her that took my breath away. She was beautiful, but I'd known beauti-ful girls before. There was something about her—in that wide goofy smile, in those sparkling eyes—that easily made her the most beautiful thing I'd ever seen.

"What about your girlfriend?"

"I don't have a girlfriend anymore." I tried out a smile, my heart racing. "For the moment, at least. Maybe you'd be will-ing to help me with that?"

She looked down at the ground for a moment before fac-ing me again. A small smile played at her lips, teasing out the dimple I loved.

"Maybe."

That word—and the smile that came with it—felt like ev-erything.

"Let's get out of here, okay? I got a room at your hotel. We can go talk. And figure out what happens next."

I held out my hand to her. She hesitated for a moment—and then she reached out, linking her fingers with mine.

It felt right.

Maggie

I had to be dreaming. That was the only explanation. Samir couldn't really be here, holding my hand, looking at me like I was his world.

I followed him through the party, my hand in his. Every once in a while, he would stop and respond to someone he knew. Each time he stopped, he draped his arm around me, holding me against his side. It was like he was afraid if he let me loose, even for a minute, I'd disappear. I knew the feeling.

Minutes later, we'd finally made it off the yacht.

"You okay to walk? Are you cold?"

"A little bit." I gestured at my dress. "I borrowed it from Fleur. There's not exactly a lot of fabric going on here."

"I can see that." His lips grazed my ear, his voice growing huskier. "I'm kind of hoping I can take it off of you later."

I flushed.

He removed his jacket and slipped it around my shoulders. I burrowed into its warmth, loving the faint scent of his cologne surrounding me.

"I missed you," he whispered. "It's been a long week."

"I missed you, too."

I barely paid attention the rest of the way back to the hotel. I didn't notice our surroundings or the people walking down the street around us. All I knew was I was with Samir. And somehow—miraculously—he didn't have a girlfriend anymore.

We walked into the hotel, heading for the elevator. I followed Samir inside, leaning back against the wall while he pressed the button. I needed a moment to catch my breath, to wrap my head around how much my life had changed in less than an hour. The doors closed and he turned to face me.

His gaze ran over my body, and warmth spread through me as he looked his fill. He walked toward me, leaning into me, pushing me back against the wall.

"Do you know how badly I want to touch you right now?"

For a moment, I couldn't think, much less speak.

"I would start here." His fingers traced the edge of the top of my dress, hovering, dipping into the hollow of my cleavage. His fingers were warm against my cool skin, his touch electric. I pushed against his hand. I didn't care that we were in an elevator. Didn't care that there were probably security cameras around. I wanted his hands and lips all over my body. I wanted him exactly as he was right now, his eyes dark with lust, tension vibrating through his body.

"I would touch you here." His fingers slipped under the dress's stretchy fabric, cupping my breast, his fingertips grazing my nipple, tugging gently.

I moaned.

Things were moving so quickly, like they always did with us, pushing me over the edge. Reason and caution gave way to want and need. Maybe I was wrong to act like he wasn't a choice I made every time his hands touched my body, every time his lips touched mine. My body chose him every time. I chose him every time.

Suddenly, he stopped, slipping his hand out, readjusting the fabric so I was once again covered.

I blinked, peering over his shoulder. The elevator doors were open on his floor.

Samir stared down at me. "I plan on finishing this." He squeezed my hand. "We have to talk first, though."

I nodded, my arms around him, enjoying the feel of his hard body against mine.

I followed him down the hall until we stopped in front of his room, waited behind him while he fumbled with his key. It was weird—I should have been nervous. But something had shifted between us. I didn't feel nervous anymore. I felt like I belonged here with him. There was power in the knowledge that he wanted me, just as much as I wanted him.

Samir opened the door, and I followed him in as he flipped on the lights. The room was bigger than the one Fleur, Mya, and I had, but I wasn't surprised. Classic Samir.

I walked over to the window, staring down at his view of the marina, feeling as if I were on top of the world. A giddy excitement filled me—an awareness that we were at the beginning of something new between us. Something I badly wanted.

I turned and faced him. He stood near the door, his hands at his sides, watching me.

"You're so beautiful."

I believed it when he said it, believed the look in his eyes, the tone of his voice. I didn't care if I was beautiful or not—just that he thought I was.

I took a step toward him.

His lips curved. "I think you should stay there."

I stopped in my tracks. "Why?"

"Because I was serious when I said we needed to talk, and I have this horrible, unavoidable habit of getting distracted around you."

I grinned. "Sorry, not sorry."

"You kind of have me by the balls and everything else."

I snorted, struggling to ignore my racing heart. "Come on, the legendary Samir Khouri? I find it hard to believe any girl has ever had you by the balls."

"They haven't." His expression turned suddenly serious. "Just you."

Gymnasts started tumbling in my stomach. "What now?"

"I like you."

"I like you, too."

"You're one of the few female friends I have. And you're definitely the only one I can't stop thinking about naked."

My lips twitched. "Ditto on the naked part."

"I'm graduating in May. The plan has always been for me to go back to Lebanon. My father's campaign for the National

Assembly will be in full force, and he wants me to start getting involved in political life."

I nodded. I'd heard this before.

"When I go back to Beirut, I'll be expected to settle down. I know it sounds weird, but my life in London is a temporary thing."

"Kind of like sowing your oats?"

"What?"

He looked so confused, it was kind of adorable. "American expression. Your last hurrah before you have to settle down."

"Something like that. I went to Beirut and negotiated with my dad. I told him Layla wasn't right for me. The rest of the school year is mine. But when I go back to Lebanon—"

I could fill in the blanks. "You have to do what your family says."

Something that might have been embarrassment flashed across Samir's face. "Yeah."

I hesitated. "Do you ever just want to say no? Do you ever think of choosing a different life for yourself? Do you even want to go into politics?"

"It's complicated. Life is different when I'm at home. What I want doesn't really factor into it. My father is the head of our family. Everyone respects him. And when he dies, someone will have to take care of my mother, to take care of the rest of the family. I'm his heir. It's my responsibility."

"That's a lot to put on you."

I didn't know what to say to him. I'd seen hints of this side of Samir, certainly known it existed. But in this moment I realized how much older he really was, how much more worldly. How much of his carefree attitude was a reaction to the massive weight he always carried on his shoulders?

"I forget myself when I'm in London. Here, life is different. Here, I feel like I can do anything." His gaze met mine. "I forget myself when I'm with you."

There was something heavy in the air between us, and suddenly I had to confront it. Had to know where I stood with him.

"What do you want with me? What is this? We talk around it, dance around it, but I need to *know*. I need to know if what's between us is real. I need to know what you want from me."

"Be with me."

My heart thudded. "How?" Everything he had just said ran through my mind. "For how long?"

"I graduate in May. Be with me until then. I know you deserve more. I wish I didn't have these strings attached. I wish I could be more for you. But this is who I am. I can't give you more. We both have to think of our futures, and I don't want you to change your life for me."

The pounding in my heart increased. I needed a moment to think, to figure out what I wanted. I needed a moment to breathe. I turned, walking toward the window. I pulled back the drapes and stared down at the marina.

"What are you thinking?"

"I don't know."

"What do you want?" His voice was urgent, as if he was waiting on my answer, as if it meant everything to him.

I felt it between us, that same push and pull that were always there. It confused me, scared me, made me want to run, made me desperate to stay. He'd broken up with his girlfriend. He was here, offering me a chance to have him—as much as he could give. I knew he wanted me. I knew we were good together. But was that enough to make it worth it? To make him worth it?

Six months. He was offering me six months. Then what? How was I going to be with him for six months and then watch him walk away? How was I going to let him go? I couldn't see a future for us either, and yet the idea of agreeing to something temporary, only to be hurt later, seemed foolish. What did "be with me" mean anyway? Was he talking about something exclusive? Was this just a fancy way of saying "friends with benefits"? It scared me how much I cared. This was so far beyond just sex for me. I was getting pulled deeper into something I wasn't sure I could get out of.

A lot could happen in six months.

22

This was not how I'd imagined things going. I didn't know what else to say. And I had no clue what she meant by *I don't know.*

Didn't know how she felt? Didn't know what she wanted?

"What do you want?" I repeated, pushing the words out. I just stood there, waiting for her answer, feeling helpless. I wanted her to say she wanted to be with me; I'd *thought* that's what she would say. But now she was quiet, and I had no fucking clue what was going on in her head.

"I don't know."

"I got that part." I sat down on the edge of the bed. "I'm just trying to figure out why you don't know."

"'Be with me' is a little vague."

"How is that vague?"

I wanted her. She wanted me. What was vague about that?

"Well, what does it mean?" For a moment, she was quiet. "Does it mean we're exclusive?"

"Are you involved with any guys I should know about?"

Did she honestly think I would be okay with the idea of her and other guys?

"No, of course not."

"Then why would you think it wouldn't be exclusive?" I couldn't remember the last time I'd thought about another girl, I mean really thought about another girl. Months, maybe? A year? Not to mention I'd broken up with Layla for her. And she was asking about exclusivity?

She turned to face me. "Let's just say I know you."

"Well, then maybe you shouldn't get involved with me at all," I snapped.

"Samir—"

"If you think I'm just some asshole who fucks a different girl every night, then why are you here?"

"I don't think that."

"Then what?"

"I don't know. I'm just not sure what you want from me. What you want me to be. I haven't really done this before, and I don't know what I'm doing. I'm trying to figure it out, but I don't know what the right decision is."

"We're the right decision." Frustration filled me. "Trust me. I know I was your first, so you don't have a lot to compare to, but I promise you, we are right. I've been with other girls—"

She grimaced.

"And it's never been like it is with you." I pushed on, ready to show all my cards, ready to do whatever I had to in order to make her say yes. "It's not just the sex. There's something between us. I know you feel it too. So yeah, when I talk about being together, I mean exclusively. No one else. Just us."

She stared back at me, still too quiet. I struggled to find the right words, to think of what I could tell her to convince her she was different. My past was working against me. I knew she was thinking of all those nights in the clubs, all the girls. And for a moment, I wished I could go back in time and change the decisions I'd made. If I could, I would have been a different person for her. I didn't know how to explain I was different now. That she made me want to be different. That I didn't want to lose her. I *couldn't* lose her.

Maggie

"I'm scared."

I wasn't sure who was more surprised to hear those words come out of my mouth—me or Samir.

"I'm not going to hurt you."

"Aren't you?"

Samir sighed. "Do you trust me?"

"Sometimes. Mostly." He wasn't the problem. I did trust him—for the most part. I just didn't trust myself. What if I got in too deep and couldn't pull myself out come May? What if I fell for him and then he left?

"I don't blame you." He ran a hand through his hair. "Just give me a chance, let me prove I can be what you need right now. I want to be that guy. I think I can be."

"What do you think I need?" I whispered, my doubt slipping away with each word that fell from his lips. He looked so lost sitting there on the bed, so unsure of himself. It was strange to see Samir unsure.

"You need someone who is going to push you outside of your comfort zone and challenge you. Someone who isn't going to give you a pass or let you run when things get tough."

Heat filled me.

"Come on, Maggie. It's me. You know it's me. As much as I'm willing to chase you—because you're worth chasing—there are so many things I'd rather do with you. Especially since time is running out. I want to fuck you up against that window, your naked body pressed up against the glass. I want to wake up next to you tomorrow morning. I want to take you shopping and shower you with gifts. I know you probably won't let me because you're you and you can be impossibly difficult, but I want to try. I want to be with you. Just you. I want to hold your hand in public and kiss you in front of everyone. I want everyone to know you're mine. I want you to be mine."

For six months.

It hung between us, unspoken. His speech was the most romantic thing anyone had ever said to me, and with each word my willpower unraveled. And yet, even the words, even the sight of his gorgeous face, of the lips I craved, weren't enough to erase the doubt.

All along I had figured Samir had commitment issues. It made sense. He was a player—at least he had been. But the reality was, whatever commitment issues Samir may have had paled in comparison to mine.

Six months. I could do six months. We could have fun, have sex. Keep things simple between us. Easy. I could lie to myself and pretend I didn't want him, that I had the willpower to stay away, but it would be a lie. I wanted him more with each word, with each moment. It wasn't going away. I'd made my choice a long time ago.

I took a deep breath. "Okay."

For a moment, he didn't speak, his gaze scanning my face as though he read the emotions playing out there.

"Okay, you'll be with me?" he asked, his voice hesitant, a thread of hope making its way through.

My heart pounded. "Yes."

"Are you sure?"

I nodded. "I'm sure."

A new tension filled the air. It occurred to me that for the first time since I'd known Samir, I was about to have sex with him without any guilt. He was free and his body was mine to explore—to touch, to taste, to tease. It felt like a fresh start for us—a chance to leave our baggage in the past. I wanted to grab on to the chance.

A slow smile spread across my face. Sex with us had always felt rushed and illicit. Now I wanted to savor it. If we only had six months together, I was going to make the most of them.

I reached behind my back—my hands shaking slightly—and slowly tugged the zipper down the back of my dress. A little wiggle and the dress pooled in a puddle at my feet.

I tossed Samir my sexiest grin, the pounding in my heart nearly deafening. "You were saying something about a window..."

23

Samir

She was trying to give me a heart attack. That was the only explanation.

In over a year I'd seen so many different sides of Maggie—playful, smart, sexy, vulnerable—but *this* was a completely new side to her. She was dressed—or undressed, rather—to seduce. She stood in front of the window in nothing but heels, a black lacy bra, a matching thong, and a smile. I could only gape at her and try to play catch-up, still reeling from the fact that she was onboard with the idea of *us*. Somehow in between trying to convince her and realizing I had, she'd taken her clothes off.

Would I ever be on my game with this girl?

"Are you okay?" Laughter and nerves filled her voice.

"Maybe. I think my blood pressure just spiked."

"Oh really?"

"Yes. Really. You're a health risk."

She reached behind her back, unhooking the bra. *Jesus*. She slipped the bra off, letting it drop to the floor next to the dress. I had to remember to breathe.

"You realize you're killing me right? Killing me."

Her eyes widened with mock innocence. "Me?"

"Yes, you." The words came out in a strangled gasp.

"Prove it," she teased.

My eyebrows rose at the challenge. In bed, Maggie was hot. But this? This was unbelievable.

I rose from the bed, my gaze roaming over her body as I stalked toward her. I stopped inches away, close enough that if I wanted to, I could reach out and touch her, far enough away to make her wonder if I would. I shoved my hands in my pockets, even though they were itching to *touch*. I wanted to take my time, wanted to savor this moment, drag it out until we were both on the verge of breaking. I wanted to go slow even though everything in my body screamed at me to rush.

Her lips parted and the urge to kiss her, to cover her mouth with mine, overwhelmed me. The first time we'd had sex had been intense, but I had restrained myself. Even our second time together, I'd tried to not freak her out too much. Tried not to push her past her comfort zone. But the girl standing in front of me, daring me with mischief in her gorgeous brown eyes, didn't look like she wanted to play it safe anymore.

I was happy to oblige.

"Turn around."

Maggie raised her chin slightly. "Kiss me first."

I groaned. "Bossy, aren't you?"

She laughed and the sound rolled over me. "You like it."

I did. I liked everything about her.

I hooked my arm around her back, bringing her against my body, her nipples brushing against my shirt. I kissed her, drawing her bottom lip into my mouth, catching it between my teeth, sucking on it, running my tongue along her flesh.

"You have an amazing mouth."

She grinned, pulling away. "Thanks. I could say the same about you."

"Turn around."

She shot me a look. "Are you going to be like this from now on? Domineering?"

I laughed. "Are you going to let me? Somehow I don't see that happening." I kissed her again, unable to resist. "But I think I'm going to enjoy trying." I broke away from her. "Turn around."

She hesitated and nerves filled her beautiful brown eyes. Then she turned.

For a moment I just stared. I was definitely a butt guy, and her ass was pretty much perfection.

My voice shook slightly. "Put your palms on the glass."

Maggie

A shiver went down my spine at the husky sound of Samir's voice. This was officially the hottest night of my life.

I placed my palms against the glass, the cold a stark contrast to my body's rising temperature. I'd talked a good game, but I was pretty sure I could last another few minutes, tops. My legs were weak, my nipples tight.

Even though I couldn't see him, I heard him move, a rustle of clothing and limbs, walking toward me until finally his body was behind mine, just barely touching me.

"Touch me."

"Where?" he whispered, his breath hot against my ear. He might have been playing hard to get, but his voice vibrated with need.

"Anywhere." *Everywhere.*

His arm curved around my waist, his fingers skimming across my stomach, his touch featherlight. I shuddered, a thrill running down my spine. He pressed against me, his lips grazing my ear, his teeth catching my earlobe. He nipped at it before drawing the sensitive spot into his mouth, his tongue working magic. His hand slipped from my waist, moving down, lower, leaving a trail of fire in its wake. He shifted between my legs, his fingers teasing. For a moment his fingers toyed with the lace on my underwear—petting, stroking, gliding—and then they slipped under the fabric and slid inside me before I even had a chance to catch my breath.

"Don't stop. Just please, whatever you do, don't stop."

Samir laughed, the sound low and throaty. "I couldn't stop if I wanted to."

With each touch, my body became boneless. My legs sagged, my skin rubbing against the cold glass. Samir wrapped an arm around my breasts, holding me against his body, supporting my weight. He leaned down, his teeth nipping at my nape. His fingers continued their torment.

He pressed kisses against the curve of my neck as I squirmed against his fingers, wanting more, wanting to be filled, wanting to feel him pressing inside of me. Needing it.

I reached back, fumbling with the button of his jeans. My hand brushed his erection, stroking it, exploring the length with my palm. I was greedy, ready to combust.

"Here, let me," Samir mumbled.

"Hurry."

He chuckled, his voice winded. "Going as fast as I can."

The rasp of his zipper filled the hotel room. It might have been the most erotic noise I'd ever heard. Then his hand slipped out of me. Followed by the sound of a condom wrapper opening.

I felt his warm body behind mine. I bent forward, my body tense, poised, waiting—he slid inside me slowly, inch by inch, filling me, his body stretching mine.

For a moment, he was still, his body buried in mine. He began to move, slowly at first, each leisurely slide of skin against skin making my body tremble. I wanted fast and rough. I wanted the heat and the fire and the passion. Still, he teased me, drawing it out in delicious agony.

I looked down at the glass, mesmerized by the reflection of our bodies, Samir behind me, thrusting into me. For one moment, our gazes met in the reflection. Heat filled his eyes. As close to the edge as I was, I wasn't alone.

Samir reached out behind me, his palm pressing against mine, his fingers grabbing mine, locking with me. He squeezed. Slowly, his thrusts began to increase, the tempo building.

I could feel my orgasm coming, just barely within my grasp. I craved that feeling, that moment when I felt like I was falling in a delicious spiral of tension and release.

Samir reached down with his free hand, teasing my nipple. I moaned.

Both of his hands came to rest on my hips, pulling my body even tighter against his, his thrusts becoming faster, deeper. He bent down over me, his teeth scraping my shoulder. Claiming me. Another shiver ripped through my body. Then I felt it, the orgasm building, my body sliding into moments of delicious oblivion. My knees buckled, but Samir held me up, his body pumping furiously into mine until finally he groaned as he came, the force of his thrusts pushing my body up against the glass.

We were silent for a moment, our bodies joined, exhaustion setting in.

He groaned. "You're going to destroy me."

I grinned, the waves of my orgasm still rippling through my body. My skin felt sensitive, each brush of his flesh against mine tantalizing.

"Let me know when you're ready for round two."

24

Maggie

Sunlight filled the room. I blinked for a moment, confusion filling me. I rolled over onto my side and stared across the pillow—at Samir's head resting there. His eyes were closed, long black lashes fanning out. For a moment all I could do was watch him sleep. I still couldn't really believe he was here. That he was mine. For six months, at least.

I leaned forward to drop a soft kiss on his lips. I aligned my body with his, curling into his warmth.

"That feels good," Samir murmured.

I kissed him again.

"Really good."

Our legs tangled together. Samir kissed me back, his hands stroking, stoking the fire within me. It was fast this time. There were no words, no joking, no laughter. Just a hurried frenzy of limbs and then the thrust of his body into mine. My orgasm came fast, the release less intense, a slow unraveling that left me sleepy and relaxed. I wasn't a morning person, but that could change if all my mornings were like this.

Samir gathered me into his body.

"Good morning," he whispered, his lips finding mine.

"Good morning."

Samir pressed a kiss to the top of my nose. "You're adorable when you sleep."

"What do you mean?"

"You make this little face when you dream. Your whole face scrunches up—like you're thinking really hard."

I considered this for a moment, not entirely sure I liked his description. "That sounds weird."

Samir stroked my cheek, tucking a strand of hair behind my ear. "It's adorable." He kissed the other cheek. "And you snore."

Horror filled me. "I do not."

He grinned. "You do. Kind of loudly, actually."

I elbowed him. "I don't snore."

"It's cute."

I flushed, burying my face in the pillow. "I definitely don't snore," I mumbled into it. I lifted my head up. "No one has ever told me that before." Surely, Mya or Fleur would have mentioned something.

"How many men have you slept with before me?" Samir countered, a knowing smile flashing across his face.

I stuck my tongue out at him. "I don't snore," I repeated, as if saying it enough would make it true.

He rolled me onto my back, his body covering mine. "You do. And I think it's adorable. You're adorable."

"I'm fierce."

He grinned. "Not even a little bit. What do you want to do today?"

I had a pretty good idea. "We could stay in the room."

"You've never been to Spain before; we're not spending the whole day in the hotel room." His hand trailed down my side, tickling slightly. "As much as I'd like to."

I pouted. "Fine. What do you want to do then?"

"I want to show you Marbella."

Samir

Our day together in Paris last year had taught me how fun it was to show Maggie around a city that was new to her. She noticed things I'd never paid attention to before and she was excited by everything. It was impossible not to get caught up in her enthusiasm.

"Where to first?"

I wrapped an arm around her, pulling her body close to mine.

"Breakfast first. I need to recharge my batteries since someone exhausted me last night—and this morning."

"You enjoyed every minute of it."

She was right; I did.

My phone beeped again. I pulled it out and checked the message with a frown.

"It's Fleur." I held the screen so she could see it. Yeah, I was becoming *that guy*. "She's been texting all morning." I grinned. "I think she wants details. You probably have a ton of missed calls and texts."

"Probably. My phone is off."

"Why?"

"Roaming charges are really expensive."

I hated that she had to worry about things like roaming charges. I wasn't stupid—I knew we lived very different lives. Even at a school like the International School, I lived in a different kind of financial reality from everyone else. But I still hated that Maggie had to budget so carefully.

If it were anyone else I would have paid her damned cell phone bill myself. But it was Maggie. I didn't want her to think I thought I could buy her, didn't want money to come between us. She was proud—her independence was one of my favorite things about her. And yet…

I wanted to take care of her.

"Do you usually share the details of your sex life with Fleur?" Maggie asked.

A smile tugged at the corner of my mouth when I heard the censure in her voice. "I don't share every detail."

"But you do share some."

"I've never told Fleur anything about us."

"Does it bother you that I did? I mean, not details or anything, just the general stuff."

I reached down and squeezed her hand. "No. I'm glad you had someone to talk to. She's one of your closest friends. Even though Fleur can be a giant pain in my ass, I appreciate her meddling. Sort of. She cares about you. I'm glad you have that. I'm glad you guys have each other."

"Since when did you become so profound?" Maggie teased.

"Are you really going to bust my balls? It's not even noon."

She laughed, the sound filling the air around us. "If I don't bust your balls, who will?"

I drew her against my body, loving the feel of her tits pressed against my arm, loving her sass. "Only you, babe."

Maggie

Samir took me to breakfast at a casual little restaurant tucked away on a quiet side street. We feasted on coffee and croissants, huddled together at a small, round table with rickety chairs and served by a waitress who spoke only Spanish.

It was perfect. Absolutely perfect.

I took a sip of my coffee. "What's next on the agenda?"

"Shopping. Then the beach, maybe? We could do a picnic. Or just get drunk on wine."

"You want to go shopping?"

"With you? Yeah."

"Aren't boys supposed to be allergic to that sort of thing?"

"I don't know. You tell me. You're the one who seems to have such firm notions about how men should behave."

I grinned. "Sorry. I didn't realize you were so enlightened."

"I'm French. French guys don't hate shopping. We understand the importance of looking good."

"Because it helps you get laid," I joked.

He gave me a look best described as smoldering. "Babe, I don't need help in that arena."

No, he certainly didn't. "Why do I put up with you?"

"Because you're the only one who can keep up with me."

He was right. I wanted to be annoyed with him, wanted to see his arrogance as a turnoff. And yet, this—his smirk, our banter, the heat that rose with each exchange—had me so turned on I was ready to go for round four. Or five.

Something rippled through my body. As much as we joked and danced around it, I could tell things were different between us. I felt like I belonged at the table with him, my hand in his. And as much as my brain told me he couldn't feel the same way, my heart saw my feelings reflected in his eyes and smile.

Suddenly I got what Fleur had been warning me against; I understood her concern.

I was falling for Samir. I'd been falling for him for a while now. And he'd told me already—this was just temporary.

25

Samir

Over her protests, I took her shopping.

I wasn't lying, I didn't mind shopping. Watching Maggie try on clothes wasn't exactly a hardship, either. I'd be lying if I pretended the possibility of changing room sex hadn't filled my mind. Especially when I convinced her to go to the lingerie shop.

I tried to buy her things—a pair of Gucci shoes, a Fendi purse, a lacy red thong that would have looked amazing on her. In the end the only things she ended up letting me get were ice cream and a ridiculously cheap scarf we bought from a vendor on the street. It wasn't anything fancy, but it made her smile. That was enough for me.

My phone beeped again. I groaned. "I need to take a cue from you and turn the damned thing off."

"I feel bad—I've blown Mya and Fleur off this whole trip."

"Do you want to hang out with them tonight?"

"Not really."

I grinned. "Good. Because I don't want to share."

"I don't either, but I still feel like a shitty friend. Maybe we should all go out tonight."

The selfish part of me wanted her all to myself, but I also wanted to make her happy.

"I'll get us on a list for a club."

Maggie stared up at me, surprise on her face. "Really? I figured you would rather stay in. Hanging out with me, Mya and Fleur doesn't exactly sound like your definition of a good time."

"Yeah, but it's yours. I want you to enjoy this trip. I'm the one who crashed it."

Her smile widened and suddenly I wanted to take her to the nicest club in Marbella—VIP, bottles of champagne, the whole bit. I wanted her there on my arm. We hadn't thrown around titles and yet I wanted to call her my girlfriend. I wanted to show her off. Not just because she was gorgeous, but because she was amazing. She was funny and smart and cool; she was so *real*—completely different from anyone I had ever met before.

More than anything, she got me. She wasn't with me because I was rich or came from a powerful family. She made me feel like I could be a different guy. Someone better. Someone I'd never cared about being before. She was special and she made everyone around her feel like they could be special, too.

"You're spoiling me."

I grinned. "I'm trying. I wish you would let me spoil you more."

Maggie pressed a kiss to my cheek. "You've done more than enough."

"What did I do to deserve you?" I asked, my voice light, teasing. I tried to act like the question didn't matter. But it did. I knew what girls saw in me; I was used to it. But Maggie didn't seem to want those things or care about them, and it staggered me.

"You aren't the guy you show to everyone else. You're different—more. I like discovering that. I like that part of you feels like a secret only I know about."

For a moment I couldn't form the words I wanted to say to her. She made me tongue-tied, twisted me into knots. I didn't feel like I had game with her. I felt raw, exposed. She was five feet, four inches of scary and I couldn't get enough of her.

Maggie

The beach was our next destination. We linked hands, walking with our shoes off, toes digging into the sand. We strolled in silence, the waves crashing against the shore the only sound around us. It was chilly between the sea air and the cold, wet ground and yet I didn't really care.

Today had been one of those days that felt too good to be true. There was a haze over it—it felt like a dream, like I had borrowed someone else's life. Maybe I had. Maybe the knowledge that this was temporary made it even more special. We felt finite, like a moment—a shooting star or the fireflies Jo and I used to chase during the summer. This feeling—the idea that I belonged, that I'd finally found a place I could be myself—I wanted to cling to it.

"You're quiet."

I turned to look at Samir, a wave of surprise crashing over me the way it always did when I saw him. He was so different from the kind of guy I'd grown up expecting to find. I couldn't imagine him in my world, eating barbecue or going to a football game. I couldn't quite see myself in his.

I loved London. I loved the International School and going to clubs and drinking champagne. I loved feeling like I was standing on the edge of a whole new world, close enough to dip my toes in. I loved the possibility of it all, the magic and the adventure of this life. But as weird as it sounded, I loved being a visitor and not a permanent resident. I saw how things were for Mya and Fleur—they had everything, more money than I could probably ever dream of—but I doubted much dazzled them anymore. I loved being dazzled—the rush of excitement, the sense that I must be dreaming, that I was living far beyond my own potential. I never wanted to lose that feeling.

"Just thinking of how we must be the perfect example of opposites attracting."

"I'm not sure I would call us opposites."

"Have you looked at us lately? I'm pretty sure we couldn't come from more different places if we tried."

"True." Samir studied me, curiosity in his voice. "You never really talk about South Carolina."

"It's not that exciting. I come from a small town—a couple stoplights." I shrugged. "It's nice, the people are friendly, everyone knows each other and people live their whole lives there. It works for them."

"It didn't work for you."

"No, it didn't."

I didn't know how to explain it to him. Maybe I didn't know how to explain it myself.

"Why?"

I pushed a stray strand of hair away from my face, staring out at the ocean. We'd stopped walking, our bodies specks in the large expanse of beach. The sand felt endless, and this late in the day, with the sun almost setting, it was nearly empty— our own private world.

"Because I didn't fit there. I tried. I wanted to. But it just never felt like home." I sighed. "When I was a kid I used to hear about my dad going to all of these cool places—Korea, Japan, Germany—and I kept waiting for him to take me with him." I laughed, the sound eaten up by the waves. "I would get these stupid guide books from the library and I would read them cover to cover. I wanted to know everything about his life there. I wanted to be ready—" I broke off, staring out into the ocean. "I wanted to be ready in case he ever came and got me."

I hated how pathetic it sounded, how much it seemed like my entire life had been defined by my father's absence, his choices, never mine.

"I'm sorry."

I shrugged it off, like I didn't need to hear the words, even though a part of me did need them. No one had ever acknowledged that I got a shit deal from *both* my parents. My grandparents made excuses for my dad's absence, but they never acknowledged he had fucked up. In all fairness, I'd never talked about it. Until now. Until Samir.

"I think I just always tried to convince myself things were temporary. That I would only be in South Carolina for a few years before he would come get me. Obviously that wasn't the case." I grimaced. "Sorry. I didn't mean to be a total downer."

"You and your American expressions. You weren't being a *downer.*"

I elbowed him in the side.

"You're going home for Christmas?"

"Yeah."

"Will your dad be there?"

"This year. Yeah. He's bringing *her* home." I didn't bother keeping the edge out of my voice. I liked that I could be myself, unfiltered, with Samir. He'd been the first person I'd talked to after I'd found out my father had married a stranger. He'd pretty much seen it all when it came to my baggage.

"That sounds pretty miserable."

"I have a feeling it will be."

He gathered me closer against his body. "I think I'm going to miss you."

Something tightened in my chest. "I may miss you, too," I teased.

"Oh, really? What's this 'may' business?"

I grinned. "I can't let you get a big head. Although I'm pretty sure we're past that point."

"Very funny." He grabbed me, his arms wrapped tightly around my body, lifting my feet off the ground. He spun in a circle, pulling me along with him. I was dizzy and breathless, completely swept away in the moment and the feel of his strong body anchoring mine.

"What are you doing?"

He winked. "Getting you back." He moved closer to the water, his eyes dancing.

I turned my head, looking down at the waves. "Don't even think about it. It's cold and we're going to get soaking wet."

"Where's your sense of adventure?" He inched closer to the shore. Water hit my calves, and the saltwater smell filled my nostrils.

"Samir." My voice held a warning note, but as far as protests went, mine were weak.

His lips swooped down and suddenly I didn't care about the water anymore.

26

Samir

The end of the winter semester snuck up on us in a wave of papers and exams and crap I didn't want to be doing. Before I knew it, I was looking at my last week in London before winter break, my last week with Maggie.

I didn't want to let her go even though I knew I had to. She would head back to her grandparents, and I was going to France. We split most of our time between Beirut and Paris, but my mother liked to spend Christmas with her family, so I usually spent the winter in Paris. Plane tickets had been purchased, plans made. But I saw the shadow that clouded Maggie's eyes every time she talked about her Christmas plans. If I could have spared her having to go home and deal with the shit with her dad, I would have.

I trailed a hand down her bare side, my fingers tracing lazy patterns on her naked skin.

"We're supposed to be studying," she protested, lifting her head from the book on my bed.

I ran my hand through her hair, tilting her chin with my free hand and capturing her lips. My tongue slipped into her mouth, teasing, devouring her. I shifted, pulling her along with me, wrapping her gorgeous legs around me, making sure she felt just how much I wanted her.

"Studying," Maggie murmured against my mouth, her teeth tugging on my lower lip.

I stroked her tits through her thin top, the fabric already bunched up, exposing plenty of pale skin.

"It's just a small break. I only need a few minutes."

Maggie laughed. "Oh, lucky me. With an invitation like that, how can I resist?"

I grinned. "Hey, I'm exhausted. I seem to remember *someone* waking me up in the middle of the night."

"I didn't hear any complaints."

"And you never will." I leaned forward, brushing my mouth against hers.

"We both have finals tomorrow," she reminded me, the words getting lost between our kisses.

"It'll be fine." I cupped my hands around her waist, squeezing, drawing her flesh against mine.

Maggie pulled back. "It will not be fine. Scholarship, remember? I can't afford to do badly. No matter how much I'd rather be doing you."

I sighed, resting my forehead against hers.

"Fine. I'll be good." I moved my hands off her, staring up at her gorgeous face.

She rolled away, grabbing the book from the floor.

"But you're going to have to put on a sweatshirt or something if we're going to keep studying. I can't concentrate—especially when you aren't wearing a bra."

Maggie laughed. "Cute, but I'm out. I'm going to head back to my room and study with Fleur and Mya for a bit."

"You sure?" I tried to keep the disappointment out of my voice. Sometimes I worried I came on too strong, that she'd get freaked out by how much I liked having her around. But with time a limited commodity between us, it was impossible not to feel like I had to make the most of every moment.

"Yeah. I'm really worried about this exam. It's all essay and the professor's kind of a dick." She gave me a look filled with mock censure. "Besides, isn't your final in the class you've been messaging me during? Maybe you should be studying, too."

I did my best to look contrite. "Yes, ma'am."

Maggie laughed.

"Are we still on for tomorrow night?"

I tried to sound casual about it. It was our last night in London before we each went home for winter break. For three weeks. Three *very long* weeks. It was possible I was dreading it as much as Maggie.

I didn't exactly talk to my parents during the school semester so the fallout from my breakup with Layla had been minimal at best. But now that I would be home for three weeks… I could already envision the lecture. Something about how I was disappointing my parents and not living up to my legacy. My father would remind me of my worst childhood transgressions and my mother would do her best to throw a series of society girls at me. The only benefit was that at least in Paris I had Fleur, so that was one family member I could stand.

Maggie grinned—that big silly grin of hers, the one that made her whole face light up—and all thoughts of my holiday fled. "I wouldn't miss it."

I pressed a swift kiss to her lips. "Good luck on your exam tomorrow."

She hesitated for a moment. "Why don't I come back after I'm done studying? I can sleep here."

A stupid grin slid onto my face. We'd slept together every night since Marbella. I'd gotten used to having her in my bed, curled up beside me. I'd never been big on sharing my space with someone—I was more a sprawl-out-all-over-the-bed kind of guy—but with her, it worked.

"Sounds perfect."

Maggie

I didn't want to leave. I was cursing my stupid decision to spend Christmas at home. I hadn't wanted to disappoint my grandparents, but maybe I should have come up with another plan. One that didn't involve being away from Samir for three weeks—or having to be around my dad.

I walked back to my room, trying to push the fear and doubt out of my mind. It was just three weeks. We could handle three weeks. I tried to ignore the part of me that worried he would change his mind about us or meet some girl in some club.

I punched in the code to my room, shifting my books around. The door swung open.

"Coming up for air?"

I grinned at Fleur. "Very funny. Where's Mya?"

"Final."

I gestured to the magazines surrounding Fleur. "You done?"

"Finished my last one three hours ago." She grinned. "I'm free."

"I hate you."

"Hey, I don't feel sorry for you at all. I've been here studying for days and you're the one getting laid all the time." Her nose scrunched up. "Even if you are banging my cousin."

"I have not been getting laid all the time."

She laughed. "You definitely have. You have that 'I just got fucked' look all over you."

My face heated.

"You're so easy to tease," Fleur said with a smirk.

"Thanks. What about George? Aren't things heating up between you guys?"

"George is a nice guy. It's not really like that with him."

"I'm pretty sure even nice guys get laid."

"Not this one."

Surprise filled me. The Fleur I knew was pretty much, *I came, I saw, I conquered.*

She was quiet.

"Okay, what's up?"

"Nothing."

I sank down on my bed. "Something is up. Look, I know I haven't been around as much as I used to be—"

"You aren't around at all," Fleur corrected.

It stung, but I couldn't disagree with her.

"I know. I'm sorry. I'm a shit friend. But I'm here now. I want to hear about you and George. Why haven't you guys hooked up yet? You've been dating for what, two months now?"

"Three."

"Okay, so what's the problem?"

A guilty look flashed across Fleur's face. "Don't hate me."

"What?"

"I don't think I can do this." The words rushed out in one quick swoop. Misery flashed across Fleur's face.

"Why?"

"I just don't feel anything. At all. He's a nice guy. And you were right; it's nice being with a guy who is sweet to me. Who doesn't play games and who I don't have to worry about fucking around on me."

"But?"

"I don't want to be with a guy because he's nice. I know you didn't get the Costa thing—I get that no one got the Costa thing. But when I was with him, I felt good. Alive. Everything was exciting and fun, and I know no one expects to hear this from me, but I got butterflies. Even months into being together I got butterflies. With George—it's nice. It's comfortable. It's safe. But it's so boring that at times I want to scream. We don't have anything in common. And I always feel like I'm walking on eggshells with him. He's *so* nice and I don't want to hurt his feelings—shocking, I know. But you know me, that's not really me."

"Maybe the up and down, the fighting, the worry about him cheating—maybe those were the things that gave you butterflies with Costa. Maybe it wasn't really him at all. Maybe you just miss the conflict. Maybe you don't know how to do easy."

"We don't seem to have chemistry, though. There's no spark. No fire. We don't banter. Do you know what I mean? There's no sparkle."

I did know. All those things she described were exactly how I felt around Samir.

"You're right—I need a good guy. I get it now. Costa was a huge mistake. And believe me, I don't want to go back to that. But I want to be with a guy who makes me look the way you look right now."

"Me?"

"You sparkle."

I rolled my eyes, trying to ignore the mad pounding in my heart. "Whatever."

"He makes you happy."

"He's fun."

"You make him happy, too. He's different with you. You guys are good together." She grinned. "I'll even admit I was wrong."

I laughed. "As shocking as that admission was, I see what you're doing. Don't change the subject. We're talking about you and George."

"I don't know that there really is a me and George."

"Yeah, but he thinks there is."

The guilty look flashed across Fleur's face again. "I don't want to hurt him."

"I know you don't."

"What would you do if you were me? You've had more experience being a nice girl than I have."

"I have no clue. I like George. A lot. He's a good guy and he's wild about you. He's smart and he's cute. He's a catch."

"I know. I feel like an asshole complaining about this, but I'm not happy. I know this isn't really a problem—I shouldn't be bitching about how much my boyfriend likes me."

"It is a problem if you don't feel the same way."

Fleur sighed. "Maybe I should give him more of a chance."

"Not a bad idea. Just don't lead him on. If you're having doubts, you need to talk to him. Maybe you can slow things down a bit."

"I guess."

"Is everything else okay? You seem kind of off."

Fleur sighed again. "I don't know anymore. I thought this year would be different. I thought I could get past everything that happened and be a different person. Better. Instead I just feel like a fucking mess."

"You aren't a mess. You're just in transition right now. It makes sense that you're going to struggle a bit. It's not going to be easy. Everything will be okay."

I could tell by the look in her eyes that she didn't believe me. I couldn't blame her—I wasn't sure I believed it myself.

"Can I join you guys?" I gestured to the empty seat at Max and George's table.

George grinned. "Of course."

It was my last exam this morning. I was sort of ready. Maybe. I'd studied last night for a few hours and then gone up to Samir's room to fall asleep. He'd woken up in the morning for his final and I still had a few hours before mine.

"Are you guys done with exams?"

George nodded. Max grimaced. "One left. Managerial accounting."

"That sounds pretty miserable."

"It is."

"Hi." Fleur sat down next to me. She leaned across the table, pressing a kiss to George's cheek, ignoring Max.

"It's nine a.m. How do you look like you just stepped out of a fashion magazine?" I asked with mock annoyance.

I was very happily rocking my standard exam uniform of sweatpants and a hoodie, and I couldn't have cared less. Fleur wore some kind of black sweater dress that hugged her body. Her hair was pulled up in a high ponytail that swung with each jerk of her head.

"It's a French thing."

Max snorted but didn't look up from his breakfast.

"Where's your better half?"

I pulled off an end of my croissant. "Exam."

"Are we still going out tonight?"

"Yeah, Samir booked a bunch of tables at Babel."

"You're in, right?" she asked George.

He nodded like he was into it, but the dread in his eyes said something else entirely.

Max continued eating, not looking up. I shot Fleur a look. I knew she wasn't a big fan of Max's, but I felt like an ass not inviting him.

She ignored me.

"Max, do you want to come? There's a big group of us going."

He laughed. "Thanks, but it's not really my scene."

Fleur smirked. "Obviously."

"Fleur!"

Max shook his head. "Believe me, there's no need to spare my feelings. I would have to actually care what Fleur thinks in order to be offended."

"It's really a shame you can't hear what I'm thinking right now," Fleur shot back with a saccharine smile, flipping him off.

"Really mature."

Fleur glared back at him.

"Are they always like this?" I asked George.

"Unfortunately, yes."

"Fleur needs to learn to play nice with others." Max smirked. "Must be a French thing."

"Ass."

I sighed. "Please. It's too early. Can we save the bickering until I've had my coffee?"

Fleur rolled her eyes. "Whatever. I'm out. Good luck on your exam, Mags." She kissed George quickly and then turned away.

Max's head jerked up, his gaze narrowed as he watched her walk away. "Explain to me again why you're with her, bro."

George shook his head. "Don't start."

"You should come out with us," I interjected, struggling to change the subject.

"It's really not my scene."

"It'll be fun. Besides, that way George won't be bored."

"Come on, man. She's right—it'll be fun. It's the end of the semester—time to celebrate a bit. Besides, maybe you'll meet a hot girl of your own."

Looking the way Max did, I was pretty sure that was a given.

"If you don't go, Fleur will think she's gotten the best of you," I teased. "She's all bark and no bite. You just have to show no fear." I echoed the advice Samir had once given me.

George nodded. "You owe me one after the last time we went out. Wingman, remember?"

Max sighed. "Fine, I'm in. I can handle a night out with the Ice Queen."

27

Samir

"I invited some people out tonight."

I tore my attention from her bare legs. At least I tried.

"What?"

"I added some guests to your little end-of-semester party."

I ran my hand up her leg, flirting with the edge of her hemline. I wished we were in private, didn't care as much as I should that we were in the back of a cab.

"Are you listening?"

"Sort of." My lips traveled to her ear, leaving soft kisses there, enjoying the shiver that ran through her body. "Not really."

Pretty much everything I had was focused on getting under that dress.

"Why exactly did I agree to a night out?" I whispered against her hair, inhaling the scent of her shampoo.

"Because we needed to celebrate. You have one semester left in your college career. It's a moment."

I couldn't have cared less.

I ran my hands over her body, cupping her curves, loving the feel of her plastered against me. "Maybe I just did it so I could see you in that dress and get you out of it later," I murmured, my lips brushing against the bare skin at her neck.

"One-track mind."

"Damn straight."

Maggie cocked her head to the side, exasperation filling her voice. "You haven't listened to one word I've said, have you?"

She was cute when she did the stern librarian thing. I struggled to look properly contrite. "Sorry. You invited people out tonight, right?"

"Yeah, Max and George."

I groaned. "Not exactly a party."

"Are you mad?"

I shook my head, shifting her onto my lap.

She pressed her lips to mine.

"I'm going to miss you," she murmured against my mouth.

"Same."

I didn't think she realized how much I wasn't looking forward to this break. Sure, exams were over, and logically I knew we should be celebrating—but I wasn't ready to let her go just yet. I wasn't sure I'd ever be ready to let her go.

The cab stopped in front of Babel. I got out, walking around and opening the door for Maggie. For a moment, I just stood there, staring down at her. It almost hurt to look at her. She was that beautiful.

She tilted her head to the side. "What?"

I shook my head, forcing a smile onto my lips. "Nothing. I was just thinking about how lucky I am."

She slid her palm into mine, linking fingers in a move that felt altogether too natural. "I'm the lucky one."

Maggie

I'd gone clubbing with Samir plenty of times. I was used to the attention, to the people who flocked to him, hoping for a chance to sit at his table and be part of the select group he called friends. In London, everyone wanted to be a VIP, and Samir was the real deal. I'd never been more aware of it than tonight, when I walked into Babel on his arm.

As Samir guided me down the concrete steps leading from the street level down into the club entrance, my hand clutched in his, I was struck by how much my life had changed in a little over a year. I'd come here my first night out in London—when he was just a guy who had seemed impossibly out of my league. I'd had my first kiss here; *we'd* had our first kiss here. As soon as we walked into the club, it all came rushing back to me.

He squeezed my hand. I tilted my head up and smiled at him, grateful for the dim lighting that would hide the emotion etched all over my face. Maybe three weeks apart were a blessing in disguise. Maybe we needed them to get some kind of perspective. I slept with him—every night. We didn't even always have sex. Sometimes we just lay together in the dark, holding hands and talking. Sometimes I woke up in the morning, my body wrapped in Samir's arms. I loved it and it terrified me at the same time. Time was running out. The end of the semester meant we were that much closer to him graduating and going back to Lebanon for good.

We had five months left.

"Maggie!"

I whirled around. Fleur, Mya, George, and Max walked toward us. Fleur and Mya were dressed to kill tonight in gorgeous designer dresses. They both greeted me with air kisses. I gave Max and George hugs. George kept tugging at the collar of a shirt that screamed "shopping trip with Fleur." Poor guy. Max was dressed more casually in a nice T-shirt and jeans. It was the kind of outfit that normally wouldn't have gotten him past a bouncer, but it seemed they had been willing to look the other way, since he looked like an underwear model.

"He wore workout trainers," Fleur hissed. I looked down

at Max's shoes and winced. It was a totally stupid, unwritten London club rule that you didn't wear workout shoes to a posh club. Max's were cooler than your average workout shoes, but still. I felt a pang of sympathy for him. I knew what it was like not to feel like you fit in.

"Shut up," I hissed back, flashing Max what I hoped was a reassuring smile.

"There's no need to whisper," Max replied, his voice dry. "I've already figured out that I've committed the unpardonable sin of wearing my gym shoes to a nightclub. I'm devastated. I can only hope no one takes my picture and this moment isn't memorialized."

Mya snorted. A grin slipped onto my face. Apparently Max could dish out as much as he took.

He turned his attention to Fleur, his eyes narrowing to a stare that would have made me flinch. "Too many big words for you, princess?"

"Fuck you."

"No, thank you."

George shifted uncomfortably.

Samir shook his head. "I'm not in the mood for this. I'm going to the table." He tugged on my hand. "Come on."

Fleur ignored us, staring back at Max. George whispered something, but she ignored him, too.

Max shot her a look that was both dismissive and cutting before facing the rest of the group. He gestured toward the bar. "I'm getting a drink."

We all watched him walk off, maneuvering through the crowd with ease.

I turned to Fleur. "What the hell is wrong with you?"

"What?"

"Are you kidding me? You're so rude to him. Look at him. He's not wearing a fucking Rolex and he doesn't drop thousands of pounds on champagne." Samir stiffened beside me, but I ignored him, the anger inside of me building. "He probably doesn't have a lot of money and can't afford Gucci loafers. Lay off him."

Fleur glared at me. "Right. Saint Maggie rides to the rescue."

Anger filled Samir's voice. "Watch it."

I turned on him. "Stay out of this. I don't need you fighting my battles."

For a moment he stood there as if deciding what to do. Annoyance flashed across his face. "Fine. I'm heading to the table. Find me when you guys grow up."

Fine. I didn't need him taking care of me. I wasn't some helpless girl who needed constant protecting.

I turned to Fleur, pushing Samir out of my mind. "What do you mean by 'Saint Maggie'?"

George shifted uncomfortably.

"We need a minute," Fleur snapped.

"Fine. We'll go find Samir," Mya said. "Come on, George."

He trailed after her, leaving me by myself with Fleur.

"What is your problem?"

"Me? You're the one who has been completely absent. You haven't shown up for anything. I've barely seen you since we got back from Spain and then you have the audacity to jump into a situation you know nothing about?"

"Fine. Then tell me. Why are you so nasty to Max? Because from where I'm standing it looks like he's not cool enough to be part of your little clique."

"We're back to that? I thought you knew me. Better than most. But you really think I'm just some shallow bitch. Fuck you."

This was all coming out wrong. I struggled to calm down. I knew most of this wasn't about Fleur. I was angry and stressed out and it wasn't fair for me to take it out on her.

"No. Of course, I don't. I just don't understand why you're always ripping into him."

"Because he's always been like this with me," Fleur snapped. "Since day one. Who do you think gave me that stupid Ice Queen title to begin with?"

I gaped at her.

"I did something to him freshman year—maybe I said something, I don't even remember—and he came up with that stupid name. And somehow, despite the fact that he barely has friends, it stuck."

I'd had no idea. I hadn't had a chance to get to know Max last year because he'd been doing some kind of finance internship in China—George had told me he spoke Mandarin and was really smart. Somehow I'd totally missed the history here.

"Ever since George and I got together, Max has been telling George I'm dumb and not good enough for him. That little comment he made tonight about how I couldn't understand the words he was using? He says shit like that all the time to me. So yeah, maybe I treat him like he's a loser, but you know what, he acts like I'm some airhead and I'm sick of it."

Tears filled her eyes. I just stood there and gaped at her. It was one of the few times since I'd known her that I'd seen Fleur cry.

"I didn't know. I'm sorry. I didn't know about any of it."

I felt awful.

She wiped at her eyes. "I know you didn't know. I'm angry you didn't know. I've missed you. You and Samir are two of the closest people in my life and you've both disappeared since Spain. I know you don't have much time together and I get it. But I miss you. I miss how things used to be. I miss my best friend—both of you."

"I know. I know I've been a terrible friend lately. I'm sorry. I promise, when we get back from winter break, we'll do a girls' night. Me, you, and Mya."

"That would be nice."

I hugged her. "I've missed you, too. And for what it's worth, I don't think you're any of those things. I love you."

"Love you, too."

★ ★ ★

We spent the night drinking champagne and dancing. Michael showed up sometime after midnight with a hot guy in tow. Mya and I wiggled our eyebrows suggestively at him.

I'll tell you later, he mouthed back with a grin.

"Having fun?"

I turned my attention back to Samir. He sat next to me at the table, his arm draped around my shoulders. We'd already made up. Turned out Samir could be very persuasive when he wanted to be.

"Yes. Thank you for this. Tonight is exactly what we all needed."

He smiled wryly. "Actually, I needed to be alone with you, but I'm taking what I can get."

I studied him for a moment, seizing the chance to take in his features, memorize the shape of his face.

"What?"

"Nothing." I made myself smile. "Three weeks just feels like a long time."

"You're nervous about being apart."

"A bit. Yeah."

"Why?"

I didn't want to admit to being jealous or insecure. It felt like such a silly thing to admit to—and yet I was.

"Maggie…"

"I'm worried you'll meet someone at a club. Some French girl or something." I chuckled nervously. "Named Claudette."

"That's her name? This fictional French girl who you think is going to catch my eye? Claudette?"

"There's no need to mock. It was a last-minute choice."

"How could I possibly be interested in someone else, when you're already such a handful?"

"I am not a handful."

"Oh yes, you are. I promise you, I spend all of my time trying to figure out what you want, how to make you happy. There's no time left for anyone else."

"Cute."

His expression was solemn. "I'm serious. There's no one else."

I wanted to believe him. My heart did funny things in my chest as each word slipped from his mouth. I wanted to trust him. But trust was the one thing that had never come easily for me.

"I need you to trust me. These three weeks are going to be miserable for us if you don't. I need you to know I won't hurt you. That I promise you I'll come back from break feeling the same way I do right at this moment—"

"And what's that?"

"Do you have to ask? You dazzle me. You make me want more. Always more with you. More time. More kisses. More laughter. More talking. More nights and days spent sliding into your body."

I flushed.

"I want more mornings with you. More goofy smiles." He squeezed my hand. "You have nothing to worry about over winter break. I want more of you. Only you."

Somehow, impossibly, I believed him.

28

Maggie

It was strange being home—almost like I'd traveled back in time. Everything about my grandparents' house was the same as it had always been. They were the same as I remembered them. But still, everything felt different. Maybe it was the stark contrast to my life back in London; maybe it was how much my life had changed this past semester. Whatever it was, I felt as if I were walking through my memories, out of place with my present. I felt like nothing fit and my father wasn't even here yet.

"I should have dusted the dining room table."

I laughed at my grandmother. She fluttered around the tiny house, her limbs a frenzy of motions.

"You dusted it two days ago."

"Do you think they'll want wine for dinner?"

I tried to ignore the butterflies in my stomach. I didn't know. I didn't know what my dad liked to drink or what his favorite foods were or how he liked his coffee in the morning. I didn't even know if he liked coffee.

"Sure."

I'd been home for a week now. My dad and my new stepmother were supposed to have arrived yesterday, but their flight got delayed and they were now coming in tonight, just a few days before Christmas. At this point, their visit was a Band-Aid I wanted to rip off.

I'd already changed outfits five times. I'd finally settled on a blue sweater dress and knee-high flat boots. I'd played with my hair a few times and ended up with a loose bun. I may have spent more time planning my outfit to see my father than I did prepping to go out on a date. Sad.

"How are my girls?"

I grinned as my grandfather gathered me in for a hug. He and my grandmother had one of those relationships that made you feel all warm and fuzzy inside. They'd been married for almost fifty years, and I would still catch them giggling together or sneaking kisses in the kitchen. They were the most solid thing in my life and as much as I complained about my family situation, I knew how lucky I was that they'd taken me in.

My grandmother beamed back at him. "It'll be nice to have the whole family together, won't it?"

"It will." His gaze traveled from her to me and back again. "You both look beautiful."

"Thanks."

The doorbell rang.

My grandmother's eyes lit up at the same moment dread settled in, a giant weight pressing down on my whole body. I would rather have had my teeth drilled without pain meds than be subjected to this. It felt like we were all in a play, cast in roles that had been written for us but didn't fit.

I knew they were proud of him. In some circles, many circles, my dad was admired—after all, he was a fighter pilot, the ultimate hero. But he wasn't to me. He wasn't my hero. He was just the guy who'd left, who didn't call, who didn't write, who didn't care.

Some silly part of me thought it would be a dramatic reunion.

That when my grandmother opened the door, my world would stop for a moment. It wasn't like that at all. It was strangely ordinary and yet it was almost like I was a spectator standing outside of my body, watching as a stranger walked through the door.

All I could do was stare at him. It was almost difficult to recognize him. He was a tall man—I must have gotten my height from my mother. I had his dark hair, though. And his eyes. It was bizarre, staring into a face that looked just like mine, and yet feeling like I looked at a stranger.

For a moment, no one spoke. Then I heard his voice, the voice I recognized from the phone—

"Maggie?"

Surprise flickered across his face. He didn't move.

I wanted to speak. Felt like everyone was looking at me expectantly. But I couldn't think of anything to say. I couldn't condense a whole dysfunctional relationship into a moment or a few words. Any words I could come up with felt fake and hollow.

"You're all grown up."

That was what happened when you missed out on your child's life. You missed things. Everything, really.

I could feel their eyes on me, the presence of a woman standing next to my father dimly registering, but I stood there frozen, stupidly staring at him, trying to sort out the jumbled emotions racing through me. Somewhere through the chaos in my head, it hit me that I wasn't nearly as prepared to deal with seeing my father again as I'd hoped to be. I no longer felt like the confident girl I was in London. I felt like a fraud, like the angry child I'd been, wondering why my parents didn't love me.

He walked toward me, a smile on his face, and then I felt his arms around me. I waited for the rush of emotion, waited for the feeling this was my father, waited for some sense of recognition, and still I felt nothing—

Hollow. Empty. Lost.

He pulled back, his expression searching, studying my face. I had to say something. This was getting awkward.

A voice spoke for me. "It's so nice to meet you, Maggie."

I'd almost forgotten all about her. Almost. I turned my attention to the woman my dad had married.

She didn't look like the stereotypical evil stepmother. She was pretty enough—blond and vaguely perky. She was dressed casually in jeans and a sweater, and I wondered if I should have dressed down a bit. Maybe I looked like I was trying too hard.

"I'm Sara."

She walked over and gave me a big hug and I thought, *I'm not sure I know you well enough for that*, but I went with it because I didn't want to seem childish, rude, or any weirder than I already did.

"It's nice to meet you," I offered weakly.

My grandmother beamed at all of us like we were one big happy family, my grandfather watching us with pride. My dad just looked like he was vaguely in shock. I had to get the hell out of there.

"I'll be right back," I mumbled, not making eye contact with anyone. I fled.

Samir

I hadn't been back a week and I was sick of being home. France was a little bit better than Lebanon at least. In Paris, I flew under the radar. Here, the weight of the Khouri name was less likely to drag me down. But still—

I missed her. At night. During the day. All the fucking time. I wanted to go back to London. It felt like I'd left my whole world behind.

My cell rang and I stared down at the number. A grin spread across my face.

"Hi."

"Hi." Her voice sounded off somehow—quiet. Then I remembered—today was the day her dad and his new wife arrived.

"Are you okay?"

"I don't know."

Her voice sounded so small. I hated it, hated the distance between us. I'd seen firsthand how much he could hurt her, and I wanted to be there with her. I wanted to hold her and tell her everything would be okay.

"I hate that you're alone right now."

"I'm fine."

"You don't sound fine."

"It's just weird. He feels like a stranger. I mean he pretty much is a stranger, but everyone expects me to have a reaction to him. Like I'm supposed to be happy to see him and act like all of the distance between us never existed."

"Do you want me to get you out of there? Just say the word. We could go somewhere. The Caribbean maybe?"

Maggie laughed. "I wish."

"Me, too."

She was quiet for a moment. "I miss you."

The words sent a funny thrill through me. "I miss you, too."

"Two more weeks, right?"

It sounded like forever. "Yeah."

"I hate this."

"Same. It's weird being in Paris without you. It shouldn't be, but it is. I went to that crepe stand by the Eiffel Tower today and it reminded me of you. I ate at the cafe we ate at. I ordered your favorite—*croque-monsieur*."

She was everywhere I turned. Memories of walking with her down the street, strolling along the river, they all chased me.

"I can't go into my father's library without thinking of that night. Without remembering how you looked. I think you're haunting me."

She was silent for a long time. "I miss you so much it hurts."

"Me, too." I would have given anything to have her here with me.

"I should go. We're eating dinner soon."

I wanted to say something to her. Something to make her feel better. Something to tell her how I felt—that her call had put a knot inside of me. But I was beginning to find that I struggled to come up with the right words with her. Everything I wanted to say seemed inadequate so in the end I just settled for the simplest thing I could think of—the absolute truth and an understatement just the same.

"I wish I were there."

"Me, too."

29

Samir

"What's wrong?" Fleur strolled into the parlor, sinking down onto a couch opposite me.

"Nothing's wrong."

"You're frowning."

I stared back down at the phone in my hand. What were we going to do in May?

"Maggie's having a hard time at home," I finally answered.

"Her dad?"

"He brought his new wife home for Christmas."

Fleur grimaced. "Someone may actually be having a worse break than we are. You have it bad, don't you?"

"What do you mean?"

A smile tugged at Fleur's lips. "Oh, come on. Maggie."

"What about Maggie?"

"You like her. A lot. It's different with her, isn't it?"

It was different with her. And I knew that was hard to explain. I didn't even understand it myself.

"She's different."

"She is. You're going to abandon me here, aren't you?"

"Maybe."

"Are you thinking about taking your father's plane to South Carolina?"

I laughed. "My father's barely speaking to me. I promise you, he's definitely not going to let me take his plane to fly to the US."

"Still pissed about Layla?"

"Still pissed about a lot of things. We're in the same continuation of 'Samir fucks up' that we've been playing on loop my whole life." I grimaced. "Your parents?"

We'd seen each other out at night—we shared a few mutual friends—but we hadn't really had a chance to catch up.

Fleur rolled her eyes. "The usual. My mother's skiing with friends in Gstaad. My father has been around long enough to complain about how I need to pick a major and then he flew off for some meeting. Allegedly they'll both be back for Christmas."

Guilt filled me. She didn't exactly have a lot of people here for her. "You could come with me, you know. Maggie would love to see you too."

"Thanks for the offer, but I'd rather not spend my break in the US. I have big plans for a day at the spa and shopping. You forget—I'm used to being alone."

I nodded. "I get it."

"What's the plan?"

"Book a flight and a hotel? No idea."

"You're flying eight hours to the US commercial? Very brave. Doesn't the hero usually go on a quest to win the heroine's hand? Flying commercial may not be on par with dragon slaying, but it's probably pretty close."

"Should I tell her I'm coming? Or surprise her?"

Fleur laughed again, and I couldn't resist feeling like the butt of a massive joke.

"Where is your sense of romance? Of course you surprise her."

Maggie

Dinner was… weird.

My grandmother made meat loaf, and I knew I had eaten it because when I looked down my plate was empty. But the taste of it? No clue. Most of the meal was like that. I knew things were happening and yet nothing really seemed to register. I was numb. Maybe it was better that way.

Somehow we muddled through a conversation.

"So how is school?" my dad asked.

It took a moment to register that he was talking to me. "Good."

"And London?"

"It's good."

Sara smiled at me across the table. "Have you made friends? Do you have a boyfriend?"

Bless her, I knew she was trying. But this whole "we're a big happy family" thing was creepy as hell and there was no way I wanted to share personal details with them.

"Yeah, everyone is really nice." I answered, evading the boyfriend question.

They tossed me a few more questions about my major, before my grandparents thankfully took over the conversation. To my dad's credit, Sara seemed nice enough. I could tell my grandparents liked her, and my dad seemed more relaxed around her than I'd ever seen him.

It shouldn't have hurt to see them together. But it did.

He looked so happy. They both looked so happy. He looked like she was the thing that had been missing in his life. Like now that he had her, he had everything he'd always wanted. I didn't blame him for that. My mom had left a long time ago.

But their smiles were a knife in my heart. This—the family dinner—this was what I'd missed. Years and years of family dinners. Holidays. Birthdays. High school graduation.

"Would anyone like anything else to eat?" my grandmother asked. "More meat loaf, maybe?"

My dad grinned. "Thanks, Mom. I would love more. It's better than I remembered."

She beamed.

"I'll have to get the recipe from you," Sara added, patting his hand.

"Of course, dear. Jay always did love his meat loaf. It was his favorite when he was a little boy."

I wondered what he had been like when he was younger. I'd never really asked my grandparents. Had he always wanted to fly? How much did we have in common? Had he joined the Air Force because he'd felt the same nagging restlessness that had made me want to leave South Carolina? Had it been his chance to see the world?

"Would you like some more wine?" my grandmother asked, holding the bottle toward my dad and Sara.

I was drinking water. In London, I drank all the time. In the US, when I came home on break, I was a kid again. It was just one more thing that made my life at home surreal.

Everyone was drinking at dinner… My gaze traveled across the table. Everyone except me and Sara.

"I probably shouldn't," Sara replied, smiling at my grand-mother.

Maybe she was an alcoholic. Maybe she just didn't drink wine. There could be a hundred explanations for why she wasn't drinking—but there was something in her smile. Something in the way my dad smiled back at her that had my stomach clenching.

Because all reason and tact seemed to have fled my body when they'd walked through our front door, I asked the question I knew floated through everyone's minds—

"Are you pregnant?"

30

Maggie

The look on my dad's face was priceless. It mirrored my own unfortunate deer-in-the-headlights expression. Apparently some traits were inherited.

Sara didn't answer me; instead, she looked at my dad. But that was answer enough.

This was so messed up.

I stared down at my plate, everyone talking around me. My grandmother was crying, my grandfather patting my father on the back.

"Another grandbaby..."

The words floated around me as I fought back tears. I had a minute tops before I too would have to smile and congratulate them. I had a minute to process this—to come to terms with the fact that my father had really and truly moved on. New family, new life.

Just like my mom.

Suddenly I felt very small; felt the same helplessness and loss I'd felt that day, sitting on the curb with my ballet teacher, waiting for a mother who'd never come. I felt as if my life were happening to me, as if I were an object people moved around, but never really stopped and noticed.

I'd never wanted to leave anywhere more than I wanted to leave now. I was stuck. Stuck here in South Carolina with people who didn't really know me and a life that didn't fit. And shit, my minute was up.

"Maggie?"

My dad's voice broke through the noise—questioning, surprisingly unsure of himself.

I jerked my head up and pasted a smile on my face.

"That's great news. Congrats." I turned my attention back to Sara. "Sorry for blurting it out. I just got excited."

I didn't blame her for any of it. It wasn't her fault that my dad had been absent for most of my life. I didn't blame her for wanting a baby with the man she loved. But I blamed him.

"I understand." She smiled warmly. "I was hoping we could spend some time together during our time here. Maybe go shopping."

"Sure."

The conversation switched quickly, to baby names and things I didn't even bother trying to follow. For tonight, we were all playing the role of happy family to perfection. When the dinner ended I excused myself and went back to my room.

And cried myself to sleep.

The next morning, I called Samir. His voice mail picked up immediately.

I didn't want to sound needy, but if there was ever a moment when I needed to talk to him, to hear his voice, it was now. Maybe it was pathetic, but he made me feel better. I wanted to talk to him before I had to open my door and go face everyone.

I shot off a quick text.

Call me. Caribbean is starting to look pretty good.

I waited a few minutes. Nothing.

Finally, I called Fleur.

"Are you dying there?" Fleur answered by way of a greeting.

I had to laugh. "Pretty much. How did you guess?"

"Samir told me."

"How is he?"

"Worried about you. He told me about everything with your dad."

"She's pregnant."

"Shut up. How old is she? Isn't your dad old?"

"She's in her thirties, maybe? I don't know."

"Are you okay?"

"I don't know. Last night…" I sighed. "It was bad. But I thought about it a lot, and now I just feel resigned, you know what I mean? Like it's happening whether I want it to or not."

"I'm sorry."

"Yeah, me, too. How's your break?"

"I've seen my father once, my mother not at all, and I bought seven pairs of shoes at Gucci today."

I chuckled. "Retail therapy to the rescue."

"It's better than eating my feelings."

What would it be like to go through life with Fleur's confidence? Would it make the bad times easier? Would I be more prepared to deal with shit like last night? Or was Fleur's nonchalance a façade she slipped on, much like my easygoing approach or Samir's arrogance? Maybe we were all pretending we lived lives we wanted.

"Have you talked to Samir lately?"

Fleur was quiet for a moment. "Why?"

"I just called him, and his phone is going straight to voice mail. He hasn't responded to my text."

"I think he had plans today. Maybe give it a few hours and try him again."

I hated the flash of insecurity that filled me, and yet I couldn't quite ignore it. "Have you seen much of him during break?"

"Yeah, a bit. Why?"

"Please don't tell him I asked you, but have there been girls around lately? Like is he going to clubs and stuff?"

Fleur laughed. "Are we seriously having this conversation?"

"Don't judge me. I'm feeling a little vulnerable right now. Besides, I seem to remember having a few similar conversations with you."

"You guys are ridiculous. I think Samir went out a couple times. Once I went with him. He spent the whole time hanging out with friends. He's not talking to other girls or hitting on other girls. In fact, honestly, he spends an awful lot of time talking about you."

"Really?"

"Yes, really. His friends here are giving him massive shit about it. You're both idiots. He's into you, really into you. You don't have anything to worry about."

I sighed. "I think I'm really bad at this."

"I think so, too. You both are. I can't decide if it's funny or sad."

I laughed. "You're such a bitch."

"And yet you still love me."

"It's a mystery."

"Well, as much as I would love to continue playing the 'does he really like me?' game, I have some damage to do at Chanel. Check in later, okay?"

"Will do. Have fun shopping."

I ended the call with a smile. That was the thing with Fleur. No matter how much she pretended there wasn't more there, she always knew exactly what to say to make me feel better.

The sounds of people waking, my grandmother puttering in the kitchen, filled the house. I wanted to stay in the sanctuary of my room, wanted to hide out here until break was over.

But then I thought of Fleur. If anyone faced challenging situations head-on, it was Fleur.

So I did what she would have done. I put on some makeup, straightened my hair, and picked out my favorite outfit.

I was ready.

Samir

Seeing Maggie was the only thing that would make this day better. The flight from Paris to Charlotte, North Carolina, was a pain in the ass. A kid screamed in my ear for about six hours and first and business class had been sold out, so I'd ended up in the smallest seat known to man, wedged in between two people who had no concept of personal space. I'd gotten drunk for the first half of the flight and then tried to sober up for the second half. When I got to Charlotte, I then had to drive another two hours to get to the town where Maggie lived. The only car they had available was some two-door American insult.

I was jet-lagged, pissed off, and so far, not so impressed with America.

As far as plans went, I could have come up with a better one. There had been a later flight with room in first class that would have arrived at a reasonable hour. It would have given me time to plan the rest of the trip and maybe rent a car that could actually get me there sometime this year. But I'd been impatient, impulsive—one of my father's chief criticisms—and eager to see her. So here I was.

I turned off the interstate, following the signs for the name of the town Fleur had given me. Somehow it was difficult to picture Maggie living here. I'd seen some grass, trees, a few cows. It wasn't bad; it was just a world away from the life we lived in London.

The closer I got to her house, the more I wondered if this

had been a bad idea. I didn't fit here. Maybe she didn't fit here either, but I *definitely* didn't.

I continued driving, passing by run-down buildings and brightly lit restaurants. I'd been to New York a few times during the year I'd lived in Boston and studied English, but the total of my knowledge of the US had been limited to major cities. This was like traveling to Mars.

There were parts of Lebanon that were remote, so it wasn't the space that surprised me as much as it was… I don't know… the absence of things I thought Maggie would love. She was so excited by London—so in love with the busy streets and the historical landmarks she could talk about for hours. She loved the adventure of it. It was hard to imagine her happy here.

I followed the GPS's instructions, turning down a little dirt road, trying to ignore the nerves growing with each mile. I had five miles to go.

As far as plans went, I didn't really have one. I'd made reservations at what seemed to be the only hotel in town. I was not looking forward to that experience. I was a little nervous to show up on her doorstep, but Fleur had insisted a surprise was the way to go.

My phone rang.

Maggie.

I hesitated for a moment before answering.

"Hi, beautiful."

"Hi."

Her voice sounded stiff, even worse than last night.

"What's up?"

"It's just been a shitty day. I've been wanting to talk to you."

"I'm sorry. Things have been hectic here."

"It's late, isn't it?"

I tried to do a calculation of what time it would be in France. "Yeah, I'm just lying in bed."

Maggie laughed. "Wish I could be there with you."

"Me, too. What are you doing right now?"

I turned the car down a tree-lined street. I could just make out the outline of a house in the distance. I knew she was home; I'd had Fleur call her to find out.

"Just sitting in my room pretending to nap. I needed a break."

"Is everyone else there?"

"Oh, yeah. They're talking about baby stuff."

"What do you mean, baby stuff?"

"My dad's wife is pregnant."

"Are you serious?"

"Just found out last night at dinner."

"I'm so sorry."

"Thanks. It's not like it's really going to affect me. They're moving to Oklahoma in a few months for their next assignment. They'll have the baby there. I was a mess, but I'm doing better now. I mean, the whole situation sucks, but it kind of is what it is. Things have been fucked up between me and my dad for a long time. I don't think the baby is going to make a big difference."

Maybe not, but it hurt her. However much of a risk I was taking by coming here, I was glad I had.

I pulled up in the driveway and stared at the house for a moment. It was smaller than I'd anticipated, but so far not much in the US was living up to my expectations. There were a few cars parked out front, and I felt my first twinge of nerves at meeting her family.

This wasn't exactly my thing. Best case I could say hi to everyone quickly and then take Maggie away for a bit. An audience was the last thing I wanted.

"Samir?"

"Sorry, I got distracted for a moment."

"It's okay. I should probably let you go anyway."

"Why don't you go outside first?"

"Why?"

"Because I sent you a surprise. You sounded down yesterday."

"What did you do?"

"Go outside and see."

I got out of the car, feeling a little stupid. I was nervous and excited and hoped I hadn't gotten this totally wrong.

Then the door opened, and she walked out, and I stopped thinking at all.

31

Maggie

I felt like I was in a dream I didn't want to wake up from.

Samir stood in front of me, impossibly, a smile on his face.

For a moment I just gaped at him. I blinked, convinced when I opened my eyes again he would be gone. But he wasn't. He stood in front of me, everything I needed. Part of my brain couldn't process that this was Samir, *my Samir*, standing in my grandparents' yard in South Carolina. The same yard Jo and I had played in when we were kids. The same yard I'd taken my prom photos in. He was here. With me. He'd flown from France. To see me.

"How are you here?"

He walked to me, and I felt my feet carrying me toward him, closing the distance between us until I was in his arms, kissing him, his arms wrapped around me like he'd never let me go.

It had only been a week and yet we kissed like it had been months. I ran my hands over his shoulders, through his hair, reveling in the feel of his body pressed against mine. I wanted him inside me. I wanted his touch, his kiss, his body to make me forget everything that had happened since I'd first come home.

I forgot that we were in South Carolina, standing in my grand-parents' front yard, my whole family inside the house. I didn't care about anything except for the fact that he was here, that he'd cared enough to come, and the part of me that had been holding its breath for a week suddenly felt like it could breathe.

Samir broke the kiss first. "Surprised?"

I laughed. "Yes. Shocked. I didn't... I never expected this." I shook my head. "Seriously. How did you pull this off?"

"Fleur helped a bit. I was worried about you." He reached down, linking our fingers, squeezing my hand. "And I missed you. I didn't want to be in Paris anymore. I wanted to be here with you."

Emotion clogged my throat. I didn't know what to say. I'd never had a boyfriend before. Never been the recipient of those grand gestures I'd only ever read about. In a month, Samir had changed all of that. He made me feel important. Made me feel like I was worth more than I'd ever imagined.

"Thank you." I searched for the words. "No one has ever made me feel as special as you do."

"You deserve it. You are special. This was all worth it, just to see the smile on your face."

I wrapped my arms around his neck, my lips once more seeking his. "I'll make it up to you later," I whispered against his mouth.

A wicked smile flashed across Samir's face. "Oh, trust me, I'm going to hold you to it."

I ran my hands over his body, loving the feel of his strong muscles against me.

"Maggie?" Samir stiffened. "I think we have company."

I whirled around and came face-to-face with my dad stand-ing in the doorway, staring at the spot where Samir's hand rested just above my ass.

Samir

I realized I was grabbing Maggie's ass in front of her dad at precisely the same moment the murderous expression came into his eyes. For a moment we all just stood there staring at each other, frozen, a ridiculous parody playing out.

It occurred to me I maybe should move my hand, but I wasn't sure if that would call more attention to the fact that it was there in the first place. Judging by the anger that didn't seem to be fading from her dad's face, it seemed like the wisest course of action. She also might have told me her dad was a giant.

"Shit," Maggie hissed, breaking away from me.

"I'm guessing that's your dad," I whispered. He had her eyes and her hair. Besides the obvious height difference, the resemblance was strong.

"Yeah."

"Are you going to introduce me?" her father asked, walking toward us.

He had a good three inches on me.

"This is Samir." Her voice was strained as she said my name.

Her father stopped a foot away from us. I waited to see if he would hold out his hand to shake mine, but instead he just stood there, his gaze pinning us.

No one spoke.

"How do the two of you know each other?"

My lips tightened. I got that he was pissed. If some guy were making out with my daughter, I'd probably be pissed, too. But come on. Maggie was at university. He hadn't exactly been around to be much of a father to her. It seemed ridiculous and unfair for him to act like he had a say in who she dated or what she did.

"We go to university together," I answered.

Maggie's gaze darted back and forth between us. I waited

for her to say something, but she seemed too uncomfortable to speak. I'd gotten so used to the Maggie that she'd become, I'd forgotten the girl she'd been when she'd first come to London. Forgotten there was a part of her that would always feel like she had to play by the rules and live up to everyone's expectations. She didn't say it now, but I could practically see the inner workings of her brain, her fear and hesitation. She was angry with her dad, but she also wanted him to be proud of her. She didn't like disappointing him, and it was easy to see he wasn't happy about me.

"Really," her father drawled.

I waited for her to say something, the silence stifling. It was a strange feeling. I realized in that moment that though we'd agreed to six months together, I didn't really know what that meant. I didn't know what she wanted from me or if this was more than just sex to her. I was the first—and only—guy she'd ever slept with. Maybe that was it for her. Maybe I'd overestimated the connection between us.

"He's my boyfriend."

The rush of relief I felt at the sound of those words stunned me.

We hadn't really had the talk. I didn't think I'd care about labels—once I would have thought her announcement to be too rushed, too official. But coming from her lips, it sounded just right.

"It's nice to meet you, sir." I struggled to sound like the kind of guy you would want dating your daughter.

Maggie's lips twitched.

"Maggie!"

An older woman—she had to be Maggie's grandmother—walked out the door, a beaming smile on her face.

Oh god, I was going to meet the whole family.

Maggie

As far as surreal moments in my life went, introducing Samir to my family may have ranked as number one.

But then again, the Samir who sat next to me on my grandparents' couch was not the same Samir I'd gotten to know in London. He was unfailingly, flawlessly polite. He laughed at my grandfather's jokes, complimented the house until my grandmother blushed, and asked Sara questions about the baby. He avoided my father, but considering the glare my father had been sporting since he'd spotted us in the front yard, I didn't blame him.

Still—it was hard to reconcile the guy who'd fucked me up against a window with the boy who now sat next to me now, his hand holding mine, answering my family's pointed questions.

Everything about this felt contrary to the progression of our relationship. We'd gone from sex in secret to meeting the family in one fell swoop and I still felt like I was playing catch-up. Maybe we both were.

This was a side of Samir I hadn't really seen before. He was trying—hard. And besides my dad, it seemed like they liked him.

After what felt like an eternity, I made up an excuse about showing him around town.

"You'll be back Christmas morning, right?" my grandmother asked him.

Yep, totally surreal.

"I would love to," Samir answered, sounding surprisingly like he meant it. "Thank you for inviting me."

His arm around me, we walked out to the car. It hit me then that in a way, this felt like a new beginning. Like we were standing on the edge of something different, a fundamental change in our relationship that would stay with us for the time that remained. No matter how hard I tried, I couldn't pretend my heart wasn't engaged anymore.

I was in love with Samir.

It had been building for so long. No matter how much I tried to avoid it, the outcome was already decided. I was going to hurt—a lot—later. When he left and went back to Lebanon, he would take a piece of me with him.

I'd played it safe most of my life. Avoided risks, looked before I leapt. It had served me well. But no matter what good sense and logic told me, I couldn't walk away from him. I'd take the hurt and the pain that would come in May in exchange for however many days of this feeling inside me—this hope and this peace.

I was done listening to my head. It was time to listen to my heart.

32

Samir

I was nervous. Which was completely ridiculous. But I felt completely out of my depth. Something had changed between me getting out of the car and her grandmother inviting me over for Christmas. I just wasn't sure what.

I'd met girlfriends' parents before. I'd practically grown up with Layla's family. But this felt completely different. I'd started off telling myself I was going to be polite and get us out of there as quickly as possible. But then I'd started trying and realized I wanted them to like me. Because it was important to Maggie and Maggie was important to me. More than I'd understood.

"Are you all right?"

I tossed her what I hoped was a reassuring smile. "Yeah."

"Are you sure?"

"Yeah. Are you?"

"It was a little weird. Kind of surreal."

"Yeah, it was. It was good, though."

"Sorry I called you my boyfriend. I know I kind of sprung that on you. I just wasn't sure how to describe you to my dad. I figured 'we have lots of sex' wasn't wise."

I laughed. "True. I didn't mind the boyfriend label. It was nice."

She was silent for a moment, and when she finally did speak, I had to strain to hear her. "Good."

"Tell me about South Carolina Maggie."

She laughed. "There's not a lot to tell. I was pretty boring."

"I find that hard to believe."

"I was pretty good in high school. Everything was about getting into Harvard. There wasn't time for much else."

"What about your friends?"

"I still have some people I keep in touch with. It's harder now that I'm living in London. You're going to have to meet my best friend, Jo, while you're here. She'll never forgive me if I don't introduce you guys."

"Good. I want to meet your friends. See where you grew up." It surprised me how much I meant it. I wanted to know her better. Not just who she was now, but the person she had been.

"You were great with my family back there."

"Your dad hates me."

"Maybe."

"Definitely."

"I wouldn't worry about it too much. It's not like he's around enough for it to even matter." She smiled. "I like you. That's all you need to worry about."

I stopped at a red light, tearing my gaze away from the road to look at her.

"Have I mentioned you look extra hot today?"

"I was channeling my inner Fleur."

"What exactly does that mean?"

"You know how she goes out with that 'take no prisoners' attitude? I asked myself what Fleur would do, and I decided to be fierce."

I laughed. "Please don't start taking life cues from my cousin.

I like you the way you are." I leaned over and kissed her before the light turned green. "I'm dying to get you alone and naked. It has been a week."

"Poor baby."

"I am a poor baby. Do you know what it's been like, waking up in the middle of the night, wanting you, and not being able to have you?"

"I have a rough idea of what that might feel like."

"Really?"

"Hey, it's been a week for me, too. We have a lot of time to make up for."

Her voice was sultry and smooth, and I swear I got hard just listening to her.

"Have I mentioned how much you turn me on? Seriously. I keep waiting for this thing between us to calm down. For me not to feel like I always have to have you. I keep expecting it to change. To not be so—"

"Intense?"

I nodded. Even now, in the car, I wanted her. Normally I'd be getting bored by now. A month was a long time to be with one girl. But with Maggie it felt like it was never enough.

"Pull over."

It took a minute for her words to register.

"What?"

"Pull over."

Her voice was husky, and it only took a second for my brain to figure out exactly what she meant. *Jesus.* It was dark out and the road was remote. I was so hard I didn't care about anything else.

I pulled the car over, my heart pounding madly. I'd had sex in my fair share of exciting places, but for some reason the sight of Maggie unbuckling her seat belt and climbing into my lap blew my mind.

Maggie

The steering wheel dug into my spine, my knee cramping as I tried to wrap my legs around Samir. An SUV would have been so much better for a roadside seduction.

"Not a lot of room."

"You're just not trying hard enough," I teased. "Push your seat back."

His eyes flared and a thrill ran through my body. Something built inside of me. Something desperate and hungry and eager for release. I wanted him like this—fast, furious, a little bit wild. I wanted to be in control, wanted to watch his dangle by a thread before slipping completely.

I reached down, pulling my sweater over my head, glad for the heat running in the car—

Shit, it was cold.

I leaned forward, my breasts rubbing against the front of Samir's coat. "Warm me up," I murmured, my lips meeting his, picking up right where we'd left off in the front yard.

He groaned.

"I can't wait much longer. I'll make it up to you later," he promised, kissing his way down my bare neck.

I was happy to oblige.

We both reached between us, fumbling with zippers and buttons.

"There's no way this is going to work," Samir grumbled.

I grinned, nipping at his earlobe. "Oh, ye of little faith. I got this." I arched, leaning back so my head rested above the steering wheel. "Did I mention I did gymnastics when I was younger? I'm very bendy."

"Fuck me, that's hot."

I laughed. I loved seeing him like this—off balance, hungry for it. For so long I'd watched Samir sail through life without breaking a sweat. If he wanted a girl, she ended up in his lap.

I loved keeping him on his toes…and knowing I was the only one who could.

"Do you have a condom?" I asked, my voice strained.

"Yeah, give me a second."

Samir reached back into his jeans pocket. He hit me in the knee.

"Ow."

"Shit. Sorry. Are you okay?"

"Yeah. I'm fine."

Our gazes connected and we both burst out laughing.

I love you.

The words flew through my head, terrifying and seemingly out of nowhere. I had to force myself not to give voice to them. Not to ruin everything by telling him the truth. I was someone else entirely when I was with him. I liked this Maggie… She was bold and feisty, and I suspected she'd always been there, lurking under the surface.

With Samir, it just felt right.

We came together in an awkward, desperate tangle of limbs and laughter. There would be time for us to explore each other's bodies later. For teasing and foreplay. For now there was just a need to be filled, to feel Samir moving inside me, to be carried away by the moment and the release I desperately needed.

I didn't want to think of love or worry about what would happen next. I just wanted to feel. So I gave myself over to the moment, to the sensation of Samir filling me.

When I came, all thoughts and worries disappeared.

33

Samir

She sat on a tree swing in her grandparents' backyard, staring out across the field. If I were a different guy—the kind who read poetry or analyzed art—I would have said the light from the rising sun illuminated her in a way that nearly blinded me. Or that the profile of her face, with the backdrop of the field behind her, was the most extraordinary thing I'd ever seen. But I wasn't that guy. Instead I walked up to her and planted a kiss to the top of her head, inhaling the scent of her shampoo and trying to ignore the fact that I was already turned on.

Maggie tilted her head up and smiled at me. "Merry Christmas."

I grinned. "Merry Christmas."

"I thought you were coming over later."

I didn't want to tell her the truth—that I'd woken up and rolled over to an empty pillow and been filled with a sense of loneliness that had surprised me. That I'd hurried over here because more than anything, I wanted some time alone with her—even if we were fully clothed.

"Do you mind?"

"Not at all."

I reached behind her, tugging on the rope, pushing the swing forward.

"Is Samir Khouri really pushing me on a swing? I'm pretty sure half the International School would pay good money to see that."

I grinned. "It's definitely a new experience."

"Too cool to push girls on swings, even when you were younger?"

"Something like that."

She stretched out her body, planting her feet on the ground, holding the swing still.

"What were you like when you were younger?"

"Charming. Incredibly handsome."

Maggie laughed. "Be serious."

"I am being serious."

"I want to know what you were like."

"Well, for one, I wasn't as cute as you were. I saw the baby pictures on the wall."

Maggie blushed. "Please don't mention those."

It was strange to see her younger self. It had been like a glimpse into another part of her life, one I couldn't help but be curious about.

"You were adorable."

"I had glasses."

"Glasses are sexy." I leaned forward and kissed her. "Maybe we'll play sexy librarian later."

She laughed. "Maybe." She elbowed me in the side. "Stop stalling. I want to know about little Samir."

I sighed. "I was shorter. And kind of a terror. I went through a lot of nannies."

"You had nannies?"

"Until I went off to boarding school."

"I can't imagine it. I used to envy you rich kids with your

fancy cars and your exciting vacations. I guess it wasn't much better for you either."

"It had its moments."

"I wonder what it would have been like if we'd met at a different time in our lives…when we were younger. Somehow I don't think high school Samir would have noticed me."

"I would have noticed you."

The look she sent me was skeptical at best. "I find that hard to believe."

"Ouch."

"I just don't think I would have been your type."

Probably not. I would have thought she was hot, no doubt about it. I may have even flirted with her a bit. But she would have firmly ended up in the category of girls I labeled *look but do not touch*.

"You would have scared me a bit," I answered, surprising myself—and, by the looks of things, her—with my honesty.

"Why?"

"Because."

"That's not an answer."

"That. That, right there. You call me on my shit. You push me. You see through me. You make me feel like I need to be better, need to work harder. You make me afraid I'm going to come up short."

She gaped at me.

"If I'd met you back in high school, I would have thought you were just as gorgeous as I do now. You probably would have made me laugh like you do now. But I would have been stupid and immature and somehow I would have fucked things up between us. That's why you would have scared me."

"And now?"

"Now you terrify me, and I just spend all my time hoping that even though I'm still stupid and immature, I won't fuck things up between us."

I expected to feel embarrassed or like I'd lost major points with her. But this had stopped feeling like a game a long time ago.

"That first day I saw you standing outside of the school, I thought you were beautiful. And later, when I saw you naked after you dropped your towel—" she flushed "—I knew I wanted you in my bed. And the kiss at Babel—that kiss haunted me for weeks. It was just a kiss. It shouldn't have been anything. I'd had hundreds of kisses, but I couldn't shake that one.

"But that wasn't what made me want you. The more I got to know you, the more I saw who you were—I wanted you even more. You don't let people in. You have these walls up, and I get that. But every once in a while you allow people glimpses behind the walls. And those glimpses made me want more—all of you. You make me want it all."

Maggie

It was too much. Emotions pushed through me, threatening to bubble to the surface. The same words kept running through my mind—

I love you, I love you, I love you.

"Too much?" he asked, a crooked smile on his face.

"No. Maybe."

"You freak out sometimes."

I nodded. "A bit."

"How do two commitmentphobes end up in a relationship together?"

"Is that what we're doing?" I asked, trying to keep the uncertainty out of my voice.

We'd been dancing around it for weeks now. Maybe it was stupid of me to have to ask, but I'd never done this before. With Hugh, things had felt different—easier maybe, less intense. It had felt like practice, and this felt like everything.

"Isn't it?"

His expression was inscrutable, his voice guarded. I wasn't the only one with walls. Part of me wished I could have met him in a few years, when I had a little more experience, when I'd worked through some of my own shit, when I knew what I was doing. I worried I wasn't very good at this—worried he would leave.

"I'm here because I want to be. Because I don't want to be anywhere else. I'm here and I'm not going anywhere." A smile slid across his face. "I like calling you my girlfriend. And I like hearing you call me your boyfriend. I don't share. I want everyone to know you're mine." He walked behind me, bringing his arms around my chest, pulling me back against him and holding me there, his head resting against mine.

"Okay?"

I nodded. "Okay."

He stood behind me for a moment, his hand lazily stroking my hair, his other arm still around me.

"How was everything last night after I dropped you back here?"

"It was fine."

"And now?"

I didn't know how to explain how I felt. Not upset, just…lost maybe. I didn't know where I fit anymore. My grandparents were getting older, and I wasn't a kid any longer. Now that I was out of the house, their responsibility to me was over—or changing at least. My father and Sara would be starting a new life, with a new baby now. I felt like everyone was moving on, and while part of me knew I had to change and move forward, I couldn't help but feel like I was being left behind.

"I feel like everything is changing and everyone's lives are moving in directions that don't include me. It's stupid, right? I mean, I moved to London, I should have expected at some point this wouldn't be my home anymore—that things would change. It just feels weird."

"It's not stupid. It's normal to be scared sometimes."

"I'm afraid I'm going to be alone." I didn't know where I got the strength to share this part of myself, only that I trusted him to understand.

"I promise you, you're never going to be alone. You have people in your life who love and care about you. They'll always be there."

The conviction in his words shook me. Hell, the word *love* surprised me. This wasn't a conversation I ever would have imagined a year ago. But we were changing too, becoming something new.

"You should talk to your father."

I looked up at Samir in surprise. "Why?"

"Because you're not over everything. He hurt you. He still hurts you. And you're stuck. You need to be able to find a way to put all of this behind you."

"Since when did you become so wise?" I teased, ignoring the pull on the thread holding my heart in place, threatening to unravel it.

A year ago, I would have done anything to avoid such a conversation and the inevitable pain it might stir up. But I was tired of clinging to the past, tired of it holding me back from my future.

"Maybe you make me wise."

I laughed. "Then you're really in trouble."

He kissed me. "Stop worrying. It'll be fine."

"I don't know what to say."

"I know you. You'll figure it out."

34

Maggie

We sat next to each other on the back porch, tension filling the space around us.

I couldn't remember the last time we'd been alone together. Not since I was little, maybe? Even then, I remembered my mother more than him. He'd been gone a lot then, too. I remembered drawing pictures for him on deployments, hearing his voice on the other end of a static-filled line. That was about it.

I leaned forward, resting my elbows on my knees, staring out at the woods behind my grandparents' house. I would sit here when I was younger, wondering at the world beyond those woods, thinking of my parents somewhere out there without me.

"Pretty view," he commented.

"Yeah. It's a little weird being back here."

"Tell me about it."

It was the first time I'd ever felt like we had anything in common. Samir's advice pushed me on.

"Is that why you joined the Air Force? Because you wanted to leave?"

Surprise flickered across his face. "Maybe."

"Did you always want to fly?"

"When I was a kid, your grandfather had a buddy who flew crop dusters. He took me up in a plane once when I was eight. It was my first plane ride, and it was the coolest thing I'd ever seen. We took off and I felt this rush, and then we were in the air, looking down below, and everything beneath us seemed so small. I felt like I was on top of the world. And yeah, after that, there was nothing else I wanted to do."

"You love it."

"I do. It gets old sometimes—the moving, the deployments, the life. But when I'm in the cockpit, everything makes sense. There's a part of me that still feels on top of the world."

It was so strange to hear him talk like this, strange to see this side of him, strange to see myself in him.

"It's the only dream I ever had. And it came at a high price." He stared down at his hands. "Other guys manage families and flying. It's tough, but they do it." He sighed. "I was young when I met your mother." I froze, shock filling me. He never spoke of her. "I was cocky and thought being a fighter pilot was the most important thing in my life." His voice cracked. "I made some mistakes. Lots of mistakes."

The words hung between us, overwhelming me. I wasn't sure how to respond or if I was even supposed to. But there were questions I wanted answered and he was the only one who could answer them.

"How did you meet?"

"I was in Vegas for an assignment and your mom was there for a bachelorette party. I saw her sitting in the audience at a show and that was it. I told my buddies I was going to marry her. I went up to her afterward and we hung out the rest of the night. The next night we eloped."

I gaped at him.

He shook his head ruefully. "It was impulsive."

"What was she like?"

He stared off into the yard and for a moment he seemed to be somewhere else entirely.

"She was dazzling. She was the kind of girl you couldn't look away from, no matter how hard you tried. You look a lot like her."

My heart caught in my throat. "Really?"

He nodded.

"I don't remember what she was like. It's been a long time."

"She was beautiful. Funny. Smart. The day she left was the worst day of my life. Your grandmother called and told me you were by yourself waiting outside ballet practice. I was in Alaska. It took me a few days to get home, but when I finally did, you just stared at me with these big brown eyes. You would follow me around the house, like you were afraid I was going to go, too." His voice cracked. "Every time I looked at you, I felt guilty. It became easier to not look at you. Easier just to leave."

There was a tightness in my chest, an aching, twisting pain.

"You deserved better than what we gave you, and I'm sorry for that. But I was young then and so was she. Even though we did the best we could, neither one of us knew what it was to be a spouse, much less a parent. We fucked up."

"Yeah, you did."

He was giving me an apology—fifteen years too late. The damage had already been done. The cracks were there, and no amount of glue was going to fix them.

"I'm sorry. I was a mess after she left. For a long time. I honestly thought you'd be better here with my parents. I couldn't give you stability, couldn't give you the kind of life you needed. I knew they would take care of you."

They had. My grandparents were wonderful. They had taken me to soccer practice and gone to parent-teacher conferences.

They'd stepped into the role my parents had abandoned. But I wondered if he'd ever thought about the burden he'd placed on them—they'd already raised one child, then they had to take care of me. Were there things they'd wanted to do with their lives? Trips they'd wanted to take? Dreams they hadn't gotten to fulfill?

It felt like we were all sacrificing for my father's dream—none of us by choice.

I understood wanting to escape; I could even understand his love of flying. But I couldn't understand the way he lived his life at the expense of everyone else around him. I was like him, and yet on some fundamental level, I wasn't.

I saw my parents differently now. I'd been angry for so long—angry with my mother, with my father. But it didn't matter anymore. I got it now. It wasn't me. Whatever had happened between us, whatever happened to my family was on them. It was their choices and mistakes that fucked everything up. There was nothing that could be done to fix the past, no words that would make it better. An apology did more for him than it did for me. The second I'd heard it, I'd realized how little it really meant. I'd never really needed it at all.

It was time to let go.

He cleared his throat. "Maybe you can come visit us in Oklahoma."

I shrugged. "Maybe."

I wasn't sure I wanted to have him in my life, wasn't sure where this relationship would lead. It was difficult to sweep over so many years of pain between us. But letting go made me feel better, lighter. I didn't want to spend my future living in the past.

"That boy…"

"Samir?"

He nodded. "Is it serious?"

It was strange to hear him asking me fatherly questions. Strange to think he cared.

"I don't know," I answered honestly.

"It seems like he's serious about you."

Surprise filled me. I didn't want to discuss Samir with my dad. Somewhere along the way I'd stopped caring what my dad thought of my decisions. If he was proud of me—great. But I wasn't going to live my life to impress anyone but myself. Not anymore.

35

Maggie

January came quickly, and soon I was walking up the steps to the International School, excitement and relief filling me. It was good to be home.

I opened the door to our room, greeting Fleur and Mya with hugs. I set my suitcase on the floor of our dorm room, shutting the door behind me.

Fleur grinned. "Tell me everything."

"There's not much to tell."

"You're just as bad as Samir," she complained. "I was expecting stories when he came back to Paris. I got nothing."

I laughed. "Why are you so fascinated with my sex life? Still nothing going on for you in that department?"

"Drier than the Sahara."

"Sorry, man."

"Why are you still with him?" Mya asked, stretching out on her bed.

"Because he's sweet. Normal. He's good to me."

"You don't seem happy, though."

Mya was right—she didn't seem happy. It was like she was

stuck in between the old Fleur and the new Fleur and neither one fit her very well.

"She has a point."

Fleur pulled a face. "Not you, too. You're the one who encouraged me to go out with him in the first place."

"I thought he'd be good for you."

"Maybe you should just take some time and be single," Mya suggested. "More than the few months you did over the summer. Maybe you need a break from guys."

"Maybe." Fleur sighed. "I guess I just want what you have."

It took me a second to realize she was talking to me. "What are you talking about?"

"You and Samir. It's cute—and a little annoying. You guys seem really happy together—like you get each other. I want that. And even though you won't dish, I'm guessing the sex is pretty hot."

I flushed.

"See? I want a guy who is my friend and is amazing in bed. I want the blushing, and the butterflies, and everything else."

I understood what she meant, but she didn't really get it. She saw one side of me and Samir, but she didn't see the rest. She didn't understand the clock running down on our relationship. Each month that passed meant we were one month closer to graduation, one month closer to him leaving.

"Don't we all want that? But don't you get that it's just temporary? I don't know where I stand with him. It's easy to be in the perfect relationship for six months." Not that I was even sure we were the perfect relationship. I was happy with him, but I was also confused. How were we supposed to turn our emotions off just because he graduated? How was I supposed to kill the feelings inside of me when he left?

"You're going to be a mess when this ends," Fleur commented, worry filling her eyes as understanding dawned. "I

see the way you look at him. This isn't casual for you, is it?
Isn't just sex."

"No, it isn't. It never was."

"Does he know that?"

"No, he doesn't. You can't tell him either."

"Don't you think he might feel the same way?"

Sometimes. Sometimes when he looked at me, I could swear
I saw the same worry and fear mirrored in his eyes. But other
times I was convinced I just imagined it.

"Okay, enough," Mya interrupted. "I can't take any more of
the drama. There's more to life than guys. We live in London.
Maybe you've heard of it? Most glamorous city in the world.
And here the two of you are, sitting in your room, moping
over boys."

"I'm not really moping," I interjected.

"You are. You're all lovesick and mopey. Both of you. Well,
Fleur minus the lovesick part."

Fleur chucked a pillow at her.

"Can we do something tonight? Something fun that doesn't
involve talking about the opposite sex."

She was right. So much of last semester had been spent with
Samir that I'd totally neglected my friends.

"Sounds good to me."

Mya grinned. "Excellent. Cafeteria, then maybe a movie?"

"Done."

We walked down to the cafeteria together. I'd missed this
these past few months. Sure, I loved spending time with Samir,
but it was nice just to hang out with the girls.

The building was still largely empty. The spring semester
started tomorrow and as usual, it seemed like most of the student body was milking their winter break for everything it
was worth. Samir wouldn't get back until tomorrow morning.

The first thing that hit me as we walked toward the cafeteria was that it was loud. Really, really loud. The sounds of people talking and yelling spilled all the way out to the stairwell.

Mya frowned. "That's weird. It sounds like a party in there."

"Maybe more people are back."

A crowd of people formed in front of the cafeteria, staring at something on the wall.

"Maggie!" Our old roommate, Noora, stood in front of me, a worried expression on her face.

"Hey." I nodded toward the crowd. "What's going on? I didn't think it would be this busy."

"You need to get Fleur out of here."

"Why?"

Noora opened her mouth to answer at the same time Fleur moved ahead of us, pushing through. In her wake, the crowd quieted, silence filling the hallway.

"What the hell is going on?"

Noora pointed, a flush staining her cheeks, and I suddenly saw what everyone was staring at—

Just as Fleur's perfectly timed "Motherfucker!" filled the air.

I blinked. Something was crudely taped to the cafeteria wall. A photo of Fleur. Naked.

"It could be worse."

Fleur glared at Mya. "How?"

"You could look bad."

"She's right, you know," I interjected, staring down at the photo we'd ripped off the wall. "I would kill to have a body like yours. Anyone would kill to have a body like yours."

"I'm naked," Fleur hissed through clenched teeth, taking a sip of her scotch.

We were holed up at a little bar off Grosvenor Square. Fleur was on her second scotch. Mya and I just stared at her, helpless.

"Where's the picture from?"

"Where do you think? Take a page from my book. Never let your asshole of an ex-boyfriend take naked pictures of you."

"Do you really think Costa would do this? Release them? Isn't he in the US?" Mya asked. "Why is he still screwing with you?"

"I don't know. Maybe he released them, maybe he didn't, but either way he shared private pictures between us with someone else."

"Were there more?"

She stared down at her glass, swirling the amber liquid around. "Yeah. He took a few."

I knew it wasn't the time to make her feel even worse, but I couldn't help but wonder what the hell she'd been thinking. Nothing about naked pictures sounded like a good idea to me.

"I know I'm an idiot."

I sighed. "You aren't an idiot. You just trusted the wrong guy."

Tears filled Fleur's eyes.

"It's going to be okay."

She shook her head. "That's just it—it isn't going to be okay." Our gazes met and I knew we were both thinking about everything else.

"You should tell her." I nodded toward Mya.

Mya frowned. "Tell me what?"

Fleur drained her glass, setting it down on the wood table with a loud clunk. "Fuck. I got an email a few months ago. It was from some dodgy anonymous email address. Anyway, whoever sent it said they knew all of my secrets and if I didn't pay them fifteen thousand pounds, they would tell everyone at the International School."

Mya gaped at her. "What did you do?"

"I ignored it. I figured it was someone being stupid or trying to get money out of me. I wasn't actually going to pay it."

"But you think the picture might be linked to that?"

Fleur nodded.

"Shit."

"I don't know what to do. I can't believe someone is actually blackmailing me."

"Yeah, but I don't understand what they actually have on you. It doesn't make sense. What kind of secret would be worth fifteen thousand pounds?" Mya sputtered.

Fleur flushed, her gaze darting toward me.

I reached out and squeezed Fleur's hand. "She's a friend and she'll understand. You need to talk about it."

"Talk about what? You guys are talking in riddles, and I have no clue what you're talking about."

"I was pregnant," Fleur began, and I watched as Mya's entire expression changed. "It was Costa's. I had a miscarriage. That's why I missed part of freshman year."

This time it was easier for Fleur to get through the story. Her voice shook, but she kept her composure. When she'd finished, silence filled the table.

"What are you going to do?" Mya finally asked.

"I don't know." She ran a hand through her hair, and I was struck by how *lost* she seemed. Her customary confidence was gone, and without the façade of strength she seemed like another person entirely—a little vulnerable, a little scared.

"Are you going to pay?" Mya asked.

Fleur toyed with the empty glass. "You know, I'm not."

"Are you sure about that?"

"Yeah, I am. If someone wants to judge me for the fact that I was pregnant and had a miscarriage, then go for it." She grimaced. "I'm not going feel bad about what I did with Costa. I loved him. At least I loved who I thought he was. And I thought he loved me. Anyone who has a problem with my choices can go fuck themselves."

"Are you sure you're ready to face the gossip and stares?" Mya asked. "People may be more vicious than you think."

Fleur nodded. "Bring it."

I almost choked on my drink. "Can I be you when I grow up?"

Fleur laughed. "Funny. I think I'd rather be you."

36

Maggie

Despite Fleur's outward confidence, I knew the first day of class was going to be bad. We walked down the hall, Fleur flanked by me and Mya. Everyone stared at us. Part of me was used to the stares—hanging out with Fleur and dating Samir meant people constantly watched us. It had been weird at first, but by now I was mostly used to it.

These stares were something else entirely.

These stares were accompanied by whispers just loud enough for us to hear—

"…got exactly what she deserved…"

"…such a bitch…"

"I wonder how many guys have naked pictures of her on their phone?"

I flinched, my temper flaring. I wanted to respond, to strike back at everyone treating Fleur like she was trash. But she'd made us promise not to engage, so instead I walked through the hall next to her, my head held high, my eyes ice. I didn't know how she did it. None of the gossip was even directed at me and yet I felt like crumpling underneath the scrutiny and scorn.

Fleur acted like she didn't hear any of it, like their words were so far beneath her notice she couldn't be bothered to respond.

Suddenly the whispers stopped. People turned away, shuffling into classrooms, and moving down the hallway. I looked up and saw him walking toward us, anger etched across his handsome face.

Samir wrapped his arms around me, his lips meeting mine in a fierce kiss. He pulled back, studying me carefully.

Neither one of us spoke. It had been a week since we had last seen each other, and the texts and phone calls hadn't nearly been enough.

"I missed you," he whispered, soft enough so only I could hear.

"I missed you, too."

His gaze shifted from me to Fleur. For a moment, her expression wobbled, and she looked like she would break.

Samir released me, giving Fleur a hug, worry all over his face. "Omar told me what happened. Are you okay?"

Fleur nodded.

"I'm going to kill him."

"It's not worth it. I was stupid. I shouldn't have taken the picture in the first place."

"You were his girlfriend. He never should have showed it to anyone." He reached out, linking his fingers with mine while he said hi to Mya. "What can I do to help?" he asked, turning his attention back to Fleur.

"Create a bigger scandal than I have, so everyone's attention will move from me onto you," Fleur answered dryly.

"Sorry, but I think my scandalous days are behind me." He flashed me a wicked grin. "Although I could possibly be persuaded to get naked with Maggie in the hall if she's up for it."

I elbowed him in the side, grateful for the smile on Fleur's face.

"What?" His expression was all innocence. "I'm just doing what I can to help."

"Ha ha." I glanced at my watch. "Class starts in five, we should probably get going."

Samir sighed. "Why do I already know the answer you would give if I asked you to skip class?"

I kissed him. "Because you know your girlfriend cannot possibly miss the first day of class." I leaned closer, my lips grazing his ear. "But if you give me an hour or two, I'll definitely take you up on the getting naked thing."

Samir groaned. "Have I ever told you my low opinion of delayed gratification?"

"Poor baby."

"Definitely, poor baby."

"See you in your room?"

He nodded. His arm snaked around my waist, pulling me up against him... He was already hard.

"We're in the hall. And we definitely have an audience." I motioned to where Mya and Fleur stood behind us.

"Don't care. Not even a little bit. That's what a week away from you has done to me." He leaned forward, not giving me a chance to protest, capturing my mouth in a delicious kiss. His hands roamed over my body as his lips plundered mine, his hand moving down, resting just above my ass, his touch possessive and triumphantly male. It was a totally inappropriate kiss for school, and it was also a claiming of sorts. The feminist in me should have been horrified. I was too turned on to care.

"See you later, babe," he whispered against my mouth. He walked away, leaving me there, frustrated beyond belief.

"Girlfriend?" Mya asked.

Fleur sighed. "I can't even."

I flushed. "Come on. Class. Now."

I sank down into one of the few remaining seats, next to Max. Luckily Fleur and Mya had class together so at least Fleur would have some moral support. She kept saying she was fine on her own, but I couldn't bring myself to leave her alone.

Max smiled at me. "Hey. How was your break?"

"Good. Yours?"

"Can't complain."

"Where are you from again?" I thought somewhere in the Midwest, but I couldn't remember exactly where.

"Chicago."

"Nice."

"It has its moments."

I wondered if he'd talked to George, if George knew his girlfriend's naked body had been seen by a large chunk of the student body. Fleur hadn't seen him yet, and I knew she was dreading the conversation.

Our professor was late. Normally I wouldn't have minded, but I was all too aware of the low buzz going around the room, and the not-so-subtle looks being thrown my way. Apparently some of Fleur's notoriety was rubbing off.

"Is she okay?" Max asked, his voice low.

My head jerked up, surprised by the concern in his tone. "Fleur?"

He nodded.

"Yeah, I think so. I mean she's pissed, but she's hanging in there."

I hesitated, unsure of how involved I should get. It wasn't really my business, but I couldn't help but wonder if George was going to break up with her over this. I wasn't sure she could handle it right now, not on top of everything else.

"Does George know?"

Max paused a moment too long before answering. "Yeah."

I wanted to ask more, to find out what George knew or thought of it. I wanted to know if George had seen the photo. I wanted more details because she was my best friend, and I was worried about her. Especially after last year.

But for one moment Max's expression met mine and a flush covered his cheeks. It hit me then that he'd seen the picture. He looked uncomfortable, and I definitely was, and the last thing I wanted to do was talk about my roommate's naked body with her boyfriend's best friend.

I breathed a sigh of relief when our professor finally arrived.

37

Samir

I couldn't believe it was my last semester of school—in both a good and bad way.

Four months stood between me and graduation. Four months left in London. Four months left with Maggie.

She sat next to me in class, her elbow grazing mine. It was such a small thing—touching elbows. I never would have characterized it as erotic, but I'd been turned on for the last ten minutes.

It was only the second week of classes, and I was already checking out. Our professor droned on at the front of the room, and while I could vaguely make out the words he said, my attention was solely focused on the girl next to me. Last year, I'd learned the hazards of sitting next to her in class. I'd been forced to sit next to her, desperately wanting to touch her, taste her. She'd been so close and yet tantalizingly out of reach.

This year was a different kind of torture. Because I knew in an hour I'd have her back in my room, legs spread, my head between her thighs, her naked body laid out like a feast on my bed. I adjusted in my seat.

"What are you doing?" Maggie hissed. "You keep staring."

"Just thinking about how I'm going to get you naked later," I murmured, nudging her foot with mine.

She glared at me. "Well, stop it. It's distracting."

I grinned. "Really?"

"Mr. Khouri."

Maggie kicked me under the table.

I jerked my head up. Our professor stood at the front of the room, his arms crossed in front of his chest, a pissed-off expression on his face.

"Sorry."

"This is a classroom, Mr. Khouri, not a nightclub. You would do well to remember that. See me after class."

Not how I'd planned on spending the rest of the day.

Maggie cast me a worried look. *Sorry*, she scribbled on her piece of paper. My lips twitched. It was seriously adorable that she had both a notebook and her laptop out in class. I wasn't sure what she was worried about, running out of pens—she had three—or her computer mysteriously crashing.

The weird thing was, I *liked* that she was smart. I'd never been a big fan of girls who were airheads; contrary to popular belief, most of the girls I dated were passably intelligent. But with Maggie it was totally different. I fucking loved how smart she was. It was one of the things that turned me on.

Her mind was a fascinating challenge, her moods ever changing. She was unpredictable, like the weather, always forcing me to readjust and struggle to keep up. She was constantly surprising me, constantly pushing me. I loved it.

The hour went by with agonizing slowness. I tried to concentrate, but it was difficult with Maggie right there. When she flipped her hair, the scent of her perfume wafted over me, instantly calling to mind the image of her hair fanned out over my pillow. Or the sensation of winding it around my hand, her silky length curling around my fingers, while she took me in her mouth.

We needed a seat between us.

She shifted in her chair, stretching out, her tits thrusting forward in her tight sweater.

Maybe two.

"Did you pay attention at all?" Maggie asked as she gathered her stuff when class was finally over.

"Someone kept distracting me." I leaned over and stole a kiss.

She flushed. It was kind of cute how embarrassed she was when we were affectionate in public. It kind of made me want to do it more. Hell, who was I kidding, I'd take about any excuse to have my hands all over her.

"You have to go talk to Dr. Abbott," she reminded me.

"I know." I reached out and tucked a strand of hair behind her ear. It had been distracting me all class. "You're very stern."

"How do you make that sound sexual?"

I grinned. "It's a gift. Besides, stern is sexy. On you. Everything is sexy on you."

"Mr. Khouri."

Maggie laughed. "Somehow I don't think stern is going to be sexy on Dr. Abbott. Good luck."

She walked out of the room, hips swaying from side to side, tossing a final glance over her shoulder at me.

Resigned, I turned away, walking up to the front of the classroom.

Dr. Abbott stared at me, a speculative look in his eyes. "You and Ms. Carpenter are dating, I presume?"

I nodded.

He shook his head. "I wouldn't have pegged that one."

I had to smile. "We get that a lot."

"I would imagine." He leaned back in his chair, his gaze pinning me. "What are your plans after graduation?"

I hadn't been expecting him to lead with that. I'd figured

something along the lines of "change seats," or "don't talk in class."

I shrugged. "I'm going back to Lebanon. My father's campaign is kicking off."

I didn't have to elaborate beyond that. He taught Middle Eastern politics. He knew who my father was.

He considered this for a moment, his gaze unwavering. It was almost enough to make me uncomfortable. Almost. But I'd been raised around formidable political figures my whole life.

I'd had a few classes with Dr. Abbott. He mainly taught upper level IR and Maggie had a bit of an academic crush on him.

"And what about your plans?" he asked me. "Have you thought about furthering your education?"

"No."

"Maybe you should. You could do a master's. I've read your papers—you have a knack for getting at the heart of the problem." He sighed. "There's an instinct to IR. It can't be taught. Some people get it. Lots don't. It would be a shame for you to waste your affinity for this discipline.

"Just think about it. I'm always happy to write a letter of recommendation or discuss your options." He nodded toward the door. "You can go now. I can tell you're dying to catch up with Ms. Carpenter. But really—consider the master's."

I headed for the door.

"And Mr. Khouri?"

I stopped.

"Stop talking in class."

Our conversation played in my mind the entire way back to the dorm.

I punched the code to open my room. Maggie lay on my bed, her legs curled up, a book in her lap. For a moment I just stood there, watching her.

She looked up and our gazes collided. Her smile lit up the freaking room.

"What are you reading?"

"*On War.* Clausewitz. How was the meeting with Abbott?"

I sat down on the bed next to her, tucking her body against mine. I ran a hand through her hair, watching the light highlight the different shades of brown.

"It was okay."

"Was he pissed about us talking?"

"I think he was more amused that you were dating me."

Maggie groaned. "I don't want *Dr. Abbott* thinking about our sex life."

She said his name like he was a god.

"I wouldn't worry about it. He was kind of cool, actually."

"What did you guys talk about?"

"My future."

She stiffened beside me. "What did he say?"

"He mentioned that I should think about doing a master's or something."

She was quiet for a moment. "Is that something you would want?" she finally asked.

"I don't know. Maybe. I've honestly never really thought about it. Not seriously at least." I kissed her, loving the feel of her mouth against mine.

She pulled away. "Stop trying to change the subject."

"I'm not trying to change the subject," I murmured, kissing my way up her neck. "It's just a lot to think about and I don't feel like thinking right now."

Turned out, neither did she.

38

Samir

It didn't take a genius to figure out what she was doing. Ever since my conversation with Abbott, she'd made me study. Constantly. On the upside, we'd worked out a pretty good reward system.

"Want to go make out in the back of the library?"

Maggie grinned. "Are you done with your paper?"

"I have ten pages left."

"It's a fifteen-page paper."

"I see you aren't impressed."

Maggie snorted.

"But what you're failing to realize is I wrote the most important five pages. The next ten will be a breeze."

"I'm not making out with you in the library."

"You say that now, but I don't think you're thinking this through. I'm giving you a chance to combine your two favorite things—sex and books. It's pretty much win-win."

"How did you get girls before me?" she teased. "You pretty much have no game."

I fucking adored her.

"It worked on you."

Her smile widened. "Yeah. I guess it did."

I reached across the table to take her palm in mine, tracing designs on her skin.

"Get a freaking room already." Fleur slid into the seat next to mine. "You guys are disgustingly cute. Since when do you hang out in the library?"

I flipped her off.

"Are you seriously studying?"

"Maggie's studying, and I'm trying to convince her to go make out in the reference section."

"Unsuccessfully."

"So far," I corrected.

She grinned, her dimples flashing back at me. "So far."

"I just threw up in my mouth," Fleur announced.

I shrugged. "Hey, you came over here."

"I'm beginning to regret that."

"Fine, we'll stop." Maggie shot me a look. "What's up?"

She was waffling on the making-out thing. I just needed Fleur to leave.

"Do you guys have plans for Valentine's Day?"

I grimaced. That was not the best subject.

"Yes."

"No," Maggie answered at the same time.

I glared at her. I wanted to take her to Vienna, had the whole weekend planned out. She wasn't having any of it.

"Well, that's helpful, thanks."

"We don't have any plans," Maggie answered, shooting me another look.

"I want to take her to Vienna."

Fleur's gaze drifted to Maggie. "What's the problem?"

"That's an excellent question."

Maggie rolled her eyes. "Chill out. I'm not going to Vienna unless I can pay my way. I can't afford it right now."

"It's my Valentine's Day gift to you," I reiterated for what felt like the hundredth time. For someone who was as smart as she was, she could be unbelievably stubborn.

"It's too much of a gift."

"It's a trip. Not a freaking diamond."

It pissed me off that she wouldn't let me buy her stuff. When we went out to eat, she always chose cheap places or tried to find some way to pay. I'd never had to fight with a girl to let me spend money on her. It didn't sit well with me.

"Get me a card. Some chocolates. Maybe some flowers."

Fleur nodded. "Roses aren't bad. I like diamonds, too, but hey, that's just me."

"She likes peonies," I interjected. "Pink."

"There goes my gag reflex."

"You can leave," I shot back.

"Children!" Maggie glared at both of us. "We don't have Valentine's Day plans. What do you need, Fleur?"

We were going to have a talk about this later. Followed by some "making up."

"Go to the school party with me and George."

I groaned. "Anything but that."

"Sure," Maggie answered at the same time.

I scowled at her. "I don't want to spend my Valentine's Day with George."

Fleur's expression clouded. "Things haven't been good with us lately. It's awkward. Please don't make me hang out with him by myself."

"You could always break up with him," I suggested.

"I don't want to hurt his feelings. Besides, he's been good about the photo thing. It's kind of hard to dump the guy who stood by you when your naked picture was plastered all over the school."

Maggie glanced down at her watch. "I gotta go. I'm running late for class." She kissed me, entirely too quickly, and nodded toward Fleur. "We'll be there." She grinned at me, and something tightened in my chest. "I'll make it up to you. See ya later, babe."

My gaze trailed after her. I wished I could go with her.

"You have it bad."

I jerked my attention away from Maggie's retreating ass. "Thanks for ruining my Valentine's Day plan."

"I didn't run your Valentine's Day plan, you idiot. I probably just saved it."

"How?"

"You don't get it, do you? She's watched girls throw themselves at you because you have money. She doesn't have money. She struggles to afford to be here."

"I know she struggles," I muttered through clenched teeth. "That's why I want to help her. Spoil her a bit."

"She's not like that. Not with you. She cares about you. It means something to her, too. She doesn't just want to be another girl you spend money on. She doesn't want you to think that's why she's here. That she cares about the money more than you."

"She's not like that. I never thought she was."

"I know. I think she does too—mostly. But come on, you're her first boyfriend. You're used to this. She's not. She's doing the best she can to figure it out as she goes along, and she's freaked out. Give her some space. Let Vienna go. It's romantic and sweet but a little too over the top."

I guessed it made sense when she put it like that.

"Since when did you get to be so smart?"

Fleur grinned. "It's easy when you're not the one involved."

I sighed. "She's not the only one who doesn't know what they're doing," I admitted. Fleur was probably the only person I would say that to, because I knew deep down she got it. We were the same in so many ways—both a little too screwed up for normal human interaction.

"I'm terrified I'm going to fuck this up."

Fleur reached across the table and patted my hand, sympathy in her gaze. "I know."

39

Maggie

"It's stupid that I'm nervous, right?"

Mya grinned. "It's your first Valentine's Day with a boy-friend. I'd say it's pretty fair to be nervous."

"And we like the dress?"

"We love the dress," Mya corrected with a smile. "You're hot."

I'd tried to downplay Valentine's Day. Something about it felt too intense, too real. I'd thought going to the school party would be a good compromise. But then Samir had sent me a dozen fat bouquets of pink peonies and my favorite cupcakes, and our room was starting to smell like a florist's shop. Trust him to take "some flowers and chocolate" and turn it into one hundred and forty-four peonies and enough sweets to fill a bakery.

I struggled to focus on my appearance. The dress was a soft pink color, so nude it almost blended with the color of my skin. I'd been skeptical, but Mya and Fleur had insisted it was perfect.

I turned back to Mya. "Are you sure you don't want to come tonight? We're going to miss you."

"I need to be home. My mom's not taking the divorce too well and I think it'll help if we hang out together. We're going to eat candy and watch movies."

"Sounds like fun."

"It should be. Valentine's Day just isn't a big deal for me. I mean, the candy is nice and everything. And believe me, I enjoyed the benefits of Samir sending you cupcakes. I just don't—"

"Obsess about it like me and Fleur," I finished for her, a wry smile on my face.

"Sorry. But yeah."

Mya was the most put-together person I knew. While Fleur was almost aggressively confident, Mya was so chill. Nothing really seemed to ruffle her.

I used to think I was like that—calm, easygoing. Jo had always teased me that I mothered our group of friends. And I had. I'd been playing it safe, holding pieces of myself back, afraid of what would happen if I ever really let go.

Here, in London, everything was different. I felt like I was living, really living, for the first time in my life. It wasn't just Samir. It was my friends, my whole life here. I'd finally found a place that fit, finally become a version of me I'd only dreamed of before. I liked the freedom London gave me, the space I'd found to be myself.

Talking with Samir about his future had made me start thinking of my own. I wasn't sure what I wanted to do after graduation—a master's seemed likely. In our field it was kind of hard to do much without an advanced degree. I had so much ahead of me, so many things to look forward to.

But it was hard to imagine a future without Samir in it.

The Valentine's Day party was held at a posh rooftop bar in Kensington. Surrounded by greenery, with a gorgeous view of the city, it was easy to feel like we were in our own little world. It was like a secret garden—an abundance of trees and hedges and flowers—that only we knew about. The stars twinkled above, giving the whole evening an even more romantic feel.

The people-watching was pretty epic. Everyone was dressed in their finest—there were more designer outfits in this room than could be seen at Fashion Week. Champagne flowed and by the time we got there at eleven, half the student body was already drunk.

We met Fleur and George at the table Samir had reserved.

Fleur looked gorgeous tonight. Her long brown hair fell in curls around her face. Her dress was a shocking pink color, with a hemline that flaunted her long legs and a neckline that showed off ample cleavage.

I whistled. "You look amazing."

She grinned. "Thanks." She leaned over, giving me and Samir air kisses. "So do you."

"Can you blame me for wanting to be alone with her?"

Fleur ignored Samir. "Come on, let's go dance."

I cast him an apologetic look. "Do you mind? I can totally stay here."

He shook his head, his expression resigned. "Go dance." A knowing smile tugged at his lips. "I'll sit here and watch."

Couldn't argue with that. I was beginning to learn just how much Samir liked to watch.

Samir

I didn't even bother trying to talk to George.

The guy was beyond boring, and I couldn't figure out what Fleur saw in him. At some point his friend Max came and joined us, but I gave him little more than a cursory nod.

I couldn't take my eyes off Maggie.

She looked practically naked, and I wasn't sure how I felt about it. Well, I knew how part of me felt about it. The other part was just confused.

I'd be lying if I didn't admit part of me got off on walking into a room with her, knowing there were a hundred guys who would easily trade places with me. She was hot. Unattainable. I liked that she hadn't been with any other guys—the British asshole didn't exist as far as I was concerned. But a part of me also felt like she was a secret I wanted to keep—not because I was anything but proud to be with her, but because she was special.

That was a new one.

I looked up and saw Omar walking toward me. He nodded before sitting down next to me.

"Your girl looks hot."

"Fuck off."

Omar grinned. "You do realize when you graduate everyone's going to try to get with her."

I ground my teeth together. Yeah. I'd realized.

"They're going to take one look at her, and the fantasies will start. They're all going to assume you taught her all of your sex tricks and they're going to be dying to test them out."

"Are you trying to piss me off?"

"Is it working?"

I flipped him off. "What do you think?"

"I think you're sitting over here by yourself like a lovesick schoolboy. It's a little sad." He nodded toward George and Max sitting a few chairs away, their backs to us. "And with those two."

"Fleur's fault."

Omar grabbed an empty glass, draining the last of the champagne. "How is she still with that guy?"

"No clue."

Omar sighed. "You're boring as hell. I'm going to go meet up with my guy. Want to come?"

My guy was code for his dealer. I shook my head. Maggie hated drugs and I cared about Maggie. Wasn't happening.

I'd found myself changing—not totally, but enough that it

was noticeable. I drank less, smoked less, went out less. I paid attention in classes. Went on dates to the movies and restaurants rather than hanging out in nightclubs. We had picnics in the park.

Omar clucked his tongue, a smug smile on his face. "See what I mean?"

Maggie

I slid into the seat next to Samir, grinning as he pulled me onto his lap. He nuzzled my neck.

"Do you have any idea how fucking sexy you are when you dance?"

"I have some idea," I teased, wriggling around on his lap.

He hissed. "Not fair."

"Since when were you concerned about fairness?"

"Omar just accused me of being whipped."

I felt my eyes widen. "Are you?"

He nipped at my lip, sucking it into his mouth. I moaned. The things that boy could do with his mouth...

"Maybe."

I shifted my body, running my hands through his hair. "I wish we were alone," I whispered.

"We could leave."

I wanted to. Badly. But I'd promised Fleur. "Let's stay for another hour. Then we can go."

He grimaced. "I'm dying here."

"You'll be fine."

"You're cruel."

I grinned. "Hardly."

I rubbed against him, loving the shudder that ripped through his body.

"Christ." Samir repositioned me on his lap, resting his chin on my shoulder. "There. Now you're not so distracting."

"Spoilsport."

"I think I've created a monster," he joked.

"Can you blame me if I'm insatiable?"

"Have I ever told you how sexy it is when you use big words?"

I laughed. "You think everything is sexy."

"On you."

I flushed. I loved him like this—playful and charming. Loved bantering with him. Loved getting to be the girl on his arm.

Samir nudged me. "Have you noticed Max?"

"Like he exists? Yes. Like I want to have his babies? No."

"Very funny. Have you noticed the way he is with Fleur?"

"Well, he hates her, yeah. Why?"

"He watches her."

"What?"

Samir nudged me. "Max. He watches Fleur."

I looked to my left. Sure enough, Max leaned against the bar, staring at something in the crowd. I followed the direction of his gaze. Fleur stood on the middle of the dance floor, her hips swaying, long hair flowing, dancing to the beat of the music. Michael danced with her. I looked back at Max. He continued staring at the crowd, and then a scowl covered his handsome face and he turned, downing his drink, and setting the glass on the bar.

"See?"

I frowned. "That's weird."

"He does it a lot."

"Are you sure about that? You may not have noticed, but they don't get along at all."

"That may be, but trust me, he wants her."

"Even though he can't stand her?"

Samir's lips quirked. "I hate to break it to you, but we're guys. We don't care about emotional shit like you do."

I elbowed him. "That's just sad."

He shrugged, gathering me close. "Fine, maybe I misspoke. Some guys don't care about emotional shit. Others, like me, are incredibly in touch with their feelings."

I grinned. "You're such an ass."

"And here I thought I was being good."

"I thought you didn't care about being good."

"Maybe I want to be good for you," he whispered against my hair.

My lips curved.

"Something like that."

"Get a room."

I turned at the sound of Omar's voice. Samir used his free hand to exchange a complicated hand gesture thing with him; his other remained firmly around my body.

"Don't get him into trouble tonight," I admonished with mock severity, remembering the last Valentine's party and the epic brawl. "Not like last year."

Omar rolled his eyes. "Yes, Mom."

Samir laughed. "Don't be jealous just because you can't get your own girl."

"I can get plenty of girls."

Samir responded in Arabic and they both laughed.

He leaned down and pressed a kiss to my cheek. "Want a drink?"

I nodded. "Thanks."

I couldn't take my eyes off him as he got up and walked through the crowd. Everything about him was beautiful—the way he moved, the confidence with which he carried himself. I wasn't the only one who noticed. Girls turned to watch him, whispering to their friends, flipping their hair, and throwing smiles his way.

"I never thought I'd see it," Omar commented.

I tore my gaze away from Samir. "See what?"

"You have him by the balls."

I blinked. "Excuse me?"

"Oh, come on. You know it, too."

My eyes narrowed. I wasn't sure if he was complimenting me or insulting me. With Omar, it was hard to tell. He was Samir's sidekick for a reason; he had all of Samir's dickish qualities and none of his charm.

"I'm pretty sure no one has Samir by the balls."

"I wouldn't be so sure about that." Omar was silent for a moment. "Just be careful with him, okay?"

Surprise filled me. *That* was not what I expected.

"He's a good guy."

I found Samir again, leaning against the bar. Just the sight of him sent a funny thrill through my body and made my heart clench.

"I know."

40

Maggie

"We're heading out."

Fleur grimaced. "Fair enough. Sorry about your Valentine's Day."

I shook my head. "It was fun."

I stared at my reflection in the mirror, wiping away a smudged corner of my mouth where my lipstick had been disturbed by Samir's kiss. Fleur stood next to me, adjusting the top of her dress.

"Are you going to be okay if we leave?"

She shrugged. "I guess so."

I looked around. Two other girls—freshmen I thought—were deep in conversation. Besides them, the bathroom was all clear.

"You need to dump him."

Fleur sighed. "I know."

"It doesn't make you the bad guy if things aren't working. You tried. You've tried really hard. But you can't force chemistry. If you don't feel that way about him, then you need to tell him. I know I encouraged you, but I just wanted to see you happy. You're not happy, and the longer you drag this out, the harder it will be for him when you dump him."

"I know."

"But whatever you do, just don't do it tonight. A Valentine's Day breakup is a terrible idea."

"I'm not that mean," Fleur protested.

"I know you aren't." I hugged her. "Hang in there. It's going to be okay." I hesitated for a moment, not sure if I should mention the whole Max thing or not. Samir wasn't exactly the most observant person I'd ever met... but he was a guy.

"Has Max been weird around you lately?"

She made a face. "No more than usual. Why?"

There was no love lost between them. And I liked Max. For all Fleur claimed to be a reformed, nicer version of herself, I did wonder if she would tease him mercilessly if she found out he had been checking her out.

I shook my head. "No reason."

Samir

"Finally alone."

I put my arms around Maggie, drawing her back against my body.

"You smell good," I murmured.

She laughed. "I've been dancing in a nightclub. Somehow I doubt that."

"You do." I released her, walking toward my room. I fumbled with the door, pushing it open. I froze.

Soft music played from my stereo speakers. Flowers covered the floor. Some sort of candle lights lit up the room.

Behind me, Maggie gasped. "Did you do this?"

"No, I didn't." I closed the door behind us, momentarily perplexed.

"This is amazing."

A bottle of Cristal sat propped up on a bucket of ice on my desk and awareness dawned. I grinned. "I'm guessing this was Fleur."

It was fucking brilliant. It was romantic enough that it would set the perfect mood, but because I hadn't arranged it, Maggie wouldn't freak out. I made a mental note to thank Fleur later.

Maggie grinned. "She's kind of incredible, isn't she?"

"She is." I looped my arms around her waist, pulling Maggie's body against mine. "You're pretty incredible, too."

"Mmm."

I pulled back, surprised by the force of the emotions coming at me. She was so beautiful—and I wasn't just talking about her face or body. There was something else about her. Something that drew me to her like a moth to a flame.

I was falling for her. Hard.

I'd never been in love before. Never really expected to fall in love. I'd liked lots of girls. Wanted them. Lusted after them. Enjoyed them. But love... I'd never counted on that.

"What's wrong?"

I struggled to keep things light between us. "Nothing."

I held her tightly, resting my chin on her head, tucking her against my body. I couldn't speak—there were no words, no jokes—I had nothing. Anything I could say or do just felt inadequate in this moment.

We had three months left.

Maggie

Something had changed between us. I just didn't know what. We stood in the middle of the room, my body engulfed by Samir's. Neither one of us spoke. It was as if we both sensed something had shifted in our relationship and neither one of us wanted to disturb it.

It was easy to get lost in the moment—in sex, in laughter, in all the little distractions surrounding us. But this? Just standing with each other, silently, brought on a whole other level of intimacy. Conversation was easy; the silence was hard.

Minutes passed with our bodies locked before Samir reached down, joining his hand with mine. He brought our linked hands up to his lips, pressing a soft kiss against my knuckles.

I stared into his eyes, surprised by what I saw there—uncertainty, maybe. And emotion. A lot of emotion. The kind of emotion I knew was mirrored in my own eyes.

For a moment, I wondered if I wasn't alone in my feelings—if he loved me too.

My hand dropped to my side and our mouths met. At first I just brushed my lips against his, but then the kiss grew more insistent, demanding. There was no slow or easy with Samir. It was desperate and hungry and before I knew it, I was losing control.

He stripped away my clothes, layer by layer, baring me before him. But this time, when he looked at me, it felt different. It felt like more, like we'd created our own little world and for a moment it felt impenetrable. I was too scared to say the words out loud, but my heart fairly screamed them—

I love you. I love you. I love you.

He laid me down on the bed, his body covering mine, pressing me down into the mattress. I looked up at him, losing myself in those brown eyes. His expression was solemn, his gaze filled with heat. This time there was no laughter, no teasing, no words.

Our bodies spoke where words would have failed us.

His lips covered every inch of my skin, kissing, nipping, licking—painting me, branding me with his mouth and tongue. My flesh was sensitive, every nerve in my body screaming for release. Heat flooded my limbs, sending a flush over my bare skin.

His hands were exquisite torture. He was rough and gentle,

his touch creating conflicting sensations I couldn't quite catch up with. Each stroke sent me closer and closer to the edge, walking a fine line between pleasure and pain. But wasn't that the heart of everything between us?

He made me feel so much it hurt.

41

Samir

"What do you want to do for spring break?"

Maggie eyed me warily, shades of the Vienna fiasco rushing back to me.

"I thought I'd stay here. Get ready for finals."

She *would* start studying two months in advance.

"That's a really boring answer."

"Well, I guess I'm boring, then." She rolled over in bed, pulling the covers up under her chin.

She looked adorable lying there, some goopy thing covering her face. I reached out, skimming my finger across her cheekbone. My finger came back covered in a weird green substance.

"You look like an alien." A pretty cute alien, but still.

"I told you I had to do a mask."

"You didn't mention you'd be green."

Maggie rolled her eyes. "This is why I wanted a girls' night with Mya and Fleur."

"And why couldn't Fleur hang out?"

"She's breaking up with George. And Mya is hanging out with her mom."

"Finally. I was getting sick of being fake nice to that guy."

"You were never fake nice to him."

"True. But I felt like I should be and that was annoying as hell."

She rolled her eyes. "Why do I like you again?"

I laughed. "Because I adore you. And you see past my shallow outer shell."

"Hmm. Maybe."

"So about spring break…"

"I'm not going anywhere for spring break."

"Why?"

"Because I can't afford it."

"What if it were free?"

"It wouldn't be completely free. There would be some cost associated with it."

"*Some cost associated with it*—are you trying to turn me on?"

Maggie snorted. "You're sick. I'm actually worried you're some kind of sex-crazed—"

"Hey, if I'm sex crazed, it's your fault. And stop distracting me. Spring break."

She sighed. "You're not going to let this go, are you?"

"Nope."

"Why? Why is this so important to you?"

I wasn't sure she wanted to know the truth. The idea had been in my head since Valentine's Day. I could pretty much predict her reaction, so like most things, I was trying to maneuver her into it. So far, not so good.

"Because it's my last spring break." That was partly true. "And we had such a great time last year. Remember?"

Her gaze softened. "Paris was fun."

Paris had been amazing. I'd loved getting to show her the city and take her around to my favorite spots. I'd never forget the look on her face the first time she saw the Eiffel Tower twinkling at night. I wanted to see that look again.

"It would be a group thing," I added hastily. I would have preferred having Maggie to myself, but her aversion to trips was still fresh in my mind. "Fleur, Omar, Mya, if she wants to come. Maybe Michael."

"That could be fun."

"You said it yourself, Fleur's just broken up with George. It would probably be good for her to get away for a bit, have a distraction away from everything that's been going on this year. The flight would be free—we could take my father's plane."

She pulled a face. "I don't think taking your dad's plane is the same thing as free."

I shrugged. "Close enough. We don't even have to spend money on a hotel."

Her eyes narrowed. "Where do you want to go for spring break?"

Here came the hard sell.

"Lebanon."

Maggie

For a second, I was pretty sure I'd heard wrong.

He stared at me expectantly.

"Well?"

I shook my head. "Sorry, did you say Lebanon?"

"Maybe."

"As in, 'go to Lebanon because your parents are going to be in France then'?"

"As in, 'go to Lebanon and my parents might be there but that's not a big deal, right?'"

"You want me to meet your parents?" We couldn't seriously be having this conversation.

Why did he want me to go meet them? Why now? He was leaving in two months. Who cared if I met his parents or not? I didn't understand where he was coming from, what he wanted or expected from me.

"It just kind of seems like a recipe for disaster," I admitted. "I mean, I'm the girl you broke up with your girlfriend for. The girlfriend they wanted you to *marry*."

The idea of him getting married was a knot in my stomach I couldn't seem to work out.

"I want you to see my home. My country."

I did, too. But it felt momentous and potentially disastrous, and I couldn't help but think this would be the final straw that illuminated how little I fit into his world.

I sighed. "It just feels like we should be slowing things down a bit."

"Is that what you want?"

I wanted to stop time. I wanted to steal more. I wanted him to stay in London, to do a master's. I wanted to figure out where we were headed without the pressure of a ticking clock.

"No. I don't know."

"Come to Lebanon. It'll be fun. I promise. I want you to see it. I want to be able to share it with you."

I wasn't sure what the right answer was; I didn't even know what I really wanted. But there was something in his voice—an uncertainty, maybe—that made my decision for me. And I'd never been good at telling him no.

"Okay."

I'd spent hours grilling Fleur on Samir's parents. It hadn't helped. In classic Fleur fashion, she hadn't minced words.

"They're probably going to hate you. My aunt especially."

"Gee, thanks. That helps loads."

"I'm not trying to be mean—I'm just being realistic."

I couldn't figure out why he wanted us to go to Lebanon so badly. It felt like an audition of sorts, which made me even more nervous. At the same time, I couldn't help wondering what the point was. I doubted they would be happy to meet me. And I dreaded it.

Samir reached across the airplane seat, squeezing my hand. "Are you okay?"

I forced a smile on my face. "Sure."

"You don't sound okay." He hesitated. "Are you regretting this?"

"Yes. Absolutely. With the fire of a thousand suns."

His lips twitched. "Tell me how you really feel."

"Like this was quite possibly the worst idea ever. Like your parents are going to *hate* me."

The idea had been rolling around in my head the whole five-hour plane ride. I could already predict his response. But I was just freaked out enough to try.

"Listen, what if we—"

"No."

I glared at him. "You don't even know what I was going to say."

"Sure I do. You were going to say we should pretend we aren't really dating and we're just friends because my parents are going to hate you because you're American and in their eyes, all wrong for me."

I groaned. "You're so annoying. I'm trying to make a point here."

"So am I," Samir replied, his expression smug. "I know you. I know what you're thinking, what you're afraid of. Maybe we look strange together, maybe we aren't expected, but we're right for each other. You know it and I know it. I don't care what my parents have to say about it."

"Is that what this is?" I asked. "You thumbing your nose at your parents? You bringing home a girl you know they'll hate?"

"Don't."

"Don't what?" I was stressed and spoiling for a fight.

I wished we'd flown commercial with everyone else. Something about us arriving together like this—on Samir's father's plane—felt too official. Like the final nail in the coffin. More than anything, I was afraid Samir would start to see me through their eyes.

"Don't assume you know what I'm thinking and feeling just because you're scared. Don't think I'm doing the worst possible thing so you can brace yourself for some unknown future disappointment. Don't push me away. Not after everything."

I gaped at him. Because yeah, I totally did that.

"I told you." His expression was triumphant. "I know you."

His words did funny things to me. He made them sound so intimate, almost naughty. He might as well have been saying, "I know you, I've seen you naked, licked Cristal out of your belly button, lost myself inside you, watched you fall asleep, made you come so hard you screamed."

Which he had.

He squeezed my hand. "Stop freaking out."

I hated when he did this, hated when he managed me. It was unfair that he was so good at it. Unfair that he always knew exactly which buttons to push.

"I'm not freaking out."

"You are. You're doing that thing you do with your hair when you're stressed."

"What thing?"

"You twist your hair around your finger."

My hand froze in midair. "This is starting to feel a little creepy."

"Why, because someone knows you—your habits, your quirks? I must be a pervert."

"Or an asshole," I muttered irritably.

Samir laughed. "Why? Because I won't indulge your neuroses?" He leaned over and kissed me. "You're not some dirty little secret I want to hide or some scheme to provoke my parents. I want you to come to Lebanon because I want you to see where I grew up." His voice was almost shy. "I got to see where you were from. I want you to have the same chance."

I felt like an idiot, or the asshole I'd just accused him of being. He tripped me up. Often. Just when I thought I had him figured out, he threw me for a loop.

"Besides, I've never gotten laid in my childhood room."

And then he was right back to his devilish self.

"I'm not having sex with you in your parents' house."

"We'll see."

"I'm not."

Samir leaned over, whispering in my ear. "Babe, I'll have you wet and moaning before the weekend is out."

I flushed. "You can certainly try," I bluffed.

He laughed, the sound low and rich, sending a shiver down my spine. "I bet you're turned on right now. I bet you're sitting there, thinking about my hands and mouth, about me between your thighs…"

"Shh. The flight attendants might hear you."

He smirked. "I think you like knowing they might hear me. I think you like that I can make you forget all those rules you set for yourself. That with me you just let go."

I tried to act like his words didn't mean anything. Like I didn't get off on the thrill of the forbidden with him. He didn't need to know how right he was. His arrogance was both my favorite and least favorite thing about him. I was a total masochist.

"You forget—I know you. Better than anyone."

"What am I thinking right now?" I asked tartly.

He grinned. "I agree. The Mile-High Club would be an excellent idea."

I elbowed him in the side. "That's not what I was thinking."

"But now you are."

42

Maggie

Mile-High Club?

Not the worst idea ever. Turned out getting laid on his dad's plane relaxed me a bit. Until I saw his house and all my fears came crashing back.

I'd thought his family's flat in Paris was impressive. This place put it to shame.

From the exterior, his parents' house resembled a Mediterranean palace—at least what I imagined a Mediterranean palace would look like. Greenery surrounded the house, immaculately maintained. Huge cedar trees provided privacy from the main road. The house was three stories tall, the entrance dominated by double stone stairways leading up to the front drive. A Bentley was parked in the driveway.

"I don't think I can do this."

Samir tugged me forward, through the massive front doors and into a whole different world. "I met your entire family. You can handle a few days with mine."

"My sweater cost ten dollars," I hissed. "My jeans are borrowed from Fleur, and I had to roll the bottoms because she's like twelve feet tall and I'm a hobbit. I promise you, I can't do this."

Samir kissed the top of my nose, ignoring my freak-out. "You're not a hobbit, whatever that is. And your ass looks amazing in those jeans." He wrapped his arms around my waist, bringing me against his body—his *hard* body—and moving his hands lower to cup the ass in question.

I jumped back. "Someone will see." We stood in the middle of his parents' entryway. It was two stories tall, full of marble, and gold, and things that looked expensive. No big deal.

"I'm not embarrassed or worried someone might see. We decided we were going to have a relationship—a real relationship—months ago. I'm not hiding this anymore. Either you're my girlfriend or you're not. I'm not doing this back-and-forth because you're scared."

I gaped at him.

"I'm serious. This is ridiculous. Either you're in or you're out."

I'd thought all along he wanted to be as casual about everything as I pretended to be, but now, seeing the anger in his eyes, I realized he expected more from me. I wasn't sure I could give it. There was something safe in the status quo. We didn't have to define our relationship and I liked that. I couldn't lose something I'd never had.

"Maggie." His voice lowered. "I need you here. I need you to be with me."

His words unraveled the tension that had been building inside me since he'd first asked me to go to Lebanon. It wasn't about whether I was scared or nervous. It was about Samir. And, as hard as it was, it was about us.

"I don't want to screw things up between you and your family."

"You won't."

His lips caressed mine, searching for something that seemed

an awful lot like reassurance. I worried I didn't have enough to give. So I kissed him back, putting everything I had into the kiss. In the beginning, sex had been the scary part, but now sex was easy. It was everything else that terrified me.

I knew it was hard for him to be back home, knew his relationship with his parents was strained. I wanted to be strong for him, wanted to give him the same kind of support he'd given me with my family in South Carolina. Doing so meant I had to grow up.

"Samir."

I froze at the sound of the elegant voice, the French accent.

Samir's hands stilled at my waist. He pulled back, putting space between our bodies. For a moment he stared at me, desire in his gaze. It disappeared before me as his face transformed into an expressionless mask. I'd never seen that look on his face, but it was enough to send a shiver down my spine. He turned, his arm looped around my waist, drawing me close. We both stared up in the direction of the stairs.

A woman stood at the top of the staircase looking down on us like a queen surveying her empire.

Samir hugged me tighter to his body.

"Hello, Mother."

Samir

My grip tightened around Maggie's waist, tension filling my body. As far as parents went, my mother was the easier one for me to deal with. I wasn't sure I could say the same for Maggie.

In one glance, my mother cataloged Maggie and dismissed her, her mouth tightening in a firm line. It was only there for a moment before it was eclipsed by one of her public smiles— cold, polite, impersonal. She wouldn't be rude; her social rules wouldn't allow it. But she would still find a way to make Maggie feel small, to convey that she wasn't welcome in our world.

I was an idiot for bringing her here. I was an idiot for hoping things would be different. I should have predicted this. I'd wanted to show Maggie Lebanon so I'd acted impulsively—ignoring the likelihood things would play out exactly as they were. I'd been stubborn, another flaw in the long list of those my father had pointed out.

My mother glided down the stairs, her gaze trained on the spot where my arm held Maggie against me. She stopped expectantly at the base of the stairs.

"Are you going to come greet me?"

I released Maggie, my legs like lead as I walked toward my mother. My mother's perfume filled my nostrils—floral, Chanel. I leaned forward, our cheeks brushing against each other.

For a moment I just stood there, my body blocking Maggie's.

"And who is your friend?" she asked.

Fuck it.

"This is Maggie. My girlfriend."

Maggie

I tried to make my lips curve into a smile. Eventually I just gave up. It wasn't a coincidence that the temperature dropped by several degrees when Samir's mother entered the room.

"You have a lovely home, Mrs. Khouri."

"Thank you." Her eyes narrowed for a moment. "American?"

For a moment I considered lying and saying Canadian if that would buy me some points with her.

"Yes."

"Interesting."

She made *interesting* sound like I'd come from Mars.

Samir put his arm back around me, kissing the top of my head.

"I'm going to get Maggie settled into her room. It's been

a long trip." He glanced at his watch. "The rest of the party should be here in an hour."

"How lovely."

I stifled the snort. I'd never heard anyone sound less sincere.

We excused ourselves and started up the staircase when Samir's mother called back to us.

"Samir, your father will be here for dinner. I'm sure he can't wait to meet your friends."

The arm around me tightened.

We walked up the staircase, neither one of us speaking. He led me down a long hallway until we stopped in front of a door.

"This will be your room. Mine's across the hall."

Gone were the teasing voice and the sexual innuendo. His jaw was clenched, his gaze hooded. I reached down and grabbed his hand, linking my fingers with his, squeezing.

He pushed open the door, leading me into the room, closing the door behind us.

"Are you okay?"

He guided me back onto the bed, wrapping his arms around me, pulling me in, burying his face in my hair. For a moment, he didn't speak. He drew back, meeting my gaze.

"I'm so sorry about that. I should have realized how horrible this was going to be. I'm so sorry I brought you here."

"It's fine."

He laughed bitterly. "It's not fine. That was my nicer parent. I can't wait until you have to meet my father." He rested his forehead against mine. "I'm so, so sorry. This was the worst idea. I should have thought about it before I made you come here. It was stupid and selfish. All I could think about was showing you my home, how I grew up. I wanted you to see Lebanon, wanted you to love it as much as I do. But it's not worth them treating you like shit."

"That's what I was afraid of. I didn't want you to see me

here, see the way your parents looked at me and realize I didn't fit in your world."

"What?"

I sighed. "I was afraid being here would make you realize how different we were. How much I didn't fit in your life."

"Are you kidding me? I like you because you're different. I love that about you. You're worth more than all of this. Don't you see that?"

I saw it when he looked at me like that. I heard it in his voice, felt it in his kiss. Deep down, even as it scared me, I knew what I meant to him. But my head always fucked it up. My fears ran through me like a lightning storm, blinding me to anything else.

I kissed him, wrapping my legs around his waist, pulling him toward me.

"We can do this," I whispered against his mouth. "We can get through this."

In that moment, I even believed it myself.

43

Maggie

I'd never been happier to see Fleur. She sat next to me at dinner, filling the silence with an endless round of chatter and stories. I owed her big-time.

Samir sat across from me, uncharacteristically quiet. Here, he was a shadow of his former self. I figured it had everything to do with the man sitting at the head of the table.

His father wasn't a big man, but he had *presence*. There was a charisma about him. Not the same kind of charisma I'd come to associate with American politicians—he wasn't charming or overly friendly—but there was something there. Power. Privilege. He looked like a king presiding over the dinner with a sort of casual disinterest. I wasn't sure I liked how much he reminded me of Samir.

This was the world he'd grown up in—gold flatware and plates, quiet servants, and all the trappings of vast wealth. This was the world he was expected to return to, to rule over someday. It was no place for someone like me.

I kept my head ducked for most of the dinner, concentrating on the food—a Lebanese feast even the company couldn't spoil—and struggling to keep up with the conversation. Samir's parents spoke a little English, but most of the conversation was in French. Anytime the conversation came to Samir, he answered in English, and I fell a little more in love with him.

Finally, dinner ended, and Fleur, Mya, and I went upstairs and collapsed on the bed in my room.

"That was a narrow escape," Mya joked.

"Please tell me they aren't always this bad."

Fleur laughed. "Sorry. This is standard."

As much as my family situation sucked, at least I'd grown up in a loving house. I couldn't imagine what it must have been like to grow up like Samir had.

"Why does his mom seem to dislike you?"

Fleur rolled her eyes. "I'm the wild one in the family. Just ask my parents. My aunt has never liked me. Thinks I'm a bad influence on Samir."

I snorted. I loved Samir, but I was pretty sure no one could be a bad influence on him.

"How did his parents meet? For all his dad's pushing hard for a Lebanese girl for Samir, I'm surprised he married a French woman."

"Our grandfather on our mothers' side did a lot of development in Beirut so that helped. He had a ton of social and financial connections here. But still, I think Samir's dad got some political shit for it. That's probably part of why he wanted Samir to marry Layla. Their families have been close since before Samir and Layla were born. It's hard to turn your back on decades of history and friendship like that."

"They hate me, don't they?"

They hadn't been rude to me; they'd just basically looked through me, like I didn't exist. I wasn't even important enough to register on their radar. They treated me like I was just another one of Samir's flings.

Mya began studying a pillow on the bed.

"You just aren't what they envisioned for Samir," Fleur replied, her voice uncharacteristically gentle.

"I told Samir I didn't want to come. He should have listened to me."

"Samir tends to not want to hear the truth when it stands in the way of something he wants. He wanted you here. And deep down I bet he wanted his family to accept you."

"I wanted that, too."

Fleur leaned over and gave me a hug. "I know you did."

"What are we going to do? There's no happy ending for us, is there? No chance of this actually working out."

Fleur frowned. "I don't know. I wish I could tell you there was. But I think there's a huge gulf between the two of you, and until one of you is brave enough to cross it, you're always going to be apart."

I heard the truth in her words. I just didn't see a way through.

Fleur stood up. "Come on, Mya. Let's go back to our rooms. I think Maggie's going to want some privacy soon."

"Why?"

"That stuff Samir's dad was saying in French?"

I nodded.

"He basically spent the whole dinner ripping on Samir." My heart thudded. That's why he'd looked so miserable. "He's going to need you tonight."

Samir

I wanted to punch something. Someone. He was such an asshole. I supposed I was lucky he hadn't said the things he'd said in French in English. And that was only because he practically refused to speak English. But at least Maggie hadn't understood it. The only thing that had made the whole dinner bearable had been having her there. As soon as the girls had gone upstairs, it had been as if the air were sucked from the room.

I walked down the hall, my feet failing to move fast enough. I wanted her. No, I needed her. I needed the kind of peace only she seemed to give me.

I stopped in front of her door and rapped my fingers against the wood, not really caring if anyone heard me. I'd been joking about the sex before. I hadn't really planned on seducing her in my parents' house—even I had limits. But that was before. Before he'd laid into me. Before he'd made me feel like a child again. As if I were nothing. A spot of dirt beneath his shoe.

Maggie opened the door, her eyes wide, dressed only in a robe. I didn't speak. Instead, I grabbed her hand, pulling her out into the hall with me, walking purposefully toward my room. She didn't say a thing. There was something inside me tonight, something dangerous, edgy. I felt as if I were dying in this house, and I wanted her to bring me back to life. I wanted her in my bed, the scent of her on my sheets, the sight of her naked body burned in my mind, so when she was gone, and I was back living a life I wanted nothing to do with, at least the memory of her would keep me company. Even if it was all I could have.

I opened my bedroom door, Maggie behind me, her body against mine, the feel of her breasts against me enough to make me throb. I closed the door behind us and whirled around, capturing her mouth in a desperate kiss, one I lost control over from the start.

Maggie

He pushed me back against the wall, his hands fumbling for my robe's belt. His lips plundered mine, his mouth possessing me, his body devouring me.

My robe fell to the floor, and I stood before him naked, my nipples tight and aching, my body shivering, catching the tinge of need that surrounded us.

"I need you. Now." His voice was hoarse, raw, his entire body tense. I saw the hurt inside him, the pain that covered his handsome features. The sight of that pain sent a knife through my heart. If I could have taken it from him and borne it as my own, I would have.

"Then take me."

He didn't hesitate. He took me in his arms and carried me to the bed, tossing me down on the plush mattress. I was only alone for a moment before his body covered mine. His hands fisted in my hair, his teeth grazed my shoulder, biting my skin, sucking on the thin curve of my neck. His hands and lips were everywhere—cupping, squeezing, tugging, stroking. He tongued my nipple and my hips shot up off the bed, my back arching with pleasure.

I pulled at his clothes, desperate to feel his bare flesh against mine.

"I can't wait. I can't go slow. I have to have you."

When he was naked he left the bed to grab a condom from his suitcase, tearing into the foil package and rolling it on. He moved forward, settling between my legs, rubbing against me, the friction sending a tremor through my body.

"I need you. Please."

His gaze darkened and he spread my legs wider, wrapping my ankles around his back. He thrust inside me little by little, filling me, stretching my body. His hips created a rhythm my own had no choice but to follow. Our gazes locked, and I swore I could almost hear his thoughts, pushing to come out. We needed no words. Instead, we spoke with our eyes and our bodies.

He'd taught me so much about sex. There were times we were playful, joking and teasing, laughter filling the space around us. There were other times when it was fast and furious, a tangle of limbs, and a joining that felt like a desperate race to the finish. Times when he taught me to embrace the power he gave me, the ability to make his body shake at the sight of me stripping before him or prancing around in something sheer and lacy. But this? This was something new. Something he hadn't taught me. Tonight I learned sex could be something else—that somewhere in between his body slipping into mine and the ecstasy and release, two people who were broken could come together and be made whole.

We made each other whole.

44

Samir

We walked down the street hand in hand. I pointed out various places to her, loving the way her eyes lit up every time I showed her something new. The Corniche, the popular street next to the seafront, was crowded today. People strolled by the water; others rode bikes on the street. A musician played off to the side, the sound mixing with all the other sounds of the city. The weather was perfect, the company even better. I'd sent Fleur and the rest of the group off with our driver to explore Beirut. I wanted Maggie to myself.

"What do you think?"

"It's gorgeous. I love it."

This was one of my favorite spots in Lebanon. I loved the water, loved the palm trees, the deep expanse of sand before the shore. There was something about this space. Something in the air made me think of freedom despite the tall buildings that bordered it.

Maggie smiled. "You look good here. It suits you."

"Why do you say that?"

"You seem at home here. It's different from how you are in

London. Different even from the version I saw of you when we were in Paris."

"I feel different here," I admitted. "It feels like home, and at the same time, with my parents, I just wish things were different, you know?"

"I do," she replied. "It hurts when you wish you could change the relationship, when you wish things could be different. I know what it's like to hurt when it feels like you can't fix it, when you feel like there's something lacking in you that makes your parents not see you the way you want to be seen, not love you the way you need to be loved..." She trailed off, her voice thick with emotion.

I couldn't say anything. I gathered her in my arms, burying my lips in her hair, holding her so close I never wanted to let her go.

"I don't know what I'm going to do..."

She sighed. "I know."

It was the thing we never spoke of—what would happen when graduation came. We'd both already purchased our plane tickets home. It was so close—

I didn't know what I'd do when it was time to let her go.

Maggie

I saw Lebanon through his eyes. Maybe that was why I loved it as much as I did. I understood now, in a way I never had before, just how much it was a part of him. I loved that part. But I knew I had to let him go.

I stood in his arms, basking in the warmth of the sun on our bodies, the sound of the waves. It was a beautiful, perfect day. It only seemed fair that we'd get as many of those as possible considering how quickly time was running out.

He leaned back, staring down at my face. "Are you okay?"

I didn't know. Time was slipping away from us, minute by

minute. I'd been so nervous about this trip to Lebanon, so nervous to meet his family. But now it had come and would go soon and then the next big hurdle would be graduation.

"Just thinking." I tried to shrug it off, like the words didn't matter.

He gathered me closer to him, letting me wrap my body around his like a vine.

"I'm glad I got to see this." I gestured to the bustling city around me.

"Why?"

"Because now I'll be able to picture you here. Be able to imagine what your life is like."

He sighed. "That sounds so sad."

"I don't think this was ever going to be anything but sad."

He was silent for a long time, the sounds of the street behind us filling a gap we both danced around.

"I wish things were different," he whispered.

So did I.

He kissed me, his lips clinging to mine. There was desperation in his kisses now. Before we had sex last year, he used to kiss me as though I were something he had to consume, possess. Now, he kissed me as if the connection between our lips were enough to bind me to him, even though I was slipping away.

I knew because I did the same thing to him.

He broke apart from me, his face flushed, his lips swollen from our kiss, his chest heaving.

"I don't know how to let you go."

My heart lurched as the words escaped his mouth. The desire to ask him to stay filled me. I wanted the happy ending, wanted him to stay in London forever. But I couldn't speak. If the roles were reversed, if he asked me to come to Lebanon to be with him—

It was an impossible situation. I couldn't throw away my future. Not after I'd worked this hard to get here. And I couldn't ask him to do the same for me. I loved him too much.

We were in this weird in-between stage. It wasn't casual. Even if he hadn't said the words, I knew there was more there. But I wasn't ready for marriage. We'd never even kind of talked about it. I was twenty years old. I had two thousand dollars to my name, two years of college left, and a mountain of student loan debt waiting for me on the other side. I didn't have a lot of options. I had a path I'd been on my whole life. So did he.

The distance between his life and mine had never seemed more insurmountable than it did now, and I wasn't sure love—if it even existed in him too—was enough to bridge the gap.

45

Maggie

When we got back from Lebanon time moved quickly, as it tended to do when an event you dreaded loomed near. Each day felt like another moment slipping through our fingers, another day together lost. It was hard to focus on school, hard to think about anything other than Samir leaving soon.

My friends began treating me carefully, as if I would explode at any minute. Between the stress of finals and Samir leaving London, my emotions were a jumbled mess.

"Are we just going to pretend everything's okay?"

I stared at Fleur sitting across from me at the cafeteria table. "Do you want to talk about your breakup with George?"

She grimaced. "Point taken."

It was kind of a low blow. But the one thing I couldn't handle right now was a deep conversation about Samir. I was skimming the surface emotionally, going through my days on autopilot. I felt safer that way. He was leaving and I had finals and I couldn't afford to mess up my future. My scholarship required a 3.5 GPA, and my GPA was shaky enough after last year. There was no way I was going to jeopardize my chances here.

"Fuck." Fleur's voice broke through my inner panic attack. "What's wrong?"

"Max."

I looked across the cafeteria. Max stood in the middle of the room, holding a tray in his hand. He flushed slightly. His gaze darted from me to Fleur and back to me again.

The problem with going to a school as small as the International School was that breakups complicated everything. Everyone knew everyone's business and it was hard to avoid an ex...or in this case, his best friend. I felt bad for Fleur, but at the same time, I couldn't exactly pretend Max didn't exist.

He didn't seem to have the same problem. He nodded at me before his gaze drifted back to Fleur. It held there and something flickered, only for an instant, but long enough for Samir's words to run through me... *He watches Fleur.* I hadn't really noticed it before—maybe he'd never done it before in front of me—but Max continued to stare at her. I watched, fascinated, as a flush rose in his cheeks before he jerked his head and turned and walked away.

"What was that?"

Fleur didn't answer me.

"Fleur?"

Her head snapped up, her cheeks pink. "What?"

"You noticed that, right? That was weird."

She shrugged. "He's a weird guy."

That wasn't entirely accurate, but I let it slide. Finally, my curiosity got the best of me. "Do you think he likes you? Samir noticed him looking at you at the Valentine's Day dance."

The color staining her cheeks deepened. "Samir doesn't know what he's talking about."

"Actually, what I think you meant to say was, 'Samir is incredibly wise.'"

Fleur snorted as Samir sank down in the chair next to mine. He kissed me.

"Hi, babe."

I grinned. "Hi."

"What did I miss?"

"Nothing," Fleur answered, rising from her chair. "I have to go to class. We're still on for the graduation party I'm hosting at Babel, right? I'm going to reserve a table today."

Samir nodded. "Yeah, we're still on."

"Good. I'll catch you guys later." We both watched her walk away.

"She's not herself," I murmured. "I'm worried about her. She just seems even more lost now that she's broken up with George."

"I've noticed." It was impossible to miss the worry in his voice.

"Have you tried talking to her?"

Samir shook his head. "You know how she is. I can't make her do something she doesn't want to do."

"I know."

He squeezed my hand. "She'll be okay. Don't worry about Fleur."

He didn't add the unspoken—*we have enough shit to deal with*—but it hung between us. He didn't know the rest of the stuff going on with Fleur, though. Didn't know about the blackmail or the pregnancy. I wanted to tell him, wanted to get his advice, but it wasn't my secret to tell. She'd stopped talking about it all, insisting she didn't want her life to be controlled by it. I understood, and yet nothing felt resolved. It felt like a storm was brewing, and I didn't know how to help her when she didn't seem to want help.

"Are you okay?"

I almost laughed at his question. I was about as far from okay as you could get. Graduation was breathing down my neck, so close I could taste it.

"I don't know."

It was the most honest answer I could give.

"Yeah. Me too." His gaze held with mine. "What are your plans this summer?"

I blinked, surprised by the question. "I thought the whole point of this was that things were going to end in May. Do you really want to do this? Talk about the future we won't have?"

Maybe I was a chicken, but I wanted—needed—a clean break. I couldn't imagine texting him, emailing him, talking to him when he was back in Lebanon, knowing we had no future. I couldn't imagine keeping this tether between us when he'd be looking for a wife. The idea of him getting *married* was already a knife to my heart and it was only an abstract concept. I couldn't prolong the agony of not having him by keeping him in my life—always unattainable, a constant reminder of what I'd lost.

"I wanted to be able to imagine you at home, so when I'm in Lebanon, miserable, I can envision what your life is like."

His words hit me like a punch. It was so close to what I'd said to him in Beirut, so close to my own thoughts and desires. I understood his wants better than anyone, but at the same time I couldn't help but worry we were both clinging to something we couldn't keep.

"Tell me."

I sighed. "Working a lot to save up for next year. Hanging out with my grandparents, Jo. Nothing glamorous."

"Are you going to see your dad? The baby?"

"Maybe. I haven't decided. Sara's due this summer so we'll see."

"What else? What kind of stuff will you do for fun?"

It was the furthest thing from my mind. "I don't know. Probably hang out with friends from high school. Go out to dinners, that sort of thing."

He was quiet for a moment. "So are there any boys in South Carolina?"

"What?"

"Just making conversation."

My eyes narrowed. "Are we really going to do this?"

Samir

I was going down a path I really didn't want to go down. But I'd have been lying if I didn't admit the idea of her with other guys had been bothering me for months now. Even more so since Omar brought it up at Valentine's Day.

I saw the way guys looked at her. I'd never really been the jealous type, but the idea of her with someone else was killing me. She wasn't going to stay single forever. She was beautiful, and smart, and funny, and there was no way I was the only guy who'd noticed. I wanted her to be happy—

I just didn't know how I'd be happy without her.

She reached across the table and squeezed my hand. "Don't do this. It just makes it harder."

The logical part of me knew she was right. But all I had to do was look at her, touch her, kiss her, and logic flew out the window.

I had no idea how I was going to let her go. Especially when it felt like she was taking a piece of my heart with her. We had a week left and then it would all be over.

46

Maggie

If someone asked me to describe Samir's graduation, I couldn't have done it. The day went by in a blur. I put on the dress I'd bought with Fleur weeks earlier. Mya did my hair. I watched Samir get ready. Took pictures with him in his cap and gown. It all felt like a dream. Or, given the way time ran down, a nightmare.

I'd never been more grateful for my friends.

Fleur ripped on everyone's fashion choices and made me laugh. Mya held my hand. It was as if they knew how close I was to breaking and were ready to step in with exactly what I needed. I'd never loved them more.

I sat next to them during the ceremony, grateful there were several rows between Samir's parents and me. They didn't acknowledge us except for a curt nod to Fleur, but I couldn't bring myself to care. They were just another reminder he would be leaving tomorrow. Another reminder of all I stood to lose.

When he walked across the stage, so sexy in his cap and gown, my heart tumbled in my chest. Pride burst through me.

It only made things worse. The pride was too closely tied to another emotion—one I was afraid to acknowledge as love.

Samir

If you'd told me the first day of my freshman year that I'd be dreading my graduation day, I would have laughed. Now, the joke was on me. Even independent of Maggie, I wasn't ready for this.

I'd miss my friends. Miss London. Even miss being around Fleur. I had a life here. One I liked; one I wasn't ready to give up.

I went through the motions—smiled when I was supposed to, took pictures with my friends, managed small talk with my parents. It was my last full day in London, and I hated how much it kept me away from Maggie. I wanted to be next to her, in bed with her, anything to keep her close to me. Even with the production that was graduation, I knew where she was always. It wasn't even intentional. It just worked out that way.

I walked across the stage, taking my diploma from the university president. It was just a piece of paper and yet it had power over me—it was a noose tightening around my neck.

I posed for the obligatory handshake picture, using the opportunity to seek Maggie out in the crowd. Our gazes locked. It was just a moment, but she smiled at me, and I saw something I hadn't seen all day—pride. She was proud of me. And suddenly I didn't care that my father had spent most of my graduation day taking business calls or that my mother was clearly bored.

She was proud of me. And really, nothing else mattered.

Maggie

I looked at my reflection in the mirror, struggling not to cry. The emotion of the day flooded me. All around me, everyone was celebrating graduation and the end of the semester. Everyone was happy. All I could think was that my world was falling down around me.

This time tomorrow he would be gone.

In the beginning, when I'd first met Samir, I hadn't thought about the fact that he would be graduating or that he would likely go back to Lebanon when he was done. How could I? I lived in a world where kids went to school and graduated and got jobs wherever they could find work, living wherever they wanted to live. Wherever they *could* live. Political dynasties and family legacies were things I'd only read about in books. They weren't real to me. Not like they were to him.

I would have given anything, everything I had, to go back in time to last year. I wished I could have told myself back then to savor every moment with him. To not waste time worrying about my feelings, playing it safe, teetering on the edge of letting myself go. I wished I could have tumbled headfirst into it. Wished I could have frozen all those moments that now slipped through my fingers.

I sank down on my bed, struggling not to cry. Pain filled my chest, bringing with it an acute sense of loss. He was still here, but in my heart he was already gone. It was just a matter of time.

I almost wished I could avoid this night altogether. At the same time, I wished I could draw out every moment, prolonging it indefinitely. Time taunted me now, the hands of the clock threatening to tear away the one person I was worried I couldn't live without.

A knock sounded at the door.

I stood up on shaky legs, making my way across the room. I sucked in a deep breath, struggling to compose myself. From the beginning, since we'd decided to be together, I'd known he would be temporary, that I couldn't keep him.

I just wished my heart had gotten the memo.

Samir

She opened the door and my heart fucking stopped.

Impossibly, she seemed more beautiful every time I looked at her. Or maybe it was just that I saw her differently every time I looked at her. Each time I saw more.

Her hair was down in a cascade of dark brown curls. Her lips were a lush, full red, her skin the color of cream. Her body, with the curves I loved, was wrapped in a black dress that made me want to stay in.

Her eyes broke my heart.

I saw myself in her gaze. Saw the same fear and pain and sense of loss that had been chasing me all day reflected in her eyes. I was supposed to be happy. I'd been waiting for this moment for four years. No more exams, no more papers, no more time spent in boring lectures I couldn't have cared less about. But I didn't feel happy. I felt… I didn't know. Off. Like I needed to take a step and didn't know where I was supposed to go.

"I don't want to go out tonight." I blurted out the words, my voice bleak. *I want to stop time. I want to stay in my room, wrapped around you forever. I don't want to leave.*

I was frozen—by indecision, fear, the weight of expectations I could never live up to.

Maggie smiled, but I knew that smile. She was trying to pretend everything was okay. Trying to pretend she wasn't as fucked up over this as I was. We both sucked at pretending.

"We have to go. Fleur planned the party to celebrate your graduation."

"I don't care about Fleur. She'll get over it."

Maggie shook her head. "We have to go." Her voice cracked a bit, her composure slipping. "I need to be out. I need the distraction of just drinking and having fun. I don't want to think about things. If it's just the two of us, we'll be depressed. We need to get out—have a good time. It'll be fun."

I'd never been less in the mood for a party. I wanted to protest, to convince her to blow it off. But I'd never been good at making Maggie do anything. I was ready to turn myself inside out to please her. I followed her out the door and into a cab.

47

Maggie

He was angry or unhappy or something. I didn't want to think about what the "something" meant.

He didn't talk. The entire drive to Babel, we didn't say a word between us. He sat next to me, my hand clutched in his, staring out the window as the lights of London passed us by. I'd always felt as if the city were magic—I'd always seen possibility in those lights. Now I just saw a flickering sadness, the last few glimmers before the magic died out.

I wanted to speak, to break the tension building between us, but each time I opened my mouth to say something, the emotion clogged in my throat kept the words inside. They were trapped there, captured within the vault where I'd locked my heart away.

We were living on borrowed time—of course we had been all along. But now time was up and I had no clue how to handle it. No clue how to handle the emotions raging inside of me. We were both angry, both struggling to make sense of things, both struggling to move forward, to understand what to do next.

It was a spectacularly bad night for a party.

"Are you okay?" Fleur asked, hugging me when we finally arrived at Babel. "You look like shit."

"Thanks."

"I didn't mean it like that. I just meant that you look like you're going to cry." Her gaze darted toward Samir. "Did you guys get into a fight or something?"

I looked at Samir, standing at the bar talking to Omar, his back to me.

"No."

At least with a fight we would talk about things—about the future. We didn't fight because that would mean we'd have to deal with whatever lingered between us. Neither one of us was much for talking about our emotions.

"Then why are you over here when he's over there?"

"I don't know."

"You guys are idiots."

Somewhere, the more mature, but often ignored, part of my brain agreed with her.

"Not helping."

"You are. You're both throwing away your best chance at happiness."

I glared at her, trying to ignore the sinking feeling in my stomach telling me she was right. I drained the glass of champagne, letting the bubbles take me over.

"Well, that answers the question of whether you're planning on getting drunk tonight." Her gaze narrowed as it traveled over to where Samir stood with Omar. "And apparently he's going to join you." She grimaced. "You may want to head over to the bar before he screws up your last night together."

I followed her stare until my gaze settled on two very pretty girls talking to Samir and Omar.

I saw red.

Samir

I knocked back the glass of whiskey, savoring the burn that shot down my throat. The rest of me felt numb. It was my fourth one, and I had no intention of slowing down any time soon.

Omar raised an eyebrow at me. "Is that really what you want to be doing right now?"

No, actually it wasn't. I wanted to be with my motherfucking girlfriend. I wanted a lot of things I apparently couldn't have.

"Fuck off."

Omar's lips curved and I could tell he was struggling to keep from laughing at me. Yeah, I was just hilarious.

I was angry and getting angrier by the second. She was impossible. I wished she would talk to me, tell me what she was thinking. I wanted everything from her—her thoughts, her feelings, her emotions. I wanted to know what was going on in her head. I'd felt her getting progressively sadder the closer we got to graduation, and yet, I had no idea what she wanted—or if she wanted to do something about it.

"Girl troubles?"

"You have no clue."

Omar grimaced. "Dude, if this is what love looks like, I want no part of it." He spat the word *love* from his lips as if it were a dirty word. If things hadn't been so desperate, if his words hadn't stopped me in my tracks, I would have laughed.

"What are you talking about?"

There was a difference between thinking about it or worrying about it, and hearing it spoken aloud. He'd just given a voice to the thing that scared me most.

"Please. You love her. It couldn't be more obvious."

"I don't love her."

"Sure you don't."

Maybe if I said it enough I'd convince myself.

"I don't love her," I repeated.

Omar shrugged. "Whatever."

"Fuck. She doesn't love me."

It hurt to force the words out.

"Maybe, maybe not."

I hated the uncertainty in my voice. Hated how much I cared. He was going to give me shit for this for the rest of my life.

"She won't talk to me. I've tried to talk to her, to see how she feels about everything, and she won't talk to me."

"Make her."

He had a point there. Except I wasn't sure I was ready for her answer. If she said she loved me, what would it change really? We still faced the same problem that I couldn't get around, no matter how hard I tried. I couldn't have Maggie without giving up everything else. And where would that take us? She was so young—she still had two years of college ahead of her. I wanted her to have a chance at her dreams. I didn't want to ruin all that.

There would be no guarantees. It wasn't like we'd be getting engaged—she wasn't even twenty-one. For me to give up everything for her meant I was taking a gamble and my odds were a complete mystery. I didn't even know what she wanted. Besides, what could I offer her? Without my family's support, my job prospects weren't great. Hell, I wouldn't be shocked if my dad blackballed me for defying him. Then where would we be? I had a little money from my grandfather, but it wasn't anything compared to what I'd be giving up.

We couldn't do long-distance. I'd done long-distance with other girls, and it never worked. With Maggie—I trusted her and yet I knew it would plague me to be with her and be worried about other guys. And she deserved to be able to have fun and not feel tied down to a guy who could only see her a few times a year. After all of that, it still begged the question, where was this going?

"It's complicated."

Omar smirked. "You've lost your edge."

"No, I haven't."

But maybe I had. I wasn't the same guy I'd been before her, and I wasn't sure I missed that guy either. I didn't know who I was anymore.

Omar jerked his head toward two girls standing to our right. "They're headed this way. Prove it." He waved the girls over, a lazy grin on his face. *Fucker.* I knew what he was doing, and I doubted he realized how pissed Maggie would be—or just how bad her temper could be.

Omar started talking to the girls, introducing me. They were hot. Tall and lean, nice boobs. They were definitely interested in us, and I couldn't have cared less. I didn't want another girl. I wanted Maggie.

"What the fuck is your problem?"

Shit. I turned around and came face-to-face with my very pissed-off girlfriend.

Thanks, Omar.

48

Maggie

I was making a scene and I couldn't be bothered to care. I knew exactly what he was doing.

"Really?"

"It's not what it looks like," Samir answered, his expression pained.

My gaze darted from the girls and back to him. I barely spared them a glance.

"I know it isn't what it looks like. That's the point. You're pissed at me, and this is, what? Your way of punishing me? Trying to get attention?"

For a moment, he almost looked guilty, but then his expression changed, and I saw the same anger there that had plagued me all night.

"Because you've been so mature."

"Me?"

He stepped closer to me, moving away from Omar and the other girls, backing me into a corner. "Yes, you. We need to talk."

We did. I'd been avoiding it for weeks. I didn't know what

to say, didn't know what I wanted. Or maybe it was just that I wanted something I knew I couldn't have.

I still couldn't see how a future between us would ever work. I didn't fit in his world. I didn't mean that in a *he came from money and I didn't* sort of way. I meant it in a *you will have no political future in Lebanon if you marry an American girl whose father is a fighter pilot* sort of way. His parents had looked at me as if I were nothing. In his world I was.

I forced a smile on my face, ignoring the pounding in my heart. "Let's just have fun tonight, okay? We don't need to talk. Everything's fine."

"I don't want to pretend everything is fine. Nothing is fine about this." He closed the distance between us, and I had to tilt my head up to meet his eyes. "Don't tell me you don't feel the same way I do. That this isn't killing you as much as it's killing me. Because I know you better than anyone and I won't believe you."

His words splintered something inside me. He did know me better than anyone and he made me happier than anyone ever had. But I was twenty. I wasn't ready to get married or even engaged. Not even close. And it seemed silly for him to throw away his life just so we could date.

"What do you want me to say? Do you want me to tell you I've been miserable for the last month? That every day has felt like a ticking time bomb I can't stop? That every morning when I wake up next to you, I think to myself, 'only two more mornings, only one more morning'?" My voice cracked. "Do you want me to cry? Would that make you feel better?"

"Maggie—"

"No. You don't get to do this now. We said it all along—this was temporary from the start. You knew that just as much as I did. Why do this now? Why drag it out and make it worse?"

"Because maybe it doesn't have to be like this. Maybe this doesn't have to be goodbye."

I hated the hope that sprang up at those words. Hated how badly I wanted him to be right.

"You don't get it. It has to be goodbye. I need to be able to move on. I need for you just to leave, so this feeling inside me, this feeling that my heart is shattering in my chest, will finally stop. I can't prolong this; I can't keep hoping things will change between us. I need to let you go. I need you to let me go."

"What if I can't?"

"You have to."

"That's bullshit. You're scared and you're afraid to take a chance on us. Why can't you trust me, Maggie? I'm not going to hurt you."

"You're hurting me now. Can't you see that? You're breaking my heart and I just need it to be over."

He froze. "What do you mean?"

"Nothing."

He was too close; everything about this was too intense. I needed a break from him, needed space to breathe.

"Do you love me?"

Everything in the club fell away. I couldn't think, couldn't react, couldn't feel or hear anything but those words, undeniable, thundering through my ears—

Horror filled me, because I knew the answer to his question. It was inside of me, shouting to get out. Of course I loved him. I'd loved him for so long it had become a part of me, a part I would have to carve out of my chest when he left.

It seemed so unfair that I would meet him now, that my life would change at nineteen and at twenty I would be pushed to choose the path my life would take. I loved him, but we had dreams of our own, plans independent of each other. I wanted to be with him—but what did that mean? Was I supposed to drop out of school? Marry him, move to Lebanon? Was that what he wanted? Did I even want to know what he wanted?

"Do you love me?"

I heard the desperation in those words, felt the anger simmering beneath them. And for a moment I didn't know what he wanted—or needed—to hear more. The truth...or the lie.

Three words, desperate for release, fought to escape.

I love you. I have always loved you. Since before I knew how to put a name to it or what it was. And more than anything, I'm afraid I will always love you. And now you're leaving, and I feel like you're taking my heart with you.

Panic rose inside my chest. "Don't ask me that."

I couldn't do this. I couldn't open my heart. I wanted to fight. I wanted to get drunk and yell at him about something stupid. I wanted to wreck this. As fucked up as I knew it was, part of me wanted to hurt him as much as he was hurting me. I wanted to push him away, because in some sad way, I knew how to deal with people leaving.

I had no clue what to do if they stayed.

Samir

I could see the indecision in her eyes, could practically hear her thoughts warring inside of her. She was scared, and she was angry, and I'd pushed her, which was the absolute worst thing to do to Maggie, and yet I couldn't apologize or even feel guilty because I felt like I was drowning and couldn't get out.

She hadn't answered my question. Maybe that was her answer.

I didn't have a plan beyond the question, didn't have an out for this mess we'd gotten ourselves into. I was an idiot, and I was screwing this up beyond redemption. I was losing her—could feel her slipping away right in front of my eyes.

Maybe I'd never had her at all.

All along she'd made me want to be better, had made me believe I could be a different person, that I could be *more*.

"I don't love you. I'm sorry."

Her words sliced through me, leaving a trail of nothing in their wake. I'd never put myself out there with a girl. Ever. And for the first time I knew what rejection really felt like. I didn't know what to say, how I was supposed to react. Should I laugh and pretend it was all a game? That I had been joking all along? That I hadn't been standing here with my heart in my hands? I tried, but my body—and my heart—wouldn't cooperate.

"I'm going home."

Surprise, mixing with hurt, flashed across her gorgeous face. "Samir—"

I shook her hand off my arm, couldn't bear for her to touch me. Not now. "I'm tired. I'm going home."

"I'll come with you."

"Stay here with Fleur."

"It's your last night in London. I want to be with you."

I couldn't. I turned and walked away.

Maggie

Maybe I shouldn't have come. But I couldn't stay away.

I stood outside Samir's door, trying to make myself knock. Two hours had passed since he'd left me at Babel. I was no closer to knowing what to do. I was lost—and yet somehow I'd ended up here.

I knocked on the door, struggling to ignore the pounding in my chest and the nerves bubbling up in my throat. Worst-case scenario, he would send me away. Or he was already asleep. Best-case scenario? I didn't know anymore.

I waited, trying to tell myself his reaction didn't matter, that the sum of us wouldn't be reduced to the way he responded to me outside his door.

The door swung open, and he stared back at me, completely unsurprised. My heart caught in my throat. I opened my mouth to speak, but no words came out.

And then he was kissing me.

His lips were on mine, desperate, hungry. Without breaking away, he pulled me into the room, shutting the door behind us, my body flush against his, his body hard against mine.
His arousal pressed against me, and suddenly I needed him inside me.

I broke apart from the kiss first, my fingers reaching behind
me, tugging at the zipper, dragging it down. Samir's eyes flared
with heat. The dress slipped to the floor.

I reached for him, our fingers tangling. I pulled his T-shirt
over his head, my hands running over the hard planes of his
chest, traveling lower, stroking his stomach, tugging at the
waistband of his pajama pants. I needed to feel his naked skin
against mine, needed the feel of flesh on flesh.

His mouth captured mine in a rough kiss—heat and fire
melding together.

"Fuck me," I whispered against his mouth, my voice pleading.

I was drowning in him—in his touch, his taste, his scent. I
expected him to maneuver me against the bed, but instead the
cool, hard wall hit my back. I sensed the desperation in him
then—felt my own sense of urgency mimicked in his desire.

It was fast, it was furious, and it was hot. One minute he
was kissing me, his hands teasing my breasts, toying with my
nipples, flicking them with his thumbs, and the next he was
thrusting inside of me, filling me completely, my leg wrapped
around his waist. Foreplay was gone. This was need—brutal
and sharp.

We moved together, to a silent beat of pain and ecstasy. We
moved together until the pressure building inside both of us
could no longer be ignored. Until we both shattered—his body
shuddering in mine before I found my own release.

We sagged against the wall for a minute, our foreheads
pressed against each other's. Our breath mingled, our bodies

one. Samir released me for a moment and then took my hand; our fingers linked as he led me over to the bed. I lay down, staring up at him, waiting for his body to join mine, for that familiar weight next to me on the mattress.

He sank down next to me, sitting on the edge, his feet planted on the floor, his back toward me. He leaned down, resting his elbows against his knees, his head in his hands

The sight of him—the familiarity of it and the pain so obviously coursing through him—rocked me. I leaned forward, my breasts brushing against his back, my arms around his body.

"Come to bed," I whispered, kissing the spot below his neck and between his shoulder blades. I pulled away, the taste of his sweat and skin on my lips. I ran my tongue across my bottom lip, his scent flooding me.

Samir turned and faced me, his expression unbearably sad. We didn't speak. Not aloud, at least. There was no need for words. In that moment, lying in bed with him, I knew it didn't matter what I said. I didn't have to tell him I loved him. On some level we both knew.

It was in the way my eyes lit up whenever he walked into a room, it was in the air between us that visibly crackled with electricity, it was in the pounding of my heart, in the heat of my skin. It was in every look, every touch, every smile he teased from my lips, every kiss.

I loved him.

There wasn't a thing I could do about it.

49

Maggie

The sunlight hit me first.

For a moment, my mind was gloriously blank. It was just another morning. I yawned, rolling over, pulling the duvet with me. I stretched my legs, just as another pair of legs rubbed against mine, the slight roughness of hair brushing against my softer skin as our feet tangled. Hands reached out beneath the duvet, pulling me closer. His scent hit me first, that hint of spice I would forever associate with Samir. He mumbled something to me, but the words disappeared in the cocoon of fluffy white surrounding us. I wiggled closer to him, our bodies tight against each other in the small bed.

I wanted to spend every morning waking up like this.

Music filled the room, the sound of Samir's radio alarm breaking through the morning silence. *Ugh.* I pulled the heavy duvet over my head, burrowing further into Samir's warmth, my lips brushing his chest, sprinkling kisses there. Lips brushed against my face, flirting with my temples, teasing the curve of my cheek, caressing my mouth.

It hit me, like a crashing wave. I stared up at his face.

Samir's eyes closed for a moment. "I know."

He put his arms around me, drawing me up against his hard body. At once his hands were everywhere—eager, demanding. There was no question, no hesitation.

It was our last time.

I rolled on top of him, my legs around him, straddling him, bringing our bodies into the closer contact I craved. Gone was the push and pull, the frustration that simmered around us as we both struggled to define what existed between us. Instead, a bleak hunger took over, fueled by the knowledge that these moments, the sheer bliss of them, were finite.

It was our last time.

There was no time for soft kisses or sweet caresses. There was only the agony of desire, filling me, fueling me, pushing me deeper. I wanted him—needed him—inside me, making me forget—even if it was just for a moment.

A tear escaped from my eyes, trickling down my cheek. I batted it away. I hated that I cried in front of him. Hated that he saw how weak my resolve was. Hated the chance that he could see through my lies.

My heart shattered into a million tiny pieces.

Samir

I wanted to cancel my flight. I wanted to stay with her forever. I was angry. So angry—angry at myself for leaving, at my family, even at her. Because even now, even as I was buried so deep inside of her that I felt as if her body were a part of mine, I didn't know how she felt about me. I didn't know what she wanted. But most of all, I was angry at myself, because I didn't know what I wanted, and I didn't know how much I was willing to give up in order to figure it out.

It was hard to think when I was inside her. Hard to think

when I was surrounded by all that warm, wet heat. She was heaven, and being inside her always felt like coming home.

I gripped her hips, pushing her down on me, reveling in the feel of her body surrounding me. I could stay here forever, watching her move, her body a contrast of pink and white.

She moaned, the sound breaking through the morning air. My blood spiked at the noise, at the sight of her biting her lip, her head falling back, exposing that gorgeous neck as she rode me. This was Maggie—completely, wholly uninhibited, wild and wanton. It was the part of her no one else got to see, the part that was hidden. The part that was mine.

Her pace increased, her hips arching, daring me to keep up with her, taunting me with her body. A thin film of sweat covered her, her skin gleaming. I wanted to run my tongue along her flesh, wanted to taste her in my mouth. I wanted to consume her, bit by bit, to possess all of her. I wanted more. Always more.

I thrust deeper, hovering on the edge of losing control. Her eyes widened in response, her lashes fluttering closed, her head falling back. She was close. I could almost time her orgasms better than my own. I wanted her to come first. Wanted to watch her slide into her release, wanted to feel her body shuddering over mine, wanted to watch her lose her tightly held control.

She'd shattered mine.

Maggie

I lay in bed, wearing the shirt he'd slept in the night before. It was one of his favorites—the cotton was soft and worn, a hint of his cologne and scent lingering on the fabric. My limbs were sore, my body deliciously exhausted. My heart was another matter entirely. It was raw, stripped bare. Aching.

Samir dressed, his motions hurried, his back to me. His suitcases were lined up by the door, his room empty. It was strange to see it like this—all traces he had ever been here simply erased.

It felt wrong.

We hadn't really talked since last night at Babel. Instead, after we'd made love, we'd lain in each other's arms until we'd fallen asleep. There were so many things unsaid between us, so many things I feared I would never be able to say.

But time was running out and all I could do was smile and pretend it was just another normal day.

Finally he turned and faced me, his expression inscrutable.

"I think that's everything." His voice was hard; gone was the sound that always surrounded me in warmth, that made my toes curl with pleasure. The things I loved about him all seemed to be slipping away.

His phone beeped, breaking the awkward silence between us. Samir pulled it out of his jeans pocket, his gaze scanning the screen.

"My car's here."

"I'll walk you to the door."

"You don't have to."

"I want to."

Lie. I wanted us to lock ourselves in this room and never leave.

"Fine."

I followed him out of the room and down the stairs, each step taking me closer to the moment I dreaded.

I stood in the hall, staring at the building's front door, my limbs frozen, my mind completely blank. I was numb everywhere. Maybe it was the only way I could handle the pain.

Suddenly I was a little girl again. Sitting on the curb of my ballet class, waiting for my mother to come pick me up. Somehow knowing she'd never come back.

Why did the people I loved the most always leave?

Maybe it was my fault for always pushing them away. Maybe I was supposed to fight more. Maybe I was supposed to let go. I didn't know. That was the thing. I knew I needed to change, knew I'd reached the point in my life where it was time to grow up. But I didn't know how. There weren't instructions to follow or rules that would tell me how to get to happy. I had to find it myself and I was trying, stumbling through my life and the mess I'd made of things, trying to figure out how to fix everything. But time was running out, taking away my chances, leaving me with a sense of panic that it was now too late to change—to save the thing I wanted the most.

"Maggie…"

I couldn't. I knew if this were a movie, this would be the moment for the big, romantic, dramatic goodbye. Samir would crush me in his arms, and we would kiss, and it would be passionate and desperate and all-consuming. But this was my life. What was left of if it anyway. Already I felt the gaping hole he had filled. I was drained, exhausted by the emotion, the months-long anticipation.

I knew I should hold on to this moment, memorize every detail of his face, the way his dark hair fell over his forehead, the sadness in his eyes. I wanted to stop time, to pause and trace the shape of his face, to run my fingers over his skin and through his hair, to capture every piece of him. I didn't want to let go.

But time moved on and I had no choice but to move with it.

I shook my head, desperately trying to block the pain in his voice. It cracked through me, creating fissures in my already crumbling resolve.

Why did he have to do this to me? Why did he always have to break through the walls? Didn't he know I needed them? Didn't he know I couldn't get through this without them?

Why did love have to hurt so much?

"Please, Maggie. Just look at me."

The pain in his voice ripped through my heart, making me feel too much and everything all at once.

There was no way I could look at him. I was worried if I did, all the love I had for him, trapped inside, bursting at the seams of my heart, would spew out of my mouth in one awful swoop.

"Have a safe flight," I managed, forcing the words out with a wobbly smile.

"Will you be okay?"

No.

I nodded. I couldn't help it—I looked up. Our gazes locked. For one horrible moment, it hit me.

I'll never get to see his face again. Never get to kiss those lips. Never get to stroke that skin.

A tear escaped from my eye, traveling down my cheek. *Damn it.*

He cursed. "Please don't cry."

Samir set his bag down on the ground, closing the space between us, wrapping his arms around my body.

Oh, god.

"I don't want to leave," he whispered against my hair, his face buried there.

Three words. Three words could have kept him here. Three words could have ended this. They wouldn't have been a lie. My love for him consumed me. It drowned me. It terrified me. But those three words would have come at too high a price.

"You have to."

Samir

I couldn't leave.

I knew I couldn't keep her. I knew she didn't fit into my life, into the future everyone had planned. But in this moment I didn't fucking care. I didn't want a future if she wasn't in it.

I wanted to ask her again, wanted to know if she'd lied last night. I thought I knew. I thought I saw it in her eyes every time she looked at me, in her lips every time she kissed me, in the way her body responded when I was inside her.

I thought I knew. But with Maggie, I never really knew at all.

I'd never given a shit about my feelings, never much thought about my heart. But last night when I'd asked her if she loved me, and she'd said no, she'd destroyed it. Now I knew what it felt like to have your heart broken; now I knew what it felt like to be rejected. Now I knew what it was like to want something you could never really have. I couldn't throw my future away on the chance she loved me, and even if she did... I didn't know anymore.

I pulled away from her, dangerously close to losing it. This— everything about it—was too much. It hurt to look at her, to touch her, to be near her. It hurt to love her if she didn't love me back. It hurt to let her go when my head shouted one thing and my heart shouted another.

"I should go."

She nodded.

"Goodbye, Maggie."

"Goodbye."

For a moment I stood there, memorizing her face and her body. Losing myself in her eyes and her smile.

Then I turned and walked out the front door.

50

Maggie

I watched him walk away, watched the door slam behind him. The noise filled the hallway and then it was eclipsed by a yawning silence, as the world held still for a moment. I sank down to the bottom step, hugging my body to my knees.

He was really gone.

I kept waiting for him to walk through again. For this to turn out to be some big joke—it couldn't possibly be real. I'd known this moment was coming for months now—imagined it, feared it, desperately wished I could avoid it. And now, he was just...gone.

My phone beeped and I stared down at the screen.

I'm here if you need anything. Shopping? Donuts? Tequila? Let me know.

Fleur. I choked back another sob. I stood up, wiping my face. My feet shuffled up the stairs. I concentrated on putting one foot in front of the other, on the mundane, concentrated on the things I could control rather than the one major thing that had escaped. Each step that carried me up the stairs took me farther and farther away from Samir. It didn't matter.

From here on out, wherever I went, whatever I did, whoever I met wouldn't matter. There would always be a piece of me standing in that hall watching him walk away. There would always be a piece of me tethered to him by a thread that could never be broken. There would always be a piece of me that loved him.

"You look terrible." Fleur reached out, enfolding me in her arms.

"I feel terrible." It felt good to be able to tell the truth, to wallow in the comfort of our room. I pulled back, offering a weak smile. "Thanks for being here."

"Of course."

I sank down on my bed.

"Is Samir okay? I texted him, but he hasn't gotten back to me."

I didn't know how to answer that one. Did he feel the same way I did—like his heart had been ripped from his chest?

"I don't know."

"What happened?"

"He left."

"Are you guys going to talk? Are you going to try to see each other?"

I shrugged. "What's the point? Can you really see me fitting in with his family or his life in Lebanon?"

For a moment Fleur didn't answer. I figured she was too good a friend to lie to me.

"You guys could still keep in touch. You could be friends."

I could tell by the tone of her voice that even she had a hard time swallowing that one.

"No, we couldn't be."

There was too much between us. I could never just be friends

with him. I didn't know how to be around him without wanting more. Maybe before we'd had sex a year ago, maybe we
could have been friends then. But maybe we were never meant
to be friends. Maybe I was kidding myself to think we hadn't
always been more.

"I just can't believe that's it. I know it's a tough situation, but
I've seen the way you guys are with each other. You're perfect
together. He lov—"

"Don't." My voice shook slightly. "I can't do this. It's over.
It has to be over. Please, let it go."

Her eyes narrowed. "You're pushing him away, aren't you?"

"I'm not talking about this."

"You are. You're pushing him away. You love him and you're
pushing him away because you're afraid to get hurt."

"You don't know what you're talking about. He left. He's
not exactly fighting for me either."

Fleur laughed. "Are you joking? I know exactly what I'm
talking about. You aren't the only one with a shitty family situation. I know what it's like to be afraid to put yourself out
there, to be afraid to let someone in. I know what it's like to
push people away better than anyone."

My heart thudded.

"But he loves you. I know Samir, better than most. He
doesn't fall in love. He doesn't let people in. Not until you. He
loves you. Fight for him. He's just like you, afraid of putting
himself out there. He's doing the same thing you are."

"I can't fight for him."

"How do you know?"

I laughed bitterly. "Oh, believe me. I know."

"Don't you think he feels the same way you do? He's spent
his whole life not measuring up to his parents' expectations for
him. Spent his whole life feeling like he's not good enough.

Until you. I never thought I would say this, but he's different with you. You can trust him."

"Everything is so fucked up right now. I don't know what he thinks or feels about me."

"What did you do?"

Guilt flooded me. "He asked me if I loved him last night. I told him no. I made him leave because I didn't want to be the reason he threw his life away."

"You lied to him. He would have stayed if you told him you loved him. You pushed him away without giving him a fucking chance."

"You don't know that he would have stayed. Or even that it wouldn't have been a mistake. I didn't want to use my feelings to control him, not when he had so much to lose. I couldn't do that to him. He has a life in Lebanon. He has a future. How could I have asked him to give that all up? What if he regretted it?"

"And what about you? What if he wanted to choose you? You took that choice away from him."

"I couldn't ask him to choose me."

"Why?"

"Because they never choose me. Because if I love him, he'll leave. Eventually he'll leave. I've been here. Every person who I've loved in my life, every person I've trusted, leaves. Don't you get it? I love him. I love him more than I've ever loved anyone. I love him so much it hurts. But I don't want to feel this way. I don't want to feel the pain of another fucking person rejecting me. I don't fit into his world. At some point, you know his parents are going to force him to choose. And he's not going to give up everything he has for me. He shouldn't give up everything for me."

"Maggie—"

"I've been here before. This isn't new for me. I have plenty of experience being left."

Fleur shook her head. "Then you're a coward. And you don't deserve him."

She was right. I was a coward. And I'd just lost everything.

51

Samir

The summer flew by in a blur of alcohol and girls. The girls were a disaster. A steady parade of petite brunettes with brown eyes and pale skin. It didn't take a fucking psychologist to figure out what I was trying to do. Emphasis on *trying*.

They weren't her. None of them. I flirted, bought drinks, thought about sex, but when I went home at night, I was always alone. When I woke, I reached for her—hard and aching—and came up empty.

The alcohol worked better. I spent most of May and some of June drunk off my ass. I was supposed to be in Beirut, but I'd lasted less than a week before my father told me to get out of his sight. Apparently he needed an heir who wasn't running his life into the ground. He was pissed and threatening to cut me off if I didn't get my life together. He'd nearly done it until my mother intervened and sent me to Saint-Tropez to "clear my head." Even the threat of losing the money didn't break through the haze. So I drank. It numbed the pain, but the feeling still lingered there. And then I woke up.

Or rather, Fleur woke me up.

"You smell."

I glared at her, bleary-eyed. Her voice was a fucking bell ringing in my ear.

For a moment I forgot where I was, her presence confusing me. "What are you doing here?"

"What are *you* doing here? I thought you were supposed to be in Lebanon assuming the throne."

"Fuck you."

"Nice to see your sunny disposition is in full force." Her gaze swept the hotel suite. I could only imagine what it looked like through her eyes—empty takeout boxes, bottles of alcohol littered around. It was a disaster. I was a disaster. "I'm surprised not to see any big-breasted bimbos lying around."

"I kick them out after I fuck them," I drawled.

Her lips curved. "Cute."

"It's none of your business."

"I love you, so yeah, it is."

"Lucky me."

"You know, she's just as fucked up as you are."

I clenched my hand into a fist, wishing I could burrow my head in the pillow and block Fleur out. "Don't talk to me about her. Don't say her name. If that's why you came here, then you can leave."

"I'm not leaving until you talk about it."

"Fine. Then I'll leave." I rose from the bed, grabbing a shirt off the floor, pulling it over my head. My clothes were strewn all over the floor—I'd given up on doing laundry a long time ago. The maids came in and cleaned when I felt like it. I tripped over an empty pizza box lying on the floor.

"She loves you. She lied."

I froze and then whirled around to face her. "I'm serious. If you care about me at all, you will drop this and leave."

"I'm not leaving. I love you and I love Maggie. I can't watch you guys throw away your happiness because you're both cow-ards."

"I'm not a coward. I asked her if she loved me at Babel and she said no. What else was I supposed to do? Hell, even with-out her loving me, I didn't want to leave. But how can I give up everything? What am I supposed to do?"

"She's scared."

"She's scared?" The anger that had been growing inside of me all summer pushed through. "Jesus, Fleur. She broke my heart. She broke my fucking heart, okay? She ripped it out and stomped on it, and I've been walking around with a hole in my chest for months. And now you're asking me to take a chance she can reject me all over again."

Something that impossibly seemed like compassion flickered in Fleur's eyes. "She won't."

"You don't know that. She might. You don't know what she'll do. Neither do I."

"You're being an idiot."

"Maybe I am, but I can't keep doing this. It's been over two months. I haven't heard anything from her."

"Have you called her? Texted? Emailed? Anything?"

"No."

I didn't want to tell her the truth. That I'd written Mag-gie dozens of emails I'd never sent, that I'd stared at her name in my phone for hours, wanting to dial her number, text her, anything. Maybe Fleur was right, maybe I was a coward. I was afraid to give her my heart when I didn't know how she felt, afraid she'd be another person in a long line of people I let down, afraid of throwing away the security that came with my family legacy for...what exactly?

Fleur crossed her arms over her chest. "Are you happy?"

"Come on. What is this? Why are you here?" I loved Fleur, but my patience hung by a thread.

"This is a fucking intervention." Her arms arced in a wide,

sweeping gesture, her gaze taking in the crap everywhere. "Is this your life? Getting drunk and fucking girls in Saint-Tropez?"

It would be easier if that were my life. If the idea of screwing some nameless, faceless girl didn't make me feel ill.

"Why are you doing this?"

"Because you have a chance. A chance to be happy. And you're so stupid, you're throwing it away. How many chances do you think you get at love? Do you know how jealous I am? What I would do to have what you have? Don't waste it, Samir. We both come from the same fucked-up place. But Maggie's different. She loves you. She doesn't care about the money or the cars or the lifestyle. She loves you." Fleur's lips quirked slightly. "Though God knows why."

"She said she didn't."

"She was scared. She lied. Come on. You're not stupid. How many girls have you been with? I would think you would know by now when a girl loves you and when she doesn't."

Each word hit me harder than the first. She was right. I'd spent the summer replaying my time with Maggie over and over in my mind like a song on repeat. Some days I convinced myself she'd always loved me. Most days I thought I was a fool. But now Fleur was here, giving me hope where there had been none.

I didn't know what to say. Didn't know what to do. I missed Maggie. I knew I couldn't keep doing this. This wasn't a life. And yet...

"My parents will disown me. And Maggie has two years of school left. If I did have a chance with her, how would it even work? I don't want to be long-distance for two years. And the odds of me getting a job in Lebanon when my dad finds out about this are nonexistent. How am I going to live?"

"You have a trust. Maybe it's not the kind of money you're used to, but it would be enough. And you aren't just Lebanese, you're also French—you have dual citizenship and an EU passport. You have options. Don't tell me you haven't considered them. Don't settle for the life they want you to have, if it's not the life you want. You're better than that. And you'll always regret it if you let her slip through your fingers. Do you really want to wake up one day, old, in a loveless marriage, realizing you let the best thing that ever happened to you get away?"

Through the haze of my hangover, I began to feel the beginnings of a plan. She was right. I'd thought about this before. But it was a risk. A chance I was scared to take.

"You get everything you want. Why should this be any different? You want Maggie. Make it happen. Fight for her."

I stared at the door, hesitating before knocking. It was after hours, the office nearly empty, only my father left. On one hand, the last thing I wanted was an audience; on the other hand, at least the presence of other people would prevent an even bigger scene than the one that was about to erupt.

"Enter."

I turned the knob, walking through the door, palms sweating.

My father's head jerked up from the paperwork on his desk, his gaze narrowing. "You're back."

"I came back to get my stuff."

Contempt filled his eyes.

"Oh, really? Where do you think you're off to now? Back to Saint-Tropez? Going to screw around Paris with Fleur? Do you think it's okay to behave like a child for the rest of your life, to never take responsibility for your actions? Do you think I'm going to keep funding your fuck-ups?"

I held his stare. "No, I don't."

He shook his head. "I wanted a son, and this is what I got. A boy who is incapable of becoming a man."

A year ago, his words would have stuck with me. A year ago, I would have believed he was right, that I would never be more than a fuck-up. But that was bullshit, and I was tired of making myself irrelevant because he saw me as such. He was right; it was time for me to grow up. It was time for me to take charge of my life.

"I'm moving to London."

"The hell you are. Absolutely not."

"I got into grad school. I'm going to do a master's in Middle Eastern politics."

I'd been lucky to get my application in by their deadline at the end of June, even luckier that Dr. Abbott had written me a recommendation and spoken to some professors on the faculty. Fortunately my grades at the International School had been good enough for me to be accepted.

My father's face turned an interesting shade of red.

"If you think I'm paying for a useless degree so you can fuck around with girls like the one you brought home—"

I struggled for calm, knew losing my temper would only confirm all of the worst things he thought about me.

My jaw clenched as I fought to control the rage winding its way through me. "I'm serious about her," I bit out. "I'm not going to marry someone else; I'm not going to date someone else. She's it. I'm going to grad school. I have enough money from my trust to pay for it. It's done and there's nothing you can say that will change my mind."

His skin turned an even darker shade of red, almost purple. "You think you can just walk away from all of this? From your family, from your duty? From your country?"

Each word lashed out like a whip cracking across my skin.

"I'm not walking away. Lebanon will always be my home. You will always be my family." As much as a part of me resented him, he was my father; I loved him, even if it was a complicated love. I wanted him to be proud of me, wanted him to respect me. But I would never get the chance to be the person I needed to be if I always followed the path he set, never making my own decisions. "I'm going. I'm sorry if you aren't happy about it, but I have to make my own future. I need to do this on my own. Whether you understand or not, I need to go."

I waited for a blessing I knew would never come, waited for him to say something, waited to see if our relationship could ever be mended. I got silence instead.

I turned and left.

Maggie

It was hot as hell in South Carolina. The whole summer had been like that—a slow heat that burned me from the inside out. It had been a blur of hot days, long hours at work, and nights spent with Jo.

"You're quiet," she commented over lunch.

"I figured I talked your ear off enough all summer. I thought you might welcome the quiet."

"I've gotten used to it by now."

Jo had listened to me through the first month of mourning the loss of Samir, helped me pick up the pieces when I'd realized there was nowhere to go but forward. It helped that she'd met him when he came to South Carolina, that she'd seen us together. She understood how hard everything was. She'd even flown with me to Oklahoma to meet my new baby brother, James. It had been an awkward visit, but when I held him in my arms I'd felt a connection I'd never expected. We weren't a big happy family, but the sight of my little brother's face had erased so much of my anger.

She grabbed a fry off my plate. "You ready to go back?"

"I hope so."

Four months in South Carolina had been long enough. The summer had dripped by, slow as molasses, and as much as I'd needed a break from London, from the memories, I was ready to go home.

"It'll be different."

"I know."

"You know, you can always transfer to Carolina…"

I grinned. It was a familiar battle.

"I can't. You know I love you, but things are different now. London's home."

"Even if he's not there?"

It was the question that had been running through my mind all summer. In a way, Jo was right—my memories of London had become inextricably linked with Samir. It was impossible not to think of him when I thought of my time there. Not to see him when I walked into the common room, not to hear his voice when I sat in class, not to see his smile across the table from me at dinner. And yet—London was Fleur and Michael and Mya. It was my dream.

I loved Samir. But I also loved London.

I pushed past the pang in my chest. "It's home."

"I want to come visit this year. Maybe spring break."

"You would love it. Plenty of hot guys for you, plenty of accents."

Jo grinned. "Sounds like my kind of place." She stared at the clock. "How long until your flight?"

"Five hours. We should probably get the check."

Jo signaled to the waitress, a sad smile on her face. "I'm going to miss you. It's weird having you drop in and out of life like this. It always feels like you're either coming or going, never just *here*."

She was right. My life felt like it had become a continuous loop of difficult goodbyes. Wherever I was, I was always away from someone I loved—Samir, Jo, my grandparents, my new brother, Mya, Michael, Fleur. But maybe that was life. Maybe as you got older, you became less able to carry people with you. Everyone went their own way, living their own lives, facing their own adventures. All you could do was carry your memories with you, clutching the pieces you shared.

I carried Samir with me now.

"Thanks for everything this summer. I couldn't have gotten through it without you."

She nodded, tears welling in her eyes. "Of course."

I reached out, giving her a swift hug. I wondered if it would always feel like this—like I was caught between two places.

But this wasn't really my life anymore.

It was good to be going home.

52

Maggie

This time, it felt different when my plane landed at Heathrow. The excitement was gone—the nerves and anticipation replaced by a sense of calm and belonging. I made my way through the airport with ease, the normal shine and dazzle replaced by familiarity.

I took a cab to the International School, welcoming the sights of my old neighborhood—the sounds and colors that would forever be London for me. At moments, I felt the whisper of a ghost dogging me, memories of walking down the streets, Samir's hand in mine, flooding me. I was torn between wanting to run from the memories and wanting to bathe myself in them—as if I could conjure him in flesh and blood straight from memory. It was a loss, one I was still mourning.

We pulled up to the International School, my heart pounding as I stared up at the building that was both my redemption and the chink in my armor. He was everywhere here—inextricably linked to my love for this place. I got out of the cab on shaky legs, paying the driver before pulling my bag up the steps.

There were new boys standing outside smoking, new voices,

new accents, new laughter. It wasn't him. I knew that. But I couldn't help but see him there, smiling at me. Just as he had the first day.

I pushed on.

I checked in with housing, got my room assignment—Fleur, Mya, and I were roommates again—and headed upstairs. I opened the door. Fleur stared back at me.

"You look better than I expected."

I dumped my bags, rushing over to give Fleur a hug. "Thanks, I think."

She grinned. "No, I totally meant it as a compliment."

"How is that a compliment?" I teased.

"I thought you'd be heartbroken, a shell of your former self." The smile slipped from her face. "Are you okay? Really?"

I shrugged, a habit I'd picked up from Samir along the way and never bothered to shake.

"It was a tough summer. But yeah, I'm okay."

It was the most honest answer I could give; for some reason I just didn't feel like explaining the rest of it. More than anyone, Fleur would probably understand that everything reminded me of him, that there was still a part of me that expected him to walk into the room or to be sitting in the cafeteria. It was hard. I missed him more than I'd ever missed anyone.

Fleur stared at me. She opened her mouth like she was going to speak and closed it again.

"What?"

"Nothing."

"I know you. That's not nothing. What's up?"

She hesitated for a moment. "I have to ask you something."

"Okay, shoot."

"If you had a chance to be happy with Samir, I mean really happy, would you want it?"

"Fleur."

I should have known it would be like this. I hadn't been back for an hour, and he was already everywhere.

"I'm serious. It's important. Do you still love him?"

"I can't…" I struggled for the right words to make her understand. "It's been hard, okay? Really hard. I don't want to talk about Samir."

"Trust me, though. You want to talk about this. This is important. Do you still love him?"

"Why are you pushing this?"

"Because he's here. In London."

For a moment, I was convinced I'd misheard.

"What do you mean?"

"He's in London. Now."

My heart began pounding. "Why? How? How is that even possible?"

"He's doing a master's."

I sank down on the bed, shock flooding my body. Emotions ripped through me. "Why? Since when? Why didn't he tell me? How could he come back and not tell me?"

"He came back for you. Well, and for him. But probably more for you."

"What? What do you mean? Did he tell you that?"

"I went to see him this summer. He was only in Beirut for a couple weeks and then he went to Saint-Tropez. I found him there."

I just stared at her.

"He was a mess, and he was miserable. Absolutely miserable."

"So how did he end up here?"

"I told him you lied. I told him you loved him." Fleur grinned. "And I told him if he loved you, he needed to fight for you."

"But his parents—"

"He has a trust fund from his grandfather. It's not huge, but it's enough."

"I didn't want him to give up his future. His legacy—"

"He'll be fine. It was his choice. No one made him do anything he didn't want to do. He wanted this." Fleur hesitated. "He wanted to get his shit together before he saw you. He was nervous."

"I don't—So—"

"He loves you. He wants to be with you." Fleur was silent for a moment. "I know you. I get it. I get why you're scared. I get why you lied to him. I get why you're afraid to take a chance on him. But you need to stop it. He loves you. He's never loved anyone the way he loves you. Don't throw this away because you're scared."

I was still somewhere back at *Samir is here in London*. I'd always known there could be a life for him in London. I'd always loved the idea of him doing a master's—he was smart enough and he loved IR. But I'd never wanted to push him into anything. His parents had done that—pushed him and tried to mold him into someone they could control. I'd never wanted to do that to him.

I'd been so scared to love him. So scared that when he left, I'd shatter into a million pieces. I'd been scared to give anyone that kind of power over me. But I'd loved him despite my fear. And he'd left. And I'd shattered. And I'd put myself back together.

The problem had never really been whether I trusted Samir. It had been whether I trusted myself.

I could be happy here in London, without him. I could graduate from the International School, do a master's, get a great job doing something I loved. I could be happy. But that wouldn't be enough, not anymore. Not now that I knew what it was like to love someone with everything I had. My life would be a shadow of its former self. *I* would be a shadow of my former self. I wanted more. I wanted it all. I wanted him.

"Okay."

"Okay?"

Excitement filled me, and I stopped caring about the chance I was taking or the risks or anything other than the fact that he was here. He loved me. It was time for me to let him and to let myself go.

"Okay." I stood, my body feeling strange, my limbs a little shaky. Adrenaline coursed through me, pushing me on. "Where is he?"

"He's supposed to be meeting me in Hyde Park in an hour. But I think I may be coming down with a cold." She did a fake cough. "So you should definitely go instead."

"In an hour?" I squeaked. "I look terrible. I just got off of a nine-hour flight."

"I think you look good. And Samir will definitely think you look amazing." She grinned. "But if you want, I may be willing to offer my hair services. For old times' sake."

I grinned at Fleur. "How much of this was you?"

She shrugged. "I just did what I could to make sure you guys ended up where you were supposed to be. The rest of it was him."

I'd never loved her more. "You're kind of like a sexy fairy godmother."

Fleur flashed me a stunning grin. "I'll take it." She gestured toward my hair. "Come on. Let's make this happen."

Samir

I walked down the streets, heading back toward Kensington, toward the place that started it all. It felt weird, being in London and not being at the International School. Felt weird not being around her.

Grad school was a different planet. I put the Rolex away—my fellow students seemed more interested in organizing a protest than going to a nightclub. It was different, but not in a bad way. For the first time in my life I was doing something that mattered, not because my last name was Khouri and it was expected of me, but because I wanted to. It felt good.

I walked down the familiar path, heading into the park. It was a bizarre place for Fleur to want to meet. As long as I'd known her, she'd never shown any interest in the outdoors. I figured Harrods was more her speed. But she'd insisted, so here I was.

I turned my head, staring down the familiar view. From where I stood, I could almost make out the top of the International School. I missed it so much it hurt.

Missed her so much it hurt.

I'd been in London for three weeks now. I knew school started back in a few days, imagined she was back in London getting ready for her junior year. I couldn't help but wonder the same thing I'd been wondering all summer. Did she miss me? Was Fleur right, did she really love me?

I knew it was a big gamble. I'd thrown my future away on the hope that Fleur hadn't totally misread the signs. But even if she had—I felt free. For the first time in my life, I felt free of my family's expectations, of the lie of living a life I didn't want.

I wanted to be someone Maggie could be proud of. I wanted to be someone I could be proud of.

I cut through the park, moving toward a tree near Kensington Palace. I glanced down at my phone. Fleur was late, big surprise. People filtered in and out of the park, as I kept my eyes peeled for Fleur's tall frame.

Then I saw her and my world stopped.

A girl entered the park from the International School side. Her strides were long, impatient even. Her head scanned the park as if she was looking for someone. I couldn't take my gaze off of her.

She stopped in her tracks, looking back at me. For a moment, we just stood there, the park between us, staring at each other. My heart pounded. She began to walk, her strides even longer, her gorgeous brown hair flowing around her. Everything around me faded away. All of the nerves and doubt of the past few months disappeared.

I knew in that moment that no matter what happened, I'd do whatever I had to in order to keep her.

She was mine. I would always be hers.

53

Maggie

He leans against a tree.

His body is lean, his hair dark. Even from a distance, I can see his clothes are impeccable—his black coat perfectly formed on his body, his long legs encased in expensive jeans. Diesel, of course.

His face is hard to read, and yet I know his every expression better than my own. That face—the one I dream of, the one I have traced every curve of, the one that no matter how hard I try, I can't forget.

For a moment, my feet are rooted to the ground. I want to make them move, and yet the sight before me has my limbs freezing up, unable to move beyond the smallest twitch. I've dreamed this moment enough that part of me wonders if that's all this is—another cruel dream, in which for a moment I have everything, only to wake and discover I have nothing.

But he's still there.

My legs move faster, not quite running—but eager now. After all, it has been four months.

As I walk toward him, time seems to shift, and I remember

the first time I ever saw him—standing on the front steps. I remember the feeling I had at the sight of him and am blown away by the journey it has taken for us to end up here.

He doesn't move from his perch against the tree. But because I know him—because I *love* him—I watch the tension leave his body as our eyes meet. He is lighter because of me.

There's no denying the deck is stacked against us, but it doesn't feel insurmountable. Not anymore.

"Hi."

I stop before him, just out of his grasp. I blink, unable to believe he's really here. I've imagined him so many times, yet the reality of him feels infinitely better.

"Hi," he echoes, his expression solemn, a wealth of emotion in that word. He's so serious, this version of the boy I have come to love. There's something different about him now—he looks as if he's in transition, halfway between his old life and his new one.

He reaches out a hand and I link my fingers with his, that meeting of flesh on flesh as natural as always.

The air vibrates with tension, a crackling energy that too feels familiar. There's something comforting in knowing no matter how much time passes, there's still a part of me that gets nervous—giddy—at the sight of him.

"What now?"

Every fiber of my being hangs on his next words.

His lips curve as he leans forward, brushing them against mine. *Finally.* It's a familiar kiss, a beginning of sorts.

And of course, a continuation—of something never abandoned.

It has always been him.

He breaks away, flashing me a smile that's all too familiar, seducing me with his gaze.

"Well, I have a year and then I'll have my master's degree. I can get a job here in London. Maybe doing something with

Mid East policy. I want to help my people, want to feel like I'm making a difference. Not because I'm a Khouri, but because I have something to contribute. I want to be more—for you and for me." For a moment he looks unsure of himself. "I can't promise it's going to be as glamorous as it was. Or that I'm going to get it right. But I promise I'm going to try."

"I don't care. I just don't want you to feel like you're giving up everything for me."

"Maggie. You are everything."

I close my eyes for a moment, his hand clutched in mine. I cloak myself in his words, bathing in their warmth, their promise. I'm afraid that if I open my eyes it'll all be a dream. But if these last few months have taught me anything, it's that I can be alone. I'd just rather have him by my side.

I open my eyes, dazzled by the boy staring back at me. I see commitment in his eyes, a promise I know I can trust. This time is different. This time we're all in. We're both making the leap and I can't wait to fall.

"I love you," he whispers, so softly only I can hear him.

But it's enough. It's everything.

"I love you, too," I answer, my heart tumbling in my chest, the words locked inside me for far too long. "It's always been you."

I stare into his eyes—Samir's eyes—

And I see my future.

★ ★ ★ ★ ★

If you've loved reading Maggie and Samir's story, check out

French Kissed

Part three of Chanel Cleeton's
International School series

Available now!

1

Fleur

I'd never spent much time thinking about men's backs. Clothes, watches, cars? Sure. Backs? Not so much. But then again, to be fair, no one's back looked like his.

I shifted in my seat, hoping the movement would keep me awake. Bad enough it was 9:00 a.m. but it was also my Project Finance class, which was a giant pain in my ass. So really, my back-ogling kept me sane and alert. At least that was what I told myself as he stretched again, and I felt things. Lots of things.

Max Tucker sat in front of me, wearing a light gray T-shirt that vaguely translated to, *I don't care what I look like.* Your clothes could say things like that when your body screamed warrior sex god. Not that I was listening or anything.

He moved forward an inch, and I sucked in a deep breath, watching, fascinated by the muscles rippling under the soft fabric.

Compared to the rest of the guys here at the International School in London, there was something about him...something that didn't fit here.

It wasn't just that he was American or that he didn't have

money, although that was a big part of it. We went to a school where labels, wealth, and appearances mattered, but more than anything, what counted most was swagger. You had to walk around like you owned the place, and at a school filled with the sons and daughters of world leaders and moguls, that was no easy feat. But even without the swagger, you noticed Max. He might have been more peasant than king, but his body was all god.

He was tall. The kind of tall that made me feel small, which at five-eleven was a challenge. His shoulders were so broad, he nearly blocked out the class. Reason number one why I sat behind him. If they couldn't see you, they couldn't call on you. And fuck if I knew *anything* about project finance. I was here because it was required for my fashion marketing major, and even though it was only the first week of classes, I was already over it.

The other reason, the one that had me squirming in my seat as I drank in Max's body, was that I *liked* looking at him. He was beautiful in a rugged way that really shouldn't have been beautiful at all. Costa had been elegance and sophistication, with eyes that hinted at wicked pleasures and dark sex.

Max didn't look like that at all. He was too open, his eyes too expressive, his face too easy to read. He didn't look like he had secrets, like he'd ever had secrets. He looked solid. And while I'd once thought solid was the most boring thing in the world, it now taunted me, sitting inches away. It said, *Taste, touch, see.* It wanted me to reach out and curl my fingers around his gray T-shirt, slip my hand under the fabric and stroke the golden skin and hard abs his shirt hinted at.

Merde.

It hit me again, like a punch to the head. I wanted—no, after over a year of celibacy, *needed* was a better word—to get laid. I knew I was hard up when I was lusting after someone like Max. Someone I hated. Someone who hated me.

Max

Fleur Marceaux's eyes bore into me like two lasers shooting at my back. Half the time I expected that when I turned around, I'd find a dagger there. The other half I thought of long, straight light brown hair and deep brown eyes, ballerina-like legs, tanned skin and more attitude than one man could ever handle...or want.

I wasn't sure if it was a French thing or a Fleur thing, but either way, she took high-maintenance to new levels.

I turned in my seat slightly, just able to make out the curve of her jaw and her soft pink lips. Because I was weak, I allowed my gaze to dip down to take in the rest of perfection.

Even at a school like the International School, where most of the student body bathed themselves in designer labels and over-the-top outfits, Fleur took the cake.

I'd been around her enough last year when she'd dated my best friend, George—before she put his heart in a blender and hit "Liquefy"—to know that the only way to manage Fleur was to not let her mind-fuck you into submission. She always had the upper hand, so I made a point of taking it from her—because I liked it, and even more, because I liked the way it teased out a little line between her brows. The girl who glided through life looked annoyed now, and as much as I shouldn't have cared, her reaction did things to me. So I looked. A lot.

She was wearing a dress today. I had no idea what the color was—something between red and orange that clung to every inch of her body. The neckline dipped low framing mouthwatering cleavage. She wasn't curvy, and her breasts were smaller than average, her ass the same, but when her hips moved as she strutted down the halls, I'd always found myself unable to tear my gaze away.

I'd hated her for three years; been in lust with her since the first day I bumped into her in the hall freshman year. Total mind-fuck.

She glared back at me, her lips slanting into a hard line, and I met her gaze with a smug satisfaction I didn't completely feel. I never felt *satisfied* around Fleur—just needy, and edgy and wanting more. It made the game of chicken we constantly played with each other that much more difficult to win. Impossible, really.

I turned in my seat, adjusting my jeans, struggling to concentrate on the professor at the front of the room and not the girl behind me.

It was my senior year of college, just weeks before I started the long process of going through rounds of interviews for my dream job. Some companies began hiring in the fall of your senior year. I'd been waiting for this moment forever, and now it was here, and it was terrifying.

I heard my father's voice in my head:

What do you need with that fancy education? You think you're too good for home now? You just wait. You'll come home and end up working with your brothers at the bar.

I tried to block it out. Block out the doubt and the fear that he was right, that I couldn't do this. I was applying to some of the best investment banks in London, one of the most competitive cities in the world. My academic record had to be perfect.

"Eighty percent of your grade in this class will be a team project you'll work on for the entire semester," our professor announced from the front of the room. "The project will involve you financing a business venture. I'll give you the parameters, and you'll have to work within those guidelines to create a successful business. You'll be graded on a variety of factors, including how well you work together, the overall quality of your project, a written paper and a presentation before the International Business faculty at the end of the semester. You can see how the individual components will be weighed on page four of the syllabus."

I thumbed through the pages, unable to ignore the feeling that Fleur was watching me again. Didn't she care about her grades at all? Rumor had it that her father was filthy rich, but what the hell was she going to do after graduation? Live off Daddy? Did she even care about her education, or was college just a series of parties for her?

The International School was a good school, but it also attracted a certain type of student. For the most part, the American kids came here to study. Some like me were on scholarship and had taken out student loans. Taking your education seriously had an entirely different meaning when you knew you'd be spending the next ten years of your life paying it back. If I got lucky, got the kind of job I'd been working for all along, I could turn ten years into two.

"Part of being successful is meeting the challenges thrown your way," the professor continued. "You may not always like your coworkers, and there's no 'fair' in business. You may be paired with a weaker group, and you can only work harder to overcome your shortfalls. So in the spirit of creating an authentic business environment, you won't be allowed to choose your partners as was done in previous years."

Groans erupted throughout the classroom. I understood his point, but the odds of me getting a good partner were just drastically reduced. Maybe a quarter of the class took their major seriously and cared about learning. The rest of the class was like Fleur; their degrees were pieces of paper to hang on walls at family companies where they had secure positions waiting for them after graduation, and an impressive title like "vice president" they would add after their name before they turned twenty-five.

I had over one hundred thousand dollars in student loans, and the offer that I could sleep on the saggy couch in my parents' living room for a couple weeks after graduation—if I paid rent.

"If you're sitting in an odd-numbered row, turn behind you. Congratulations, you've just met your new business partner."

Wait, what?

I counted the rows, dread filling me when I came to mine. *Fuck.*

There was a moment when I thought about saying something to the professor, a stupid wistful moment that vanished as soon as it came. I turned slowly, as if my body could prolong the inevitable. But it couldn't, and it didn't, and the next thing I knew, I was face-to-face with my nemesis-slash-crush.

Fleur's lips curved, and her eyes filled with a knowing glint as if she recognized my discomfort and loved it. Her voice came next, that hint of a French accent some masochistic part of me gravitated toward like a sailor caught by a siren's song.

"Hi, partner."

Fleur

We faced off at a little French café around the corner from school. Professor Schrader had released us early so we could go over the project with our partners. Normally, I would've been thrilled—thirty minutes less of class was always a win—but at the same time it meant thirty minutes of my life spent with Max.

He scowled at me across the table, and I got a little preview of what the next three months would hold. Fabulous.

I plastered on a saccharine smile completely at odds with my tone. "Are you always like this, or is it just me?"

Max jerked his head up from the notebook he'd been scribbling in—he had freakishly small handwriting—and stared at me blankly as if he'd almost forgotten I was there.

My eyes narrowed. "Believe me, I'm no happier about us working together than you are."

Okay, that was an outrageous lie. My GPA hovered dangerously around a 2.0, and I needed to pass this class to graduate. Max was allegedly a genius. I had the better end of the deal here. Unfortunately, he was just *so* Max.

I leaned in closer, trying to sneak a peek at the notebook in front of him. "What are you doing?"

He looked back down at the page, his face hidden, his voice barely over a mumble. "Coming up with a plan for the project."

"Aren't we supposed to talk about it?" I asked, torn between annoyed and hurt that he didn't even ask what I wanted. He probably figured I wasn't smart enough to contribute. "Shouldn't we come up with a project together?"

No way was I going to end up with something boring. If I was going to have to stare at numbers all day, then at least give me something pretty to look at—besides Max. A fashion label, something I could handle.

"Hello?" I waved my hand in his face and was met with silence. He wasn't particularly talkative on an average day, but this was ridiculous.

Max let out a little huff of air as he leaned back in his chair, his palms behind his head. I was treated to the view of big, tanned biceps, and long, corded arms. His shirt rose with the motion, displaying an inch of his abs before it snapped back into place as he slouched forward in his seat.

"Fine. What kind of project do you want to choose?" He stared at me expectantly as I struggled to transition from that hint of ab to finance. "Well?" There was a challenge in his voice we both knew I couldn't rise to, and a gleam in his eyes that said what I already knew. He'd written me off as an airhead a long time ago.

This was what I hated most about Max. He always made me feel like I was an idiot. To be fair, compared to him, I probably was. I didn't like school, found most of it to be a giant waste of time. And I didn't love my major. The fashion part was great, but the rest of it? Business was my father's thing, not mine.

It would have been easy to blame the language barrier—English, after all, was my second language—but it wasn't that. Boarding school in Switzerland had been in English and French, and my grades had still been dismal. I'd spent more time hooking up with Costa than studying.

And now, at twenty-two, with less than a year between me and graduation, I regretted it. Regretted all the times I'd blown off studying to go clubbing; all the time I'd wasted on things that didn't really matter, and on the one person who didn't.

I didn't like the way people like Max looked down on me, but it was all so far beyond me. It felt like I was constantly playing catch up, starting a story in the middle when everyone else had begun at the beginning. I got Cs and Ds occasionally and skipped class when I could get away with it, because sitting in classrooms listening to subjects everyone else so easily understood was sheer torture.

I had no clue what I wanted to do with my life. No clue who I was supposed to be.

It hadn't really bothered me until now.

I blamed Samir. He was my best friend, and thanks to our French mothers, my cousin. But most of all, he was my partner in crime. When I'd been slinging back Cristal at clubs, he'd been right there next to me. It was what everyone around us did. It was normal. And there was safety in numbers; it was how you knew you were doing what you were supposed to, that your life was going according to plan. Eventually, we had to grow up, but I'd always thought I'd have more time. But then Samir had graduated and enrolled to get his master's, and he'd given everything up for his girlfriend, my other best friend, Maggie.

He was more serious, more driven, just *more*. So was Maggie. They were talking about getting a flat together next semester and making all these plans, and I was happy for them, really I was. I just wasn't sure where that left me.

I didn't have a future to get excited about. Didn't have someone to make plans with. I had a past I wished I could forget and a blackmailer obsessed with making me remember.

Copyright © 2014 by Chanel Cleeton